# Chasing Hope

## By

## Elizabeth Castle

Name: Castle, Elizabeth, author

Title: Chasing Hope

Publisher: In The Air Publishing

Identifiers: ISBN 9781967731008 (ebook) | ISBN 9781967731015 (paperback) | ISBN 9798305098266 (amazon hardcover)

Cover Design by Chiara Design

Chapter One

Matt Henney pulled up in front of the newly finished ranch house. He slammed the door of his pickup and breathed in the fresh spring air, taking in the woods and canyons in the distance. Behind the canyon, snow-capped mountains set the backdrop to what he would now call home. The snow was melting, and summer wasn't far away. Every tense muscle in his body loosened as peace settled in. Of all the places he'd been in the world, he felt most at peace in Utah. Mountains, canyons, deserts, heat, and snow could all be found within its borders.

He looked around the vast property. He finally had the stake he needed to buy into his friends' business. No more traveling. No more open roads. No more scraping together every penny.

His gaze wandered off into the distance toward the canyon, far past where the ranch house stood. The cabins, horse trails, barns, and stables were quiet. He could see horses and cattle grazing. The Waters Ranch was a combination working ranch and retreat that was open year-round to guests, but the start of the busy season was still a month away. Guests could enjoy the luxurious hotel or rent one of the many guest cabins with the canyons and mountains in the background. They could go climbing, hiking, camping, or horseback riding.  From the working ranch side, there was a small herd of cattle, goats, and chickens.  The vast fields and orchard grew a variety of fruits and vegetables.  Matt was content doing whatever was needed, whether it was working at the barns or taking guests out.

He turned to the house as the screen door opened. Allie Waters came down the four stairs of the porch and launched herself at him.  Her strong arms held him tight as he caught her up.  "I can't believe you're finally here."

A tall, dark-haired man followed at a slower pace. "She was worried you might not make it before dark."

Matt hugged his other friend.  He and Jeremy Waters had been friends since childhood.  "I wanted to see the sunset.  Nothing like it on Earth."

Allie hugged him again.  "It's so good to see you."

Matt set a hand on Allie's stomach.  When she'd told him she was pregnant, he'd been thrilled for her. They'd been friends since they'd served as medics in the army.  When Matt had brought Allie home for a visit while on leave, Jeremy had taken one look at her and had fallen in love.  It had amused him to see his ladies' man best friend become tongue-tied around the forceful Allie.  Allie hadn't been particularly interested in marriage, but time and patience had worn her down.

Matt followed his friends inside, thinking about how different they were, yet how they complemented each other.  Jeremy was much taller than his five-foot-eleven frame and dwarfed his five-foot-five wife. Jeremy's hair was almost black, whereas Allie's was shades of brown and red. Allie was the spitfire; the one who would always tell you exactly what she was thinking. Jeremy was just as forceful but did it in a quiet way.

"I see you two have been busy. Last time I saw this place, it was still bare drywall." Matt gazed around the now-completed space. The open space was painted in light desert colors but filled with lush plants. The oversized glass windows and skylights brought the outdoors in. The tile floors were a jarring turquoise but somehow fit the space.

Allie settled her palms across her full belly. "Who knew Jeremy was so good at interior design?"

Jeremy came up behind her, wrapped his arms around her, and his hands settled on top of hers. "One of us had to be. Matt, your new trailer arrived last week. We've got it all up and running for you."

Allie had wanted him to build a house on the property, but Matt had declined. It wasn't his land yet, and his money was better spent helping build up the ranch. But neither did he want to spend all of his time camping, nor take up space in one of the cabins. So, he'd compromised and let them hook up a trailer for him.

Allie leaned into her husband. "Your furniture arrived, what little there was of it. Jeremy ordered a few extra pieces, and I stocked the kitchen, though you're welcome to eat with us."

"How about a tour?" Matt was impressed by the space. It was homey, something neither he nor Jeremy knew much about. They'd both been in the foster system and had grown up in the same home. And while he had fond memories of his foster parents, neither he nor Jeremy were what you'd call home bodies.

Allie showed him around their finished home. He envied his friends. They had found each other and had built a business from the ground up. Matt accepted the cup of coffee when they settled into the kitchen. "It's hard to believe what this place used to be."

Allie inhaled the coffee before handing her husband his. "We've hired more staff. And with you finally settling in and buying in, we'll have more groups going out. Rock climbing is big business out here. I'll feel much better keeping Jeremy closer to home and letting you take the groups out."

Jeremy finished his coffee. "No rest for the weary. Hope you're ready, Matt. Allie has a new stud arriving tomorrow. Travis is going to take a new group camping at the mesa. Mike is taking out a newbie group of rock climbers. The renovations on the older cabins are finished, and we're going to start listing them to rent."

Matt rose and stretched. "Wherever you need me."

"Mmm. First problem might be in your trailer finishing cleaning it up."

Allie glared at her husband over her shoulder.

"Cut her some slack. She's trying."

Jeremy released her and went to rinse their cups. "That woman hasn't worked a day in her life."

Matt glanced at Allie's pinched lips. "Problem?"

Jeremy replied. "Hope Whitfield. The woman is useless. Allie refuses to let me fire her. She showed up here last month along with a dozen other women looking to get hired. She had no job experience at all. Allie felt sorry for her and gave her a job anyway."

That surprised Matt. Allie was a firm believer in hard work and earning your way. She had to be tough leading a team of medics in the army. "Going soft on me?"

Allie gave him a dirty look. "There has got to be something she's good at. She's a body, and she's willing to work."

Jeremy shook his head. "I booted her out of the kitchen. She couldn't seem to manage taking reservations and answering phones. Now she's the slowest member of our cleaning staff. The woman can barely make a bed. The other housekeepers are complaining. I'm going to assign her to the barn. Because, Allie, if the woman can't rake out a stall, then she's gone."

Allie relented. "All right. You made your point. School is out soon, and we'll have some new applicants."

Matt yawned, the long trip catching up with him. "Why don't I go check out the trailer and settle in."

Jeremy set a hand on Allie's shoulder. "I'll take

him. You need to put your feet up."

Allie lifted her mouth to his. "Yes, dear."

Jeremy kissed her. "Come on, Matt. Hopefully, she didn't burn the place down."

Matt followed Jeremy in his truck as his friend led him down the dirt and gravel road. It took a couple of minutes to drive to where the trailer was nestled near some large boulders. He grabbed his bag from the passenger seat. "This is a lot nicer than I told you to get."

Jeremy agreed. "It is. But Allie said there was no way she was letting that eyesore of a trailer you picked out anywhere near her property."

The trailer was single-wide, but from the length of it, it likely had a couple of bedrooms. A large window, along with smaller windows, ran the length of the trailer. A small deck held a table and chairs, as well as a grill, and there was a large fire pit nearby.

"Allie wanted to be sure you stuck around. And she said to think of it as a retreat when you come back from taking a bunch of greenhorns camping or climbing."

Matt opened the door and took in the space. There was a large kitchen to the right with plenty of cabinets, full-size appliances, and a small island. To the left, there was a full living room, a massive television, an empty bookcase, a couch, and a wood-burning fireplace. There was a short hall that led to three doors.

Jeremy let the screen door shut behind him. He

called out, "Ms. Whitlock."

A woman came from the back room, rubbing her palms on her khakis. She was about Allie's height, with chin-length auburn curls around an oval face. The pants were loose on her frame, the dark blue polo shirt tucked in. The clothes were baggy, but he could see hints of curves underneath. She was pretty enough, but he agreed with Jeremy. There wasn't much to her, and she didn't appear sturdy enough to tackle the jobs on a retreat or ranch this size. She didn't look like she could weed a vegetable garden.

Her voice was soft when she spoke. "I finished up. The bed is made up, and I washed the bathroom down. I made sure everything was stocked in the kitchen like Mrs. Waters asked."

The woman's turquoise eyes glanced at him. He could tell from the expression on her face that she was nervous.

Jeremy poked his head into the bathroom and bedroom. "All right. You can go. We'll talk tomorrow."

Turquoise eyes once again held his. It was disconcerting. The anxiety had faded, and there was nothing else in her gaze, not even relief that she could go. She quickly brushed past the two men and was out of sight by the time he went to the window. "Not much to her."

"No. Allie took a shine to her. No clue why. Allie swears she knows her. But she doesn't recall knowing a Whitfield or a Hope. But I don't have time, and neither does the rest of the staff, to tolerate someone who can't pull their weight."

Matt tossed his duffle bag next to the couch. "Can't or won't?"

Jeremy scrubbed a hand over his face. "Can't. I can't put my finger on it, but there's something wrong with her. The only reason I haven't fired her yet is that she puts in the hours. She works hard. It's just that nothing seems to get done. I don't know. For Allie's sake, I hope she can handle a rake, feed bags, or something. I will have to let her go."

Matt dropped onto the sofa. "Why don't I show her the ropes tomorrow? It's been a while since I've worked with the horses. Worse case, she can clean up after the goats."

Jeremy just shook his head. "In addition to the goats, Allie got a pair of alpacas. She also got some sheep. At the rate we're going, we could open a petting zoo. I didn't mind the cows and goats. The small farm Allie runs over on the east part of the property makes her happy. Milk and cheese fetch decent prices. Costly though. The apple and cherry orchards had a good harvest last year, and we're hoping for a repeat. Despite the small oasis we have here, we've got the desert to the south and canyons and mountains surrounding us. We're blessed this land has plenty of water to sustain our operations. Honestly, though, the sheep and alpacas are a bit much, even if they earn their keep. Can't say the same about Hope Whitfield."

Matt saw Jeremy off and checked out the rest of the trailer. The large king bed was met with approval and appreciation. The bathroom was spacious. It had a soaking tub and shower combo. The double vanity was more than he needed but was nice. There was a second empty bedroom tucked between the utility room and the master, though it would only hold a twin bed and a small dresser. Maybe he would tuck a desk in there. He didn't own much and didn't need much room. This place was a palace in comparison to some of the places he'd lived. But it afforded him privacy, a roof over his head, and a place to settle down.

It had taken him the last five years to finish saving up the stake he needed to buy into Allie and Jeremy's business. Allie had inherited the run-down retreat from her aunt on her mother's side of the family. They had wanted to bring him in years ago, but he wanted to be able to contribute to the operation, not just be an employee. They were his best friends, and they understood his need to own something of his own. He came during the busy summer season and spent the rest of the year in some of the coldest, harshest land out there, saving every penny. He'd survived, but this time he was staying for good.

* * *

Hope shivered as she poured the last of the jug of

water over her head and rinsed out the shampoo. The temperature dropped at night, but it was just as cold in the mornings. At least this way her hair would be dry by the morning. When she'd first arrived and had to start taking camp baths, she'd cropped her longer hair to her chin. It was harder to control the shorter curls, but easier to wash and rinse.

She tossed a few more branches on the small fire as she blotted water out of her hair. She combed it out as close to the heat as she dared. She'd gotten good at camp baths and learned to use the least amount of water possible. Water was scarce on this side of the river. Her camp was surrounded by rocks and boulders, the lower level of the canyon surrounding the borders of the property. The river was a good mile or more from where she sat. Thankfully she was able to fill water jugs each night after work. If she was lucky, she could sneak some food out, as well. Tonight she had been cleaning the trailer, so she had missed dinner. Her stomach growled, but she ignored it.

She sat for a while with her flannel nightgown wrapped around her legs and let the fire warm her. The tarp she had staked into the ground kept the dirt and sand off her. Her work clothes were airing out on a nearby fence, and she idly thought it was time to make a trip into town. But not tonight. Millions of stars lit up above her as she felt her eyes start to droop. She yawned, knowing it was getting late, but too tired to grab her watch and look at the time.

Hope opened the flap to the tent she'd pitched near the run-down house. After her first night inside the house, she hadn't slept in it again. Spiders, bugs, rats, and who knew what else had made what was left of the house their home. She hadn't intruded again.

"Ready for bed, Trixie?"

The massive dog raised her head. She didn't know a lot about dogs, but the vet who treated Trixie for a skin condition told her the dog was expensive. The vet's best guess was that she was likely a purebred Boerboel, a type of mastiff. Hope had been terrified the first time she'd laid eyes on Trixie. But the poor dog had been abandoned and left to starve. She had been so thin, her skin mottled, and her fur missing. Once fed and medicated, the dog slowly healed. She still had some scars, but the beautiful gold of her fur was now thick and healthy.

Hope doused the remainder of the fire and crawled inside the tent. The dog followed her inside, and Hope zipped them in. The dog lay down on the bed Hope had set up for her, and Hope climbed onto her air mattress. The dog immediately began snoring, but sleep eluded Hope. Her body was exhausted, but her mind wouldn't shut off.

"We'll talk tomorrow." That didn't bode well. Hope was surprised Jeremy Waters hadn't fired her yet. But Hope was desperate. She prayed he would give her another chance to prove she could be useful. Without the job at the Waters Ranch, she didn't know what she'd do. They were miles from a city. Miles from a town, even. Her car got her back and forth to work, and into town now and again, but it needed maintenance. She simply didn't have the money to put into it. The oil change last month was all she could afford.

She rolled onto her side, pulling the sleeping bag higher over her shoulders. By morning she'd be completely inside of it. Hope wasn't sure she was looking forward to the heat that would soon be heading her way, but it had to be better than the frigid temperatures she was currently experiencing.

She watched Trixie as she shifted to get more comfortable. Other than feeding Trixie and giving her affection, the dog took care of herself. When Hope came back from work each day, Trixie was still there. Hope didn't dare tie her up. There were wild animals, and tethering the dog could prove fatal.

Burrowing deeper, Hope closed her eyes. Matt Henney. Now he was a fresh drink of water. He was tall, likely around six feet, though he was a bit shorter than her employer. His hair was too long, longer than hers, and the gold, wavy locks went past his shoulders. The beard needed a trim but added to his rugged appearance. His biceps bulged at the edges of his t-shirt, and his chest and shoulders were broad. His eyes were a deep brown against his tanned skin. He was older than her; she'd put him close to forty. Fine wrinkles framed his eyes, but there was no gray hair at his temples, though a few sprinkled his beard and mustache. Dark wash jeans worn through the knees hugged muscular thighs.

She'd heard from one of the women who worked at the retreat tell some other women that he spent his summers here. He was a rock climber and survivalist. He took groups hunting, fishing, and camping, as well as taking advanced climbers to the nearby canyons. There was also a lot of feminine speculation about him. Rumors were that he was single. From some of the comments Hope had heard, even if he were in a relationship, that wouldn't stop some of the women from pursuing him. But gossip was that he was here to stay, and a couple of women were looking to be the first, or perhaps the next, Mrs. Henney.

He had a rugged appeal, and she wasn't immune now that she'd seen him for herself. She didn't know what possessed a person to pit themselves against nature, though these past two months living outside had given her a new appreciation for those who did. Give her a soft bed and a hot shower any day. And what she wouldn't give for hot running water. The hotel she stayed in from time to time had tepid water at best. But it had a coin-operated washer and dryer, the beds weren't full of bugs, and the price was right. And it rented by the hour, so she was able to get a room, have a nap, and wash her clothes before heading back to her "home."

It was hard to remember what home used to be. As a young girl, home was a two-story brownstone on the east coast. She'd seen pictures but didn't have real memories of it. As an adult, home was a garish mansion on the West Coast. She'd rather live outside for the rest of her life than ever set foot inside that marble entryway again.

Hope curled up tighter inside the sleeping bag as she shivered. She'd rather wear secondhand clothes than ever wear another designer suit. In a rage, she'd tossed out every article of clothing, every shoe. She'd had enough sense to sell the jewelry she owned. She still had a few pieces left to sell for emergencies. Likely the diamond bracelet would soon pay for her car. But only if Jeremy Waters didn't fire her in the morning. She'd need that bracelet to eat and to keep Trixie in kibble if he did.

## Chapter Two

Hope wandered into the barn after leaving her boss's office. Jeremy Waters had told her this was her last chance. She either pulled her weight or she was fired. When she realized she wasn't fired, at least not yet, she promised him she'd work harder. She couldn't say she felt relieved that he was giving her one last chance; she had no illusions that she could do this job any better than the others. But at least she would have another couple of days' wages under her belt before he fired her.

Hope inhaled the familiar scent of the barn. In her eyes, the horses were beautiful animals. The horses that made the Waters Ranch home were working horses, not the purebreds she knew she had grown up around. These horses were meant to take travelers up the long trails that wound into the nearby canyons. Some could herd cattle, some could pull wagons, and others were saddle horses. She saw two new horses out in the smaller corral. She took a step closer to examine the larger of the animals. This one was a beautiful black stud. He no doubt cost a fortune and would sire magnificent horses one day.

A large man emerged from one of the stalls. "Hope, right?"

She nodded and tucked her hands into her

pockets. She tried not to stare. Matt had taken the time to shave. The smooth lines of his jaw revealed chiseled cheekbones that framed a handsome face. He'd pulled his hair back into a ponytail. It should have looked feminine, but it did quite the opposite. "Mr. Henney, correct?"

"Just Matt. I don't stand on formality. Ever worked in a barn or with animals?"

Hope wanted to say yes, but honesty prevented her. While she had recollections of being inside a barn, she had no memory of ever cleaning one or taking care of the animals that called it home. "No. But just show me what to do, and I'll do it."

Matt jerked his head and headed outside. "Figured we'd start with the goats. There's a shovel over there, and a wheel barrel. Just fill it up, wheel it over to the trailer, and dump it to be hauled out for fertilizer. All there is to it."

Hope was almost relieved when he went back inside. The goats were in the pasture, but the pen they slept in was where Matt had left her. She smiled at the goats as they bleated and romped around the grass. Some played while others grazed. She couldn't recall goats in her past, but they couldn't be so different from the horses, just smaller.

She pulled on the too-big work gloves left on the wheelbarrow. She grabbed the shovel. It was heavy, but not as heavy as she feared. She got to work. Filling the wheelbarrow was easy enough. She had to work to keep her arms steady and had to use both hands to keep the shovel from tipping, but she got the hang of it.  She hummed a tune in her head as she worked.

She'd been out there more than an hour when Matt approached.  She tensed.  Then she was startled when he pushed a large cowboy hat onto her head and handed her a bottle of water.

"Take a break.  You're going to need a hat to work outside.  And make sure you're carrying water with you.  At least you're smart enough to wear sleeves and pants.  But your face is getting burned.  Sunscreen is a must for someone so fair."

Hope drained the bottle, not realizing how thirsty she was.  She didn't own a hat, though she did have a mostly empty bottle of sunscreen somewhere.  She let him take the empty bottle from her.  "I didn't know I was going to be working outside.  I'll be better prepared tomorrow."

Matt glanced around the yard.  "Looks good.  The goats are friendly, so go ahead into the pasture when you've finished emptying the wheelbarrow."

Hope realized he wasn't going back inside.  She didn't want him watching her struggle with the bulk of the wheelbarrow.  She struggled to remember if she'd ever used one.  Certainly, she'd seen one used.  Pulling up the oversized gloves on her hands, she reached for the handles.  Matt quickly jumped behind her when she would have dumped it over.  She felt tears sting her eyes.  She couldn't even maneuver the thing. Her hands simply wouldn't cooperate.

She felt the press of his chest against her back. She could smell his cologne under the scent of sweat and horses. His arms were firm around her. She stiffened in his arms, and her breath caught. She released her breath when Matt slipped around her and released her from the circle of his arms.

"I've got it. Go inside the barn for a minute."

She watched, feeling helpless, as he easily maneuvered the wheelbarrow, rolled it up the ramp, and dumped it. The barn was a few degrees cooler, but her shiver wasn't from a chill. She kept the hat and work gloves on and waited for his decree.

He stepped back inside. "Give me a holler when you finish the pasture. I'll load it up."

She gaped for a minute, then realized he wasn't going to tear into her. Matt grabbed another bottle of water and pressed it into her hand. She gave him a slight smile and practically ran out of the barn.

* * *

Matt watched the swing of her hips as she rolled the empty wheelbarrow into the pasture. She stopped when the goats swarmed her, and she took a moment to pet them. She smiled when the alpacas rambled over. She was comfortable around the animals, which was good. People not familiar with them could get nervous when being that close. The goats and alpacas were harmless, and once they realized she didn't bring food, they ignored her.

He could see what Jeremy had meant about something being wrong with her. She held the handle of the shovel close to the shovel end and bent to lift the load. She was sure to have a sore back tonight. But she'd managed to do the job. Yes, it had taken her longer than it should have, but she'd tackled the task and did it as best she could. There were no complaints about the smell or the task being menial.

He wasn't sure if it was her balance, weak muscles, or something else that caused her to struggle. As she held the shovel, her arms trembled and shook a little as she kept it flat while she lifted it. He hadn't thought she was going to be able to move the wheelbarrow, and he'd been right. He'd stayed close to help, which she inevitably needed.

Matt went to the fridge and pulled out a bottle of water for himself. He needed to cool off, in more ways than one. When he'd wrapped his arms around her to stop the wheelbarrow from falling over, he'd felt the press of her bottom against him as she struggled to keep it upright. She smelled good. Lilacs or something in her hair. She was petite, likely a couple of inches shorter than Allie, now that he'd had her pressed up against him. But she'd fit up against him perfectly, her body conforming to the hard lines of his.

Silently cursing a bit at his unruly body, he finished the bottle and tossed it in the recycle bin. No doubt it had been way too long since he'd enjoyed the company of a woman if that tiny woman made his body respond like this. There weren't a lot of women up in the northern parts of North Dakota where he'd spent the last six months. There were a few women who worked the same jobs as the men, and a bevy of prostitutes. And while he didn't judge them for their choices, he had no desire to purchase their services.

He glanced back at Hope as she continued to struggle with the shovel. She had stiffened up in his arms, her whole body rigid against his. She hadn't liked his arms around her, even if it was unintentional. She had off-limits written all over her. The retreat would be filling up soon. Maybe he'd find some single ladies and try his hand at flirting. It had been a while, and he hoped he'd remember how.

"How bad?" Jeremy came up behind him in the shadows of the barn.

Matt realized he meant Hope's performance, not his randy reaction to her. "Not as bad as you are likely thinking. She's slow going, but she's getting the job done. I saw what you're paying her. It's less than the others. I'd say you're getting a day's pay out of her. She seems comfortable around the animals. I'll have her fill the feed buckets once she's done. Frankly, I don't think she's strong enough to clean out the stalls. But she can wield a hose, and I'll show her how to feed the chickens and collect the eggs. If you're bent on keeping your wife happy, there are enough small things to keep Hope busy."

Jeremy pushed the brim of his hat back. "You're staring at her, buddy."

Matt knew it. He didn't have the desire to stop. But something was nagging at him. "I think I get what Allie meant about knowing her. There's something familiar about her. I can't put my finger on it."

Jeremy shook his head at that. "Not you too. Maybe she looks like someone you two knew back in your army days."

Matt hummed. "I don't know. Maybe."

Jeremy left Matt to keep working. Matt wasn't a stranger to manual labor. He was not a desk job type of guy. He much preferred being outdoors. Matt inhaled the scents of the barn and got back to work.

Matt heard his name called. Hope was at the fence line. "All done?"

Hope nodded as she absently petted the goat that was trailing her around the yard.

Matt took care of the wheelbarrow and then had her join him on a walk to the chicken pens. Hope's auburn curls stuck to her damp cheeks. The hat was too big for her, but she managed to get most of her hair tucked inside. His fingers itched to see if her hair was as soft as it looked.

Hope kept her distance from him. Her legs were short but kept up with him as they walked. She didn't seem winded and seemed to be enjoying the breeze.

He indulged his curiosity. "What city are you from?"

Her mouth twisted into a slight smile. "Don't I look like a country girl?"

Matt contemplated her for a moment. Today she had on a pair of tight jeans and a button-up chambray work shirt. "The clothes are right. But the rest of you is wrong."

Her brows furrowed as she took in that statement. She crossed her arms protectively across her chest. "I was living in Los Angeles for a while. I wasn't born there, but that's where I spent eight years. I was barely out of college when I moved there."

Matt held in his derision. "Let me guess, you wanted to be an actress."

Hope stumbled a bit but kept on her feet when her eyes flew to his. "Sure. Why not?"

Matt shrugged as they got to the door of the pen. He held it open for her. "I don't mind spending time on the couch watching television at the end of the day. But not much is worth watching out there these days. I certainly can't imagine making a living off pretending I was someone else."

Hope preceded him. She was eyeing the chickens as if they might attack.

The chickens were a lively bunch, so he quickly closed the door behind them. "Don't feel bad, Hope. I grew up in a city. I just got out as soon as I could."

Hope tugged the work gloves back on. "So there's hope for me? For a city girl?"

Matt didn't want to discourage her, though he sincerely doubted it. Like Allie, she tugged something inside him. He knew what it was like to not belong. She certainly didn't belong here, though she was trying. He'd seen her this morning sitting by herself with a cup of coffee and breakfast before her shift started. He knew she was waiting on Jeremy. Other staff were gathered at the tables, laughing and relaxing before the beginning of the long work day. She had been alone. In more ways than one.

Matt showed her where everything was, and then showed her how to gather eggs. She gripped the bucket with both hands, much as she had done the shovel. It was an easy enough task, though a couple of the hens were as likely to peck you as they were to run away. The gloves protected her hands more than once from an angry chicken.

Matt glanced up at the sun as she finished up. "We should take a rest. Come on, let's go get lunch."

Matt took the bucket from her. She trailed behind him as they walked back to where they had come. He offered her a ride back up to the mess hall, but she declined. Shrugging, he let her be and headed back to wash up and get a bite to eat.

* * *

Pretending to be someone else. It struck a chord with Hope. When Matt had asked her if she had gone to Los Angeles to be an actress, it wasn't a complete lie when she said sure. Her acting hadn't been on the silver screen. But she had been an actress. A good one, as far as she could discern. She had been whatever those around her wanted to be. First her father, then her grandfather, then her husband.

And isn't that what she'd been doing for the past two years? Pretending to be someone else? It wasn't hard to do when you couldn't remember who you used to be. Or when you were whoever you needed to be in the moment.

She took the filled water jugs and put them in the trunk of her car. She glanced at the mess hall where everyone was gathered to eat. Her stomach rumbled. She'd barely eaten her breakfast; she'd been nervous about meeting with Jeremy. Knowing she wouldn't be able to sneak back in later, she walked up the path. The building was crowded. There were at least a hundred people on staff. The Waters would usually eat at their house, so she didn't figure she'd run into Jeremy. She avoided him whenever she could. She spotted Matt talking to some of the horse handlers. The retreat had guests, and the men would have spent the day taking groups out on walking tours.

Hope filled a tray and found a quiet corner, or at least the quietest one she could find in the filled room. As she ate, she massaged her temples and tried to ease the headache that had formed behind her eyes. She wasn't used to working in the heat. The hat had helped, but she was feeling a little dizzy. She should have taken Matt up on his offer to drive her to the hall, but she had needed to fill her water jugs while no one was watching. She knew Matt watched her. She could feel his eyes on her back as she had worked. She hadn't wanted to show any sign of weakness, or that she was struggling to do the job he'd assigned her.

She unbuttoned the top buttons on her shirt and rolled up her sleeves, letting some of the air from the fans cool her down.  On her days off, she either went into town or spent time lounging under the large tree that hung over the old house like a looming monster. The gnarled branches creaked in the wind.  There were nights she counted the creaks until she fell asleep.  It looked like a good storm would snap it in half.  It hung directly over the house.  When it finally broke, it would take the house with it.  It would be the best thing that could happen to the old house.  No one had lived in it for decades.  And as it stood, no one ever would again.

She finished her meal, trying not to be hurt when the women who walked past her mocked her.  She heard the things they said about her. Lazy. Useless. Helpless Hope.  Probably sleeping with one of the bosses. How else could she keep her job?  She tried to brush off the comments, but they hurt.  Not because they weren't true, but because the women made sure she heard them.

"Thank goodness they put her somewhere else.  I can't believe she's still here.  The woman can't even tuck in a decent corner. Mira had to go back over all the rooms she cleaned."

"At least she didn't burn them down.  Denise said she burned an entire pot of chili.  Had to throw the whole thing away.  If Denise had her way, she would have taken it out of her paycheck."

"I hear she's stuck cleaning up crap from the goats and chickens. About all she's good for."

The women giggled, glanced her way, and kept going. Hope was aware they made sure she heard every word. Face flushed, she tossed the rest of her food and put the tray with the others. She headed to the ladies' room. She took a moment to dampen a paper towel and wipe off the morning's sweat and grime. She then locked herself in a stall and took a moment to get a grip.

*It's all you're good for, Jaclyn. You might as well earn your keep the old-fashioned way.*

Hope closed her eyes and forcefully pushed back the memory of being grabbed by her husband. Catty women she could handle. The ugly snatches of memories that worked their way to the surface, she couldn't. This memory faded to black, the same as all the others. She used the facilities and made her way back out. She took the water bottle she'd grabbed from her car and filled it to the brim with lemonade. She then snagged a couple of individually wrapped pastries and a banana and tucked them into the pouch she used as a purse. She slipped out of the mess hall.

The rest of the day went okay, at least she thought so. She had filled all the water troughs for a second time that day. As the day grew late and the horses were brought back to their stalls for fresh oats and a graze in the pasture, Matt walked her through how to clean and put away the tack. He took care of the saddles, but she was able to handle the rest.

Matt came out to meet her as she stood gazing out at the sunset. "Not a bad day, huh?"

Hope felt her lips curl into a smile. It had been a good day. She'd done everything he'd asked her to do. He hadn't said anything to her about not being able to manage the saddles or the wheelbarrow. "Not bad."

Matt tipped the hat back on her head. "Do you have a hat?"

Her smile dropped. "I can get one."

Matt pushed the hat further down on her head. "Keep it. I've got others. And take this."

Hope automatically took the round tin can from him. "Horse liniment?"

"Works just as well on people as it does horses. You're going to be sore tomorrow. It will help. This one doesn't smell so bad. I'll see you here first thing tomorrow. Want a ride back?"

Hope tucked it into her shoulder bag. "Yes, please."

Matt started off and she followed him. His large truck was parked a few yards from the barn. He opened the door for her. She stiffened when he helped her up into the cab but scooted in as he started to close the door. She saw the old turn handle for the window and rolled it down.

Matt started up the old truck. "Sorry, the air conditioning doesn't work."

Hope buckled in. "I think this truck is older than I

am."

"What are you, twenty-five, twenty-six?"

Hope glanced at her face in the side mirror. Freckles were prominent across her nose; her face was bare of cosmetics. No sophisticated dressing. Yep, all in all, she looked young. But she didn't feel it. "I'll be thirty-two soon."

Surprise changed his features. Then he shook his head. "Yes, this truck is older than you are. Older than me, but I'm fond of it, so I keep fixing her up. Bessie and I have driven a lot of roads and a lot of miles together."

Hope relaxed in her seat. "Bessie?"

"Yeah, fits her, don't you think?"

Hope thought of Trixie. "Yes, it fits."

Matt drove her to the lot where the employees parked.

"Just stop here. No reason to drive me to my car."

Matt stopped the truck, the idle loud as he watched her unbuckle her belt.

She slid from the seat to the ground. It jarred her a little, and she was already feeling an ache in her back now that she'd stopped moving. "Thanks, Matt. And not just for the ride."

Hope slammed the door, hoping he understood what she meant. He'd been kind to her. He'd shown her how to do what he needed her to do. He didn't pass judgment. He didn't get angry with her. Yes. It had been a good day.

She climbed into her fifteen-year-old Mercedes

and drove back to her property.  She found it amusing that her car was nicer than his, considering she was essentially homeless.  Trixie barked in greeting.  Hope didn't know what she did all day, though she left the door to the house open in case Trixie needed to get out of the heat.  Hope grabbed a gallon jug and filled the dog's bowl.  She then filled the food bowl to the top before heading to the tent.  She had set up her tent on the backside of the house so no one could see her. From the front of the house, there were roads in the distance.  No one came out this way.  There was no reason to.  But she didn't want to accidentally attract attention.

Once Trixie was done eating, she came to sit by Hope.  Hope had stripped and washed.  Then she grabbed the can of liniment.  It didn't smell bad, but it didn't smell great, either.  But she slathered it on her lower back, her arms, and her hands.  Trixie sniffed her and sneezed.

Hope giggled and hugged the dog.  "I had a nice day at work today.  Let me tell you about my new boss, Matt."

Chapter Three

May flowers were blooming, and the retreat was full of guests. Matt had settled in and was back from taking a group out camping for the weekend. It had been nice, except for a couple of teenage boys who were hell-bent on mischief. He'd checked the register, and the family was going to be here another week. He sincerely hoped they found something to do away from the retreat for the rest of their stay.

But today he was officially off duty and had business in town. Allie and Jeremy had already met with their lawyer and the bank. Allie could have the baby any day, so they had not waited for him to come down to the bank to sign everything. At the end of the day, he'd be one-third owner of the Waters Ranch.

He pulled the truck up in front of the bank. He paused when he saw a familiar face. Hope was digging in her purse and hadn't seen him right away. He took a step up onto the sidewalk.

"Good morning, Hope. Day off?"

Hope stopped in her tracks; her eyes widened until she realized who was in front of her. "I, ah, yes."

Matt took her elbow and led her to the door. She was stiff under his hand, but he pretended not to notice. She was a tense little thing. When they had been working with the animals together, he'd done everything he could to get her to relax. But she was one high-strung filly.

She murmured her thanks as she headed to the teller. He kept his eyes on her until the receptionist got his attention.

Pulling his eyes from Hope, he turned back to the woman. "Matthew Henney to see Mr. McMillan."

Out of the corner of his eye, he saw Hope watching him as the teller counted out her money. Hope signed the paper in front of her, then gave him one last glance before she scurried out.

An hour later, Matt took a deep breath as he stepped out into the parking lot. He took another deep breath for good measure. He might now be a broke man, but he was a happy one. He looked over and saw Hope's car was still parked two cars down. The car looked nicer than his, though it was an older model. And hers had a much fancier label on it. But the Mercedes had seen better days. He wondered about it, and her. He wondered about her a lot. He was a single man. Occasionally a lonely one. She was a single woman. At least as far as he could tell. She wore no ring. No jewelry at all. Today she was wearing a pair of worn jeans and a yellow tank top. The state was heating up as summer crept in. But despite the tank she wore in deference to the heat, she wore the same work boots she wore every day at work.

He glanced around. It had been a while since he'd been in town. There were some pretty waitresses he could flirt with. Or there were a few stores if he were inclined to shop, though he couldn't think of anything he needed. Allie kept his kitchen and anything else he might need stocked for him. She claimed that since she was buying for her and her husband, she might as well grab double.

Where would his pretty auburn-haired lady have gone? There was a library across the way. It seemed as likely as anywhere else. If nothing else, it wouldn't hurt to renew his card and pick up a couple of books. He crossed the road and climbed the stairs. The cool air was welcome as he looked around. And there she was. She was seated at one of the library's computers.

He rambled up to the front counter. A woman who looked to be at least eighty renewed his card. As he browsed the shelves, he kept an eye on Hope. She looked upset. At that moment, her eyes rose and caught his. He'd been caught staring like an awestruck teenager mooning over the pretty girl.

Hope rose from her seat, tucking her bag under her arm. She started making her way out.

Matt set the book down and followed her. "Hope. Stop."

She slowed her pace but didn't stop. "Are you following me?"

Matt denied it, though it was a lie. "It's a small town. Figured while I was here, I'd renew my library card. I thought we could have lunch since we're both off. I'm celebrating."

Hope stopped and looked up at him. She had a

suspicious look on her face. "Celebrating what?"

"I just signed the papers, and now I'm part owner of the Waters Ranch."

She nodded and resumed walking. "That's nice. There was chatter that you were buying in."

He didn't touch her but herded her toward the restaurant, even though she hadn't agreed to join him. There was only one restaurant to choose from, and she didn't seem to be resisting. "It's been a long time coming."

Hope stopped as he reached around her to open the door. His arm brushed hers, and he caught her slight shiver. The waitress seated the two of them, took their drink orders, and left.

Hope sipped her glass of water. "You must know Jeremy and Allie very well."

Matt handed Hope a menu. "I've known Jeremy since I was a kid. We grew up together. I met Allie in the military. When I introduced them, it was love at first sight. Allie inherited the ranch a few years ago, and she and Jeremy decided to give it a go. I didn't have the cash, but they invited me to buy in. Just took a little while."

Hope thanked the waitress and traded her water for the sweet tea. "It's good land. From what I understand, the orchard has been there for years. But the farm is all new."

Matt sipped his coffee. "Allie is a farm girl at heart. How long have you lived here? You said you were living in Los Angeles, but Allie and Jeremy have only lived out here for five years.”

Hope’s eyes drifted as two women came into the restaurant. Her eyes darkened as she spoke. “I’ve only been here for a few months. But people talk. Some too much.”

Matt turned to look at the women. “They work at the ranch, don’t they?”

“Lydia manages the front desk for the cabins. That’s her sister, Nadine. She manages the front desk at the hotel.”

Matt turned back to Hope. “I don’t spend any time on the retreat side, except to take groups out. Hospitality is not my thing.”

“Jeremy’s either.” Hope turned wide eyes back to Matt. “I’m sorry. I shouldn’t have said that.”

Matt shrugged as the waitress came back and delivered their salads. “He’d be the first to admit it.”

When the waitress was out of earshot, Hope continued. “Seriously. I shouldn’t. And truly, I shouldn’t be here with you. Socializing with the boss will cause talk.”

Matt finished his coffee as he contemplated her. She had a point. But he didn’t much care what other people thought. “Are you that concerned about what people will say?”

She looked him in the eye. “Yes. I don’t like being the center of gossip. And those two are some of the worst. It’s a small town. And the retreat is a town unto itself. But the damage is already done.”

Matt could hear the women whispering, though he

couldn't make out the words. The restaurant was loud as it filled with the lunch crowd. "I wouldn't worry about those two. Some people can't help themselves."

Hope turned in her seat so her back was fully to them. "So what is the plan now? You've bought in. You've been busy, I hear. Mrs. Waters's baby is due any day. The baby is starting to drop."

Matt thought it an odd term, but just like other animals, you could tell when the baby was getting ready. "I'll be doing whatever needs to be done. Jeremy is staying close to home. The nearest hospital is a good fifty miles away."

When the waitress brought their food, they were quiet for a time. He was glad to see Hope was eating her meal. The BLT and fries might not be the healthiest meal, but she seemed to be enjoying it. He'd been where she was now. Her clothes were worn; she didn't wear makeup or have a fancy haircut. Though he liked the auburn curls that framed her face and chin. Allie and Jeremy let the staff come in for a free breakfast and lunch, and he'd seen her slip food into her bag. He knew Jeremy had too. Matt could tell he disapproved, but Jeremy let it go.

The waitress refilled his coffee, but Hope declined another glass of tea. Matt leaned back and watched her face. It was hard to tell what she was thinking. "Do you camp or hike? Climb?"

Hope's mouth twisted into a small smile. "I camp.

I guess I hike simply because of my job. But, no, the only thing I climb is into bed. What's the appeal?"

For a brief moment, Matt imagined climbing into bed with her. She had the softest-looking lips. Her mouth was lush; her lower lip made to nibble. But she gave no indication of reciprocating his attraction. He wasn't even sure she thought of him as a man. It occurred to him that perhaps she wasn't attracted to men. And not that he was egotistical to believe all women were attracted to him, but most of them at least gave him a look over. He might as well be sexless where Hope was concerned.

He realized he hadn't answered her question. "I learned in the military. There's something about pitting your strength against nature. I've seen firsthand how hard it can be to survive. I like to think I'm a survivor. And somehow, I think you are too."

She didn't dispute his assessment. But she didn't confirm it either. Hope finished her tea and got to her feet. "We should probably get going. I've got some errands to run, and I'm sure you've got work to do."

Matt gestured for the check. He walked them to the counter, and he saw Hope biting her lip. She didn't offer to pay her half of the bill. Not that he would let her, since he'd corralled her into eating with him. And it went against his principles for a woman to buy his lunch. His last foster mother had called him old-fashioned. Allie still did.

Matt took her hand and led her outside. He

walked her to her car. "Thanks for joining me."

Hope put on her sunglasses, shielding her eyes not only from the sun but from him. "Congratulations, Matt. Not everyone gets to fulfill their dreams. I'm glad you are."

She didn't give him a chance to respond before she slid behind the wheel. She had a habit of doing that, saying something meaningful and then shutting him out. He could still hear her thanking him. Thanking him for being kind. There was a lot of mystery surrounding Hope. He always loved a good mystery.

* * *

Hope finished folding her laundry. She'd found a bag of clothes someone had thrown away, and she'd been thrilled when some of the shirts and a pair of jeans fit. She tossed them in with her laundry. The clothes looked to have belonged to a teenage girl, so not everything fit. What didn't fit, she folded without washing, and she'd drop them off at the donation center at the local church before she left town.

She held up the sundress to her body. The pale-yellow dress with bright pink flowers was very feminine. She had tried it on. It was snug in the bust, but not overly so. The lone pair of jeans in the bag was a bit snug in the bottom, but they would stretch. Whoever the young woman was that tossed them had fewer curves than she did. But she was grateful she had found the bag lying on top of the dumpster. She hadn't even had to dig.

She'd stopped being surprised by what people threw away. She didn't take much with her, but over the past two years, she'd managed to salvage some dishes, water bottles, sunglasses, and even Trixie's dog bowls. The leash and collar she had bought were new and had cost her a pretty penny. But the toys Trixie played with, even the stuffed teddy bear she slept with, were dumpster finds.

She set the clothes into the worn suitcase and zipped it up, along with her toiletries. She might be essentially homeless, at least the home part, but she couldn't abide being dirty if she could help it. The dingy hotel room's bed beckoned, but she had already wasted a good part of her afternoon having lunch with Matt. Matt of the golden blond hair, a chest that she wanted to curl up against, and arms strong enough to hold the world at bay.

She tried to push thoughts of Matt away, but they persisted. She didn't want a man in her life. Technically she already had one; more if you counted her stepson and her father-in-law. Which she didn't.

She turned the keycard in at the front desk and carried her suitcase to her car. One of the wheels was broken off, so it was easier to carry it than drag it on one wheel. It had been new once. The suitcase had traveled with her to Paris, London, and Venice. The city she remembered pieces of was Venice. Something about the old city had appealed to her. If her funds ever allowed it, she wanted to go back to see if her vague memories were real or just imagination.

The car started up, something for which she gave thanks each time, and headed back to the library. She'd read the email, and she'd been so upset; she couldn't handle it anymore. Matt had proven to be a great distraction from her troubles. But ignoring her problems didn't solve anything.

She nodded at the librarian who was used to seeing her come and go. She'd transferred her funds to cover the taxes on her property. She now officially owned that useless piece of land. And she was determined to hold onto it. It would make finding Marlon harder. It made paying the attorney harder, but she was stubbornly refusing to sell the small parcel that was hers.

In her email, there were no new ones, just ones she was ignoring. The attorney's office sent her another bill. This time they threatened to drop her as a client if she didn't pay them. But that was hardly a threat at this point. There were plenty of other lawyers out there. And she would find a new one when she could afford one. But she would pay the attorney the money she owed him. It was pride and principles that demanded she pay every penny she owed. She just wished she didn't owe so much.

She searched her name and scanned through the sites she'd already visited. They didn't tell her much. Most of what she learned upset her, so she could only handle it in small chunks. She searched for Marlon

Turner, but there was nothing new to find. He could be anywhere, she supposed. Even Paris, London, or Venice. He had business dealings all over the globe. Maybe Shanghai. The last time she spoke to the private investigator, that's where Marlon had been booked to go.

Hope clicked on a video she'd bookmarked, downloaded it, and saved it to her files. The woman was five-four. Her hair was black and hung to her shoulders in a sleek bob. The fitted dress was designer. The hat she held in her hands came from a store on Rodeo Drive. The heels were so high it was a wonder the woman didn't topple over.

Hope shook her head and went to the next one. The man was maybe five-nine. In heels, the black-haired woman was almost the man's height. His suit was wool. Neither of them wore a coat. Even in winter in L.A., wearing a coat was a rare occurrence.

Hope spent the next couple of hours searching, but not finding anything new. She had footage of the trial. She already knew the outcome; the charges had been dropped. Marlon had walked away a free man. A woman was dead, and no one seemed to care. No one was being held accountable. Hope wasn't naïve. Sometimes justice was a myth.

The library was closing. She grabbed a couple of books, not that she was likely to read them, but it gave her an excuse to come back. The librarian bid her good night and locked up behind her.

Her last stop was to pick up a few food items.

Thankfully there was still some money left over after paying the taxes. She grabbed the essentials. First was a giant bag of dog food. Then a loaf of bread, some peanut butter, protein bars, cereal bars, and powdered milk. The powdered milk was nasty, but it wasn't as if she had a fridge. The condensed milk was worse. The last item was a bottle of multivitamins. The way she figured it, they filled in the nutritional gaps.

Her car started up. A testament to the fact that it had once been a very expensive car. Her next check, she would have to get the car the tune-up it so desperately needed. And Trixie was due for her vaccines. Rubbing her brow to ease the headache, she headed home.

Trixie greeted her the second she stepped out of the car. The large dog bounced around her as she unloaded the groceries and put them inside the tent. She spent the next half hour wrestling and playing with the dog.

Dinner was a quick affair. Trixie gobbled her kibble while Hope ate a banana she'd snagged at work yesterday. She'd eaten every bite of her lunch, and she wasn't hungry.

She tied the tent flaps open and lay down inside. Trixie came and lay next to her. She idly stroked the dog's fur. "I had lunch with Matt today. I know, I know, it was a bad idea. And of course, those women I told you about saw us. Tomorrow it's going to be all over the retreat that the new owner is consorting with Helpless Hope. You'd think after all these months, people would get more creative. I'm not helpless. Just challenged."

The dog made a grunting noise and snuggled closer.

Hope stared at the top of the tent, shadows of the trees moving across the dark green fabric. "I didn't learn anything today that I didn't already know. I did get a final email from the private investigator. His advice is to leave it alone. He thinks it's a waste of time chasing ghosts. I would like to add that I didn't pay him for his advice."

Hope closed her eyes, fatigue dragging at her. Tomorrow was another day. And maybe the investigator was right. Maybe she shouldn't be chasing ghosts. The more she learned, the more she wished she'd never started looking. She had wanted answers. But so far, she hadn't liked the ones she'd gotten. If she had any sense, she'd let it go. But her common sense seemed to have been lost, along with her memories.

Chapter Four

The two teenagers were cussing and making rude comments to every woman who had the displeasure of walking past them. Hope looked around but didn't see any of the security staff, Jeremy, or Matt. Their lewd comments were bad enough. But they'd gone past words.

Teenager One looked her up and down as Hope walked past. They weren't blocking the exit, but close enough. "She's a nice piece. Think she needs a good bangin'."

Teenager Two grabbed at her, yanking her arm when she tried to get past them. "Isn't much to her. Wouldn't last long. You'd have to do her fast."

Hope yanked her arm free. "You talk to your mother with that mouth?"

The two boys followed her outside. "I know what I'd like to do with yours. Or rather, what I want you to do with yours."

Teenager One grabbed his crotch while the second one got close enough to grab the pocket of her khakis. She heard the fabric tear as she yanked away. She was on the early shift today, and there weren't many people around. Normally that's how she preferred it, but today she'd give anything to have someone, anyone, around.

Teenager Two spun her and grabbed her breast. Instinct kicked in, and she kicked him where it would hurt the most.

Teenager One laughed and grabbed her from behind, his arms like steel bands around her. She thrashed, but he was much stronger than she was. He started dragging her toward the back of the building.

Teenager Two got to his feet. "Bitch kicked me in the balls."

"Better hope they still work. We're going to teach this one a lesson."

Desperately, she fought them. With all her strength, she twisted, then bit him until she tasted blood.

The kid hollered and dropped her.

Hope was fast on her feet, and she dashed for the main office in the distance. She could hear obscenities being shouted at her, but she didn't dare turn back. She had a stitch in her side from running so fast, and her leg muscles were beginning to burn as she neared the main office. She turned back and didn't see the boys anywhere. While still walking, she kept scanning the area, but they must have given up.

She turned just in time to see the flannel shirt before she ran into it. She looked up into Jeremy's face.

"Aren't you late for your shift? The animals can't take care of themselves, Ms. Whitfield."

Hope was out of breath, but she took a step back and nodded. She managed to get her words back.

"On my way."

Hope could feel his eyes on her. She desperately wanted to tell him what happened. But his eyes were hard as they dismissed her. Her stomach clenched, and she hurried off toward the barn. She could only hope those boys would be leaving soon and that they wouldn't harass any of the guests or other women on the staff. She certainly couldn't go to the police. She tried to stay as far away from them as possible.

She got through the first half of her day. But even the goats and horses couldn't relax her. Adrenaline was still surging in her system, and her hands were still shaking. Those boys had scared her. Bad. It had taken all her strength and concentration to dump the wheelbarrow. While Matt had been willing to take care of it for her, the other staff members were not.

A female voice chastised her. "Hope. God, could you be any slower? The horses. They need to be fed before we can take them out."

She dumped the load, rolled the bulky wheelbarrow down the ramp, and headed to the barn. Kathy Rhodes was one of the women who led guests up the mountain paths for a horseback tour. Hope glanced at her watch and winced. She should have fed them half an hour ago.

With an exasperated sigh, Kathy helped. Between the two of them, the horses were fed. The hands came and led the other horses out to pasture.

Mucking out the stalls was Hope's least favorite thing to do. She struggled with the pitchfork. But she did her job and got out of the barn as quickly as she could manage. Looking at her watch, she was already late for lunch, so she opted to skip it. She headed straight over to the chicken pens.

She liked the chickens, now that she was used to them. They were simple creatures. She had been leery at first, but now she loved watching them flock to her while they ate. But today she quickly spread the feed and went to collect the eggs. She filled the bucket more than she would normally. It was heavy, but all that was left was to carry them to the kitchen. A good amount of the food the retreat guests ate was fresh.

Hope was halfway to the kitchen when she saw the two boys driving by on a golf cart. They didn't notice her, but her hands trembled in a visceral response to seeing them. She heard someone call her name. When she turned her head, she tripped. In horror, she watched the bucket hit the ground, spilling and breaking most of the contents.

Kathy snickered behind her. "Now you've done it. And Matt's not around to save you. Everyone knows you're screwing him, but he's up at the mesa with a group. And trust me, there are plenty of women around here to take your place."

Kathy trotted off as Hope saw Jeremy heading her way. His hat was pulled down low over his forehead. His lips were in a stern line. His temper was in check, but just barely.

"That's it, Hope. I've given you a dozen chances.

Pick up your final check."

Hope knelt in the grass, her knees aching and broken egg yolks soaking into her pants. Somehow, she'd known the day would end like this.

* * *

Matt was exhausted but felt good. He'd led an experienced team of climbers out today. None of them were staying at the retreat, but he'd take anyone out who wanted to sign up and pay the fee.

He was coming around the bend on horseback when he saw two teenagers harassing one of the staff members. Cursing, he quickly rode over. The two boys saw him and hightailed it out of there. But he knew who they were. It was the same boys whom he had taken camping with their parents. Jeremy had a no-tolerance policy. Being annoying and disrespecting their parents and everyone around them was one thing. Assaulting staff was another. They'd be out by nightfall.

He didn't know the young woman, but she was kneeling in the grass and crying. Her long brunette ponytail partially hid her pale cheeks streaked with tears. "Are you okay? Did they hurt you?"

She turned big brown eyes up at him. She was maybe eighteen at most. "They were trying to assault me. Said I'd do since they couldn't have the woman they wanted."

The sleeve of her blouse was torn, and there was a

bruise already forming on her cheek. Her name tag read Jessica. "Come on, Jessica. We'll get you back up to the office, and we'll file a police report."

Jessica clung to him. "I saw them earlier. They've been threatening women on staff all day. This morning they assaulted someone else. The woman got away, and I thought maybe they were just messing around. They're just kids. But they're not messing around."

Matt knew Jeremy was up to his eyeballs in paperwork today and would be in his office. He called him out. "We need to call the police. Those two teenagers I told you about assaulted Jessica."

She turned shy eyes up to him. "Just Jessie."

Jeremy pulled out his cell phone. He gave the officer on the other line a brief description. "They'll send an officer out."

Matt helped her into a chair. "She said they were harassing someone else this morning too. We need to figure out who it was."

Jeremy squatted in front of her. "What did you see this morning?"

Her voice was shaking as she wiped tears from her cheeks. Matt grabbed the nearby tissue box off the desk.

"I was leaving the mess hall. I was on an early shift early this morning. I was covering; one of the girls is sick. I was coming out of the mess hall, and I saw them grabbing at a woman. They were too far away, so I don't know who it was. I was going to go get help, but then she got loose and ran from them. I don't know, I figured they were just messing with her, or something. Some of the younger men like to do that."

Matt stood off to the side. "Where did she run off to?"

Jessie sniffled into her tissue. "Here. The main office. Quite the run too."

Matt handed her another tissue. It was a bit of a distance between the mess hall and the main office. Most of the staff had access to golf carts, as did the guests.

Jeremy swore as he rose. "Hope."

"What about her?" Matt didn't like the sinking feeling in his stomach.

"I found her early this morning walking over. She was looking over her shoulder. Almost walked right into me. I told her she was late for her shift. She took off to the barn. Didn't say a word about being harassed."

Matt's stomach tightened. "We'll have to find her. The police are going to want to talk to her. She should be finishing up her shift about now."

Jeremy scrubbed his hand over his face. "I fired her about two hours ago."

Jessie shrugged. "No loss. She's nice and all, but Helpless Hope needed to go."

Jeremy glanced at Jessie. "Stay here. The police are on their way. I need to talk to Matt in private."

Matt closed the door behind them so Jessie

couldn't overhear.

Jeremy opened up the filing cabinet drawer. "I was mad and a lot frustrated. Allie is driving me batty. Keeping that woman from doing too much is going to be the death of me before this baby finally comes. The order for our new bull is delayed. Our equipment supplier brought the wrong shipment. I found Hope on her knees, an entire bucket of eggs broken all over the ground. I fired her and told her to go get her last paycheck."

Matt's hand fisted, but he understood why Jeremy fired her. "There's something wrong with her hands. You can see it. It's like they don't want to work."

Jeremy opened her personnel file. "I noticed, but there's no mention of any sort of disability or work limitations in her file. She was probably still jumpy from being assaulted by those two boys."

"Have an address?"

"Boarding house across town. Miss Lily rents out rooms, usually to people staying and working here over the summer. Not unusual for applicants to use her address. Let me call."

Ten minutes later, Jeremy hung up. "Hope hasn't been there in months. Miss Lily says a young woman named Hope had inquired about a room but didn't book one."

Matt took the paper. "Where else could she be staying?"

"Our retreat is one of the only places to stay around here. There are some apartments a town over where she could be staying. There's a dumpy hotel on the outskirts too, but it's the type of establishment that rents by the hour. No place for a young woman, at least not Hope's kind."

Matt set the paper down. "Maybe the cops can find her. They'll want her statement."

But hours later, the cops hadn't found Hope. Nor had they found the boys. It was getting dark, and the boys' mother was frantic. Further inquiries by the police said she was their stepmother. The father was no help. He didn't care two licks for those boys. Matt tamped down his anger.

Jeremy had gotten Jessie a ride home with a couple of the waitresses and told her to take tomorrow off. "I need to get back up to the house. Allie will be worried."

Matt waved and headed to his trailer. He'd made a few phone calls, but he hadn't had any more luck finding Hope than the police. The officer did say that the hotel had Hope's signature on the register. According to the attendant, she rents a room for a few hours every two weeks like clockwork. As far as the man could tell, she came alone. But the police weren't going to spend a lot of resources looking for Hope. They had Jessie's statement, and they would arrest the two boys if they found them.

Matt wasn't holding out hope. In a place like this, people came and went. Likely those boys and their parents were already halfway home. Local police wouldn't, nor could they, chase them. It made Matt sick that they'd get away with it.

Matt thought of going up and visiting with Allie and Jeremy but opted against it. It hadn't gotten past Jeremy's notice that he was attracted to Hope. And it bothered him that Hope had been assaulted by those two young men, ones he should have tossed out days ago, and hadn't said a word.

* * *

Hope was in town the next day. She needed a job. And fast. She didn't have a phone, so the internet at the library was the best she could do. It was hard finding a job without an address and no phone number where one could be reached. But she filled out applications online and crossed her fingers. Unfortunately, Waters Ranch was the biggest employer in the area. She already knew she couldn't be a waitress, even if the restaurant was hiring. She couldn't manage the oversized trays.

Hope wanted to cry but forced back the tears. She'd already cried all over Trixie. She'd lost her job, easy access to water, and two free meals. No matter who hired her, she would have to drive longer distances to get there. She kept telling herself she'd survived worse, but it was hard to remember. She let out a silent laugh. The irony of that statement wasn't lost on her.

The library was closing when she left. She was opening her car door when someone called her name.

A petite brunette was waving at her. Unsure, and not caring what she wanted, Hope opened her car door. The woman shouted her name again.

"Hope. I'm glad I found you. The police are looking for you."

Hope thought the girl's name was Jenny or something like that. Bile rose in her throat. "Why are the police looking for me?"

"Those two boys at the ranch. They attacked you, didn't they?"

Hope was confused. "How do you know about that?"

The girl wiped at fresh tears. "Matt found them attacking me. He called the police. I told them I'd seen them harassing someone else, and Jeremy said it was you."

Hope was starting to understand. "So Mr. Waters told the police I was the girl they were harassing?"

"Yeah, he said it had to be you. He'd seen you at the main office that morning around the same time I saw a woman running from those boys."

Hope wanted to cry but figured the young woman was crying enough for both of them. "Tell them they're mistaken."

The girl took her arm when Hope turned her back on her. "You need to tell the police what happened. And the boys are missing."

Hope leaned against the open car door. "Missing?"

She nodded. "Their father was at the police station this morning when I was there signing my statement.

His wife went out looking for them. She thinks they're up in the canyon hiding from the cops. Jeremy and Matt are organizing a rescue. But the old trails they think the boys took are only accessible by horseback. The mom has been missing since last night, and the dad went to the police this morning. I heard their baby sister went missing too. She's only ten. Matt and Jeremy think she might have tried to find her mom. Jeremy is looking for anyone who can ride to help in the search. There's a big storm coming. Rare this time of year, but it's being forecast as a big one."

Hope's stomach was sick at the thought of a ten-year-old girl lost in the canyons. She couldn't find any sympathy for the two boys, who were hiding from the police. But if the mom was gone and the girl was missing, that was four people Search and Rescue were looking for.

"Thanks for telling me."

The girl tried for a smile through her tears. "Jessie. My name is Jessie. Please, tell the police what happened. When they're found, I want them arrested. Between the two of us, they can't deny it happened."

They could, but Hope didn't bother to tell her that. With enough charm, you could get away with murder.

* * *

It was already getting dark. Matt looked at the small group. Jeremy couldn't leave Allie. Not that he would. Not all of the staff who could ride were willing to go off in search of the missing family. Matt agreed. Knowing how to ride and being able to traverse the terrain were not the same thing.

Jeremy held his wife's hand as he finished helping map out the area. "We're not going to be able to ride out tonight."

Matt disagreed. "We can head up to the line shack, shelter there, and get an early start. We need to beat the weather. If the storm is as bad as it's predicted, we'll need every minute to find them and get back to stay ahead of it."

Jeremy didn't like it, but he stayed quiet. "You've got the training. I don't. But don't do anything stupid. There's only seven of you."

A soft voice came from the back of the crowd. "Eight."

Matt knew that voice. "Hope?"

She had a pack over her shoulder. "I can ride. And I can camp. I can help find her."

Jeremy looked more than skeptical. "We don't need a hindrance."

She straightened her shoulders and looked him in the eye. "I can ride. I'm going."

Matt felt his lips curl. "She can ride with me. We'll pair off and head up the trail before it gets too dark."

Hope hitched her backpack higher. "I just need one thing."

Allie leaned into her husband, her face as skeptical as his. "What?"

Hope glanced back at her car. "I need someone to watch my dog."

Jessie stepped forward. "I can watch your dog."

Hope turned and went to her car.  A huge dog jumped out of the back.

Jeremy swore. "That's not a dog.  That's a horse."

Jessie turned white as a sheet. "I, uh, don't know."

Hope turned to Allie. "Trixie's a good girl.  I've got her food, her bed, and her toys.  She just needs a place to sleep and someone to feed her."

Jeremy relented. "We'll take her.  You guys go."

Hope squatted down in front of her dog, talking softly. "Be a good girl for me.  I promise I'll be back."

Jeremy took the leash from her while Hope kissed the top of the dog's head.

Hope turned back to Matt.  "I'm ready when you are."

*  *  *

Hope's butt was sore when they finally stopped. They made it to the shelter shortly after sunset.  She was alone with seven men, but since one of them was Matt, she wasn't as nervous as she thought she would be.

One man went about starting a fire.  The others took care of their horses.  Hope was trying to unfasten the saddle when Matt came over. "I got it. Why don't you grab the feed bags and set them up?"

Hope released the saddle, grateful he took over.

The horses had been saddled by the time they'd gotten to the barn, so she hadn't had to worry about it. She murmured to them while she tied up the bags. The horses were hobbled and started eating as soon as she hung them. The shelter was designed to shelter horses and humans.

She was the last to grab her sleeping bag. She glanced at Matt, who gestured to the spot next to him. She shook out her tarp and rolled her bag out.

Matt relaxed. "Ladies' room will be on the right. Men's room on the left."

One of the men smiled at her. "I can't get my wife to camp with me."

She gave him a half-smile back but didn't encourage any further conversation. She got up, stepped over Matt's legs, and sought some privacy. She washed up a little and brushed her teeth. She didn't want to sleep in her jeans, so she swapped them for the sweatpants she'd packed. Keeping her bra on, she changed the dusty flannel for a t-shirt.

Conversation had lulled by the time she came back. She stepped over Matt again and climbed into her sleeping bag. Used to sleeping outside, though certainly not around so many people, it didn't take long for her to fall asleep.

Chapter Five

Morning came too soon.  The sun wasn't fully up yet as Matt passed around the maps Jeremy had given them.  He assigned each of them a quadrant.  They had satellite phones so they could stay in communication.  They ate a quick breakfast, saddled up the horses, and broke up into pairs.  Matt led him and Hope further north.

Matt was looking for signs that anyone, or even anything, had passed through this area.  This area was flat, but soon they'd be following rock trails higher into the lower mountain range.  Hope's eyes were scanning the distance, the same as his.  She had binoculars she was using, but there was not a sign that anyone had been this way in a while.

Matt was impressed with how well Hope rode. He'd caught her massaging her backside this morning, but who among them wasn't?  It had been a while since he had spent this much time in a saddle.

Matt halted his horse, took a drink from the canteen, and held it to her.  She took a swallow and handed it back. "Doing okay?"

Hope dug into her saddlebag and pulled out a tube of lip balm. "I forget how dry it can be here."

It wasn't an answer, but he let it go. When she held her lip balm out to him, he took it.  "The benefits of traveling with a woman."

She smiled at him and tucked it into her pocket when he handed it back. "Never leave home without it."

Matt nudged the horse, and they continued north. "So Trixie, huh?"

Hope glanced at him, remembering her comment about his car. "Fits her, don't you think?"

Matt laughed. "It does. That dog is bigger than you are. She has to outweigh you by a good thirty pounds or more. I think Jessie almost fainted when she jumped out of the back of your car. Where'd you get her? She's a fine-looking dog."

Hope brought her horse even with his. "I found her. Someone had dumped her. I had about the same reaction as Jessie the first time I saw her, but she's just a big baby. She'd never hurt a fly. Took some training, though. You're right, she outweighs me by a good thirty pounds. She was never house-trained, no training of any kind. But she took to me, and I fell in love with her."

He had seen the way Hope had baby-talked and kissed the dog as she'd left her with Allie and Jeremy. "She's in good hands."

She looked at him from the corner of her eye. "I know. And so am I."

He looked at her, but she wasn't looking at him anymore. Her eyes were back on the landscape.

They rode in silence for a while, only the chatter on the phones interrupted from time to time.

Hope halted her horse. "I need a minute."

Matt dismounted. Hope had her hands on the reins, but she didn't move.

Hope stretched her hands, then she let out a frustrated groan. "I need help getting down."

Matt helped her balance as she dismounted. Her hands slipped off the pommel of the saddle, but he had a good grip on her and eased her down.

Hope stripped off her gloves as she thanked him. "Sometimes my hands don't always want to work."

Matt took one of her hands in his. They were half the size of his, delicate and smooth. "What happened?"

Hope frowned and pulled her hand from his. "Nothing. They just don't always work."

Matt knew there was more to her story, but he didn't press. He gave her privacy and found a spot of his own. They met back up at the horses. They walked them for a time.

Hope eventually tugged her gloves back on and mounted on her own. "Doesn't seem like anyone has been up this way in a long time. I'm scared for that little girl, Matt."

Matt was trying not to think about it. He had spent a few days with the family. The youngest child was ten; she had curls not so different from Hope's and had bright green eyes. She smiled a lot and liked to tell stories. Her older brothers clearly didn't like her, and she stayed out of their way. She'd even sat next to Matt and told him all about her favorite teacher, her orange tabby cat at home, and how this was the best place she'd ever been.

The other problem was he'd been a medic. He'd been in war-torn countries. He'd seen the mangled bodies of children. He prayed that they didn't find the little girl's body, but the child whole and alive.

They split off and looped around, but neither found any trace. When they met back up, Matt's frustration was palpable. "They're not here. No one has been up this way. I think we need to go east. There is no way a child could climb the rocks to the west of us."

Hope pulled out her copy of the map. She pointed to the eastern section of the map. "There is water here, likely some trees. It seems like as good a spot as any to try to make camp."

Matt leaned over to look where her finger was pointing. "Us or them?"

Hope tried to ease the pressure off her backside. "Either. Were any of the Edgertons experienced campers?"

Matt bumped his heels on the horse, and they turned east. "Some. Not survival stuff like this. But they would have a better shot than some."

They were getting ready to stop for the night when Jeremy's voice came over the radio. "I've got some good news and some bad. The mother made her way back down the canyon. The little girl is still missing, and the two boys haven't been spotted. Mrs. Edgerton says the little girl, Meggie, likes water.

They had taken the hiking path closest to you two. Head east and north, and you'll find the river. I pray you have better luck tomorrow."

Matt looked up at the darkening sky. Another night didn't bode well for the little girl. "How is Allie?"

"Worried. But otherwise okay. She's getting restless, though. I think the baby is closer than we're ready for."

Hope waited, but Jeremy didn't say anything else. She looked at Matt.

Matt got the message. "How's Trixie holding up?"

Jeremy paused for a second. "She's plastered against Allie. Mighty friendly dog. Probably didn't help that Allie fed her some of her dinner. I'll have the phone by me all night."

Matt tucked the phone back in the saddlebag. Hope's eyes were scanning the area.

Hope pulled a knit cap out of her backpack and pulled it over her head. It was getting chilly. "It doesn't feel right to stop looking."

"No. It doesn't. We'll keep going a bit further until we have to stop for the safety of the horses."

An hour later, they came up to the river. Though Matt thought it a little optimistic to call it a river. They crossed it on the horses and then stopped to walk them. He could tell Hope was getting tired, but she didn't say a word. She just kept on.

Matt grasped her arm. "We need to stop for the night."

Hope nodded but didn't say anything. They traveled a little further until they found a space near a rock outcropping. It would help to buffer the wind.

They set up camp. They didn't talk much, simply ate their meal. Matt watched as Hope climbed into her sleeping bag in her clothes. Her eyes closed as soon as she was covered.

Matt put out the fire and lay down.

* * *

Hope woke. She wasn't sure what had woken her, other than a full bladder. The sounds of the night creatures didn't bother her, though she would much rather be inside her tent than out in the open. She rolled and saw that Matt was sound asleep.

Careful not to make any noise, Hope unzipped her bag and slipped out. She shivered, but it wasn't as cold as it had been in previous months. But it was cold, too cold, for a little girl. Hope made her way around the rocks to find some privacy. Her eyes scanned the rocks around her. An owl was in the tree above, looking down at her.

When she was finished, she kept walking to stretch her legs, careful not to go too far. Her legs ached. Her back ached. And her backside ached. She knew she could ride a horse. She just couldn't remember how long it had been. Her sore bottom told her it had been a while.

The owl flew down and caught an unsuspecting

critter. Hope heard the creature screech. Then she heard something else screech. Hope's heart began racing as she tried to listen for the sound again. It was faint, but she swore she heard crying. Hope cursed, realizing she didn't have her flashlight. The moon was full, but the scattering of trees cut off the light.

Hope heard the sound again and knew it wasn't wishful thinking. "Meggie. Meggie, honey. Where are you?"

"Momma?"

The sound was faint, but Hope was able to pinpoint where it came from. She scrambled through some brush. "Meggie? Talk to me, sweetie."

The crying began in earnest. Hope looked around, but she didn't see the girl. She came around a cliffside and looked up when small rocks fell onto her shoulders. The girl was halfway up the side of the cliff. The outcropping wasn't much bigger than she was. There was no way Hope was getting her down on her own.

"Hi, Meggie. My name is Hope. My friend Matt and I are looking for you. Your mommy sent us. But I'm going to need help to get you down."

The girl was sobbing now, and it broke Hope's heart. She needed Matt but was afraid to leave her. Hope talked softly to her, trying to calm her. When the girl's tears started to subside, Hope looked back toward camp.

"Meggie, I need to get my friend Matt. He's a

really good climber, and he can get you down. But I need to go get him. I need you to be brave and sit completely still until I get back. Can you do that?"

The girl began crying again. "I don't want to be by myself."

Hope took a few steps back and pointed. "I'm just going right over there. Okay? I won't be gone long. I promise."

The girl tucked her head to her knees. Hope, knowing she had no choice, started heading back to camp. She stuck sticks into the ground so that there was no way she was going to lose her way back.

Hope wanted to shout for Matt but was afraid she'd scare Meggie. The girl was in a precarious spot. Once she spotted the horses in the dark, she sprinted to Matt.

She knelt and shook him. "Matt. I found her."

Matt rolled onto his back. "What?"

Hope was breathing hard, and her words were broken. "Meggie. I found her. Grab your stuff."

Matt kicked his way out of his sleeping bag. He grabbed his gear and followed.

Hope picked her way through some bushes. "Meggie. I'm back. My friend Matt is here. He's going to get you down."

Matt cursed as he looked up. "How in the world did she get up there?"

Since he didn't seem to be looking for an answer, she stood next to him as he pulled some rope out of his backpack. He then pulled off his boots and put on climbing shoes.

Hope stood helplessly as Matt started talking to Meggie, much like she had.  Meggie was crying and got to her knees.  Now that rescue was a few feet away, Meggie was no longer listening.  Hope tried to calm her while Matt focused on getting to her.  She grabbed the flashlight and tried to light up the rock so he could see.  She let out a sigh of relief when Matt reached her.

Matt held the girl to his side.  "The easiest way to get you down will be to lower you with this rope.  See, I'm going to make it into a harness, and then I can lower you to Hope."

The girl nodded and let Matt adjust the rope.  Hope could tell it was difficult from his position to get enough leverage to lower her over the edge.  Matt somehow maneuvered her so that she was between his knees and could start to lower her down.  Hope was sure to keep the flashlight out of Matt's eyes as he started to turn Meggie around.

The owl that had been watching them screeched again.  Hope watched in horror as Meggie screamed.  She jerked in Matt's arms and started going over the edge.  Matt managed to get a grip on her, but the loose rocks they were sitting on shifted when Meggie threw her arms around Matt's neck.  The pair started to slide down the rocks.  Matt shifted until he was on his back.  Hope screamed as the pair tumbled off the ledge.

Hope threw herself toward the cliff wall, some

vague idea of helping to break their fall. The impact of Matt hitting her square in the chest knocked all the breath out of her. Her back hit the ground as Matt and Meggie landed.

Meggie was sobbing. Hope's head hurt from where she had hit it on the ground. Her ribs hurt from the impact of Matt landing on her. He had somehow bounced off her and was lying on his side.

She was dizzy but made herself crawl around. Matt's eyes were closed. Hope grabbed Meggie to her, holding the girl as she shook from the terror of the fall. Hope looked Meggie over. She had some scratches on her face and hands. Her clothes had tears in them. But thankfully, she otherwise looked okay.

Hope brushed her hair back and wiped the tears. "Are you okay? Do you hurt anywhere?"

The girl was watching Matt, who hadn't moved. "We fell."

Hope got to her feet, not feeling too steady. Her heart was racing, and she found it difficult to take a deep breath. "Yes, you did. But you're okay."

Hope grabbed Matt's pack and fumbled for the phone. She punched in the code.

"Waters here."

Hope could have wept. "Jeremy. I found Meggie. She's banged up, but she's okay. But Matt's hurt; he's not moving. I don't know what to do."

Allie's voice could be heard over the line, but Hope tuned her out.

Jeremy's voice came back over the line. "Where are you?"

"We went east to the river like you said. We rode another couple of hours from there. I'm not sure how far north we are. Meggie was up on a cliff. Matt went up to get her, but then they fell."

"Is your camp by the river?"

Hope nodded and then realized she hadn't actually spoken. "Yes. We camped alongside it behind a large pile of boulders and an overhang. The horses are grazing there."

Meggie took a step toward her and then cried out. Hope dropped the phone. "Meggie, what's wrong?"

"My arm hurts."

Hope could hear Jeremy. She shouted back at him. "I need a minute."

Allie's voice came over the line. "Is Matt moving?"

Hope silently cursed her uncooperative hands as she carefully removed Meggie's jacket. Hope turned to face the phone. "Meggie's arm is broken. Matt isn't moving. I don't know what to do."

Allie's voice was calm as she walked her through what to do. Meggie was barely conscious by the time Hope got Meggie's arm stabilized. The branches and Hope's socks might not be pretty, but her arm wasn't going to bend tied up the way it was.

Allie had already told Hope to cover Matt with the survival blanket. She had tucked it around him as best she could to keep him warm. Allie warned her that he might go into shock.

Hope was quietly crying as she checked Matt over, relaying to Allie what she could see.  She didn't feel anything broken, but something was wrong with his arm.  It hung limply at his side.

Allie's voice was still calm on the line.  "He might have dislocated his shoulder in the fall."

Meggie was quiet as she leaned up against the cliff.  Her huge green eyes watched her as she looked over Matt.  Hope concentrated on what Allie was telling her.  It was dark and hard to see, but she managed to cut the shirt off his shoulder despite her shaking hands.

"Um, I think it's dislocated."

Allie's voice was odd as it came over the line.  "Okay.  You're going to need to get the shoulder back in the socket.  You have to be very careful and listen to exactly what I tell you."

Hope listened to the instructions.  She heard Allie groan over the line.  "Allie, are you okay?"

Jeremy came on the line.  "She's in labor.  She's also refusing to budge.  Let's get this done."

Allie slowly walked her through the steps.  Hope was crying and shaking, but she somehow managed to get the shoulder back in.  When she leaned back, Matt's eyes were open.

Hope bent over him.  "Matt?  Can you hear me?"

Matt groaned.  He tried to move, but Hope pressed her arms on his chest.  "Don't move.  You fell."

Matt stayed still.  "Meggie?"

Hope pointed to where Meggie was sitting.  "She

broke her arm in the fall.  But otherwise, she's okay. She's going to be fine.  I need to get her back to camp and get her some food and water."

Matt groaned again and closed his eyes.  "Go.  I'll be fine."

Hope wiped at fresh tears.  "I can't leave you here."

Allie's voice came over the line.  "Meggie is in shock, Hope.  You need to get her to camp.  Get a fire going.  Jeremy has men ready to set out at first light to walk up the river."

Jeremy's voice came back.  "Matt, how do you feel?"

Matt's hand shook and couldn't hold the phone when he tried to take it from Hope. "Concussion.  My shoulder hurts, but I don't think it's broken.  I've got some deep cuts on my back; I can feel blood seeping."

Allie calmly told Hope what to do, but advised her not to move Matt yet.

Jeremy's voice came back.  "I'm passing the phone off to Mike.  Our baby has decided he wants out."

Matt moaned softly, but Hope could see him smile. "She always did have terrible timing.  I can help Hope. Just get someone up here on the double."

The radio went silent.  Hope sat on her knees beside Matt.

Matt took her hand.  "Get Meggie to camp.  Get her to drink some water.  But slowly.  If the water stays down, try to get her to eat.  There is some ibuprofen in the medical kit.  That will help with the ache in her arm."

Hope wiped more tears from her cheeks. She gathered Meggie and headed back to camp. She made sure every stick was still firmly in the ground.

Hope was able to get Meggie to drink some water and swallow the pills. She didn't eat much, but Hope wasn't surprised.

Meggie sniffled as she rested on Hope's sleeping bag. "We can't leave him there, can we?"

Hope couldn't remember ever feeling this helpless. The sky was dark, and clouds were starting to roll in. The storm wasn't going to hold out for long. She shook her head at Meggie. "No, we can't leave him there. The horses will be okay. When the sun starts to come up, we'll start heading down the river. We'll meet the men coming for us. But for now, let's go back to Matt."

Hope rolled up her sleeping bag and the tarp, then grabbed Matt's saddlebag. There were first aid supplies inside. He would need the ibuprofen as much as Meggie did. There weren't many pills in there, so Hope ignored the pain in her ribs from when Matt had landed on her.

She wrapped her jacket around Meggie and led them back to Matt. She let out a sigh of relief when he opened his eyes as they approached. He didn't say anything, and she was grateful. She laid out the tarp and rolled the sleeping bag out for Meggie. Without a word, the girl climbed inside with Hope's help. Hope turned to Matt and dropped the bag. "I'll be right back."

By the time she got back to Matt and Meggie, she was exhausted. She rolled out her spare tarp and laid Matt's bedroll out. She grabbed his pack. "Do you think you can roll over?"

Matt started to nod, then groaned. "I can wriggle my toes and arms. My shoulder and head hurt the worst. Help me sit up. We'll go slow."

Hope had to get behind him and push. She wasn't strong enough to pull him up, but he was able to use her as leverage to sit. He was breathing heavily, and she knew he was in pain. Figuring his shirt was already ruined, she grabbed the knife and cut the rest of his shirt away. Her eyes stung at the deep cuts on his back.

Matt pointed to the canteen. "Use the shirt to wash the cuts. There's antiseptic in the first-aid kit."

Hope followed instructions as best she could. Once she was satisfied that the wounds were clean, she smeared the antiseptic on the cuts. She then dug into his bag for a fresh shirt. She managed to get it on him but couldn't get his injured arm into the sleeve.

Matt slumped and struggled to stay upright. "Just leave the arm inside the shirt. It's not my dominant."

Hope helped him get into his bedroll. "You dislocated it in the fall."

Matt's eyes held hers. "You did a damn fine job. You'd make a great medic."

That made her smile. She took a strip of his shirt she'd cut up and washed the cut on his forehead and in his hair. She smeared antiseptic as best she could.

"This would be easier if you had shorter hair."

Matt reached out a hand and touched the ends of one of her curls.  His voice was faint, and his eyes started to close.  "So soft."

Matt's hand fell to his side, and she hoped he'd fallen asleep and not passed out.  Hope got to her feet and winced.  Her ribs were throbbing, and she felt close to collapse.  She checked on Meggie.  She roused the girl long enough to take a few more sips of water and a couple more bites of a protein bar.

She looked between the two.  She took the survival blanket and folded it in half.  She laid it down between Matt and Meggie and was within arm's distance of both should either of them need her.  She climbed between the layers and reached out so she could hold Matt's wrist.  She set the alarm on her watch to wake her.

Chapter Six

Matt woke to his shoulder throbbing in time with his head. He could smell rain. The storm was not far off. His internal clock told him it was close to five. The sun was just starting to peek over the horizon.

He glanced down and saw Hope's hand holding his wrist. Her face was pale. Too pale. But she was going to need to get Meggie out of the canyon. His world was spinning, and there was no way he was going to be able to walk them out of here.

The beep of Hope's watch was loud in the quiet of the morning. Her fingers tightened on his wrist. He could see her wince when she tried to sit up. Her turquoise eyes landed on his. His voice was rough. "Where are you hurt?"

Hope eased into a sitting position. "Just sore. Rain is coming."

Matt kept his eyes on hers. "Yes. You need to take the horses and get you and Meggie out of here. I don't think the men are going to beat the storm."

Hope got to her feet. "I don't know what to do. I can't leave you here."

Matt's eyes hardened. "You damn well are going to leave me here. I'll get myself back to our camp. The overhang will keep me dry and warm enough until I can walk myself out of here."

Hope started to argue, then her shoulders drooped. "Okay."

Matt watched as Hope gently woke Meggie, who began to cry. Hope held the girl, crooning soft words to her as she got her to drink some water and take a couple more pills. As the sun was coming up, he saw the splint on Meggie's arm. He vaguely remembered Hope telling him that Meggie had broken her arm.

Matt's head hurt something fierce, and every time he turned his head, he was dizzy. But everything was working; he didn't seem to have any cognitive issues, so he was sure he didn't have a brain bleed or any other major trauma. At this point, even if he did, there wasn't much he could do. Hope needed to get the girl back to her mother, and he wasn't going to hold them back.

Hope kept glancing back at him. He wanted to sleep but was worried Hope might choose to stay if he did. Rain was coming. And it was coming soon.

Hope got Meggie to her feet and got her bedding and supplies wrapped up. "The canteen is full. The food is at the top of your bag, so you won't have to rummage for it. The survival blanket is next to you. If it starts to rain, it should keep you dry."

Matt waved her off. "Go. Just follow the river downhill."

Hope shook her head. "You'll need the horse. Meggie and I can ride double. She's not going to be able to ride down on her own."

Since it was the smartest thing, he let Hope bring

the horses back. She fed them and sheltered Matt's horse as best she could. He was relieved when the pair finally mounted up.

"I've made a marker where we camped. The rescue team should be able to find it if you can't make it down on your own."

Matt stopped her when she started to turn the horse. "Hope. Be careful. Just follow the river."

She nodded and spurred the horse.

Matt closed his eyes. He prayed they made it down the canyon safely. The sky was leaden, and the promised storm was coming. He was under the trees, but he doubted they'd keep much water at bay. The tarp and survival blanket would help, but the water would run downhill and likely flood him out. Or at a minimum, would soak him through. He wrapped himself up. He needed to sleep. And then he'd get himself out of the canyon, one way or the other.

* * *

Meggie was quiet and leaning against her chest as they rode. Hope didn't dare go any faster. She followed the river and kept the horse on soft ground where she could. It had started to rain, thunder rumbled in the distance, and Hope wrapped them in the tarp. The last thing she wanted was for Meggie to catch a chill.

They had been riding almost half the day when she came upon a mud and rockslide. The pile was blocking the water, and the river was starting to fill as they got closer. The rain was falling steadily, and the river would only get deeper.

"How are we going to get through that?" Meggie's eyes were once again filled with tears.

Hope didn't know. The water was muddy, and she wasn't sure how deep it was.

"Hello?" A male voice came from the other side.

Hope shouted back. "It's Hope and Meggie. Meggie needs help."

"Wait there."

Hope wanted to cry back that it wasn't like she could go anywhere, but refrained. She could hear two distinct voices. It took some time, but one of the men reached the top of the rockslide. She knew how dangerous it was for him to have climbed it, but it was that or risk the water.

"Let's get the girl first. Get her into the harness. We'll pull her up. Dennis is below watching the pile to make sure it isn't about to give way."

It took longer than it should have, but Hope got Meggie secured in the harness. She then wrapped her up in the tarp. It would make it easier to slide her body over the pile. Meggie kept her eyes on Hope until the dark-haired man got a hold of her and slid her down the other side.

"Now you."

Hope knew she was more than double Meggie's weight, and rocks were already sliding as the steady rain became a downpour. "I'm going back to Matt.

He's hurt badly, but we have supplies. When the rain stops, we're about a four-and-a-half-hour ride straight up the river. I've got wooden markers tied to a tree."

The man took her measure and nodded. "All right. We'll get Meggie back to her mamma. Keep Matt and you as dry as you can. You have the phone. The battery should last a couple of days if you shut it off and only call if you have an emergency. We'll find an alternate route around on our way back to you."

"Do you have extra first-aid supplies?"

The man shouted to the man below. It took a few more minutes, but he was able to toss her a fresh kit, and she managed not to drop it when she caught it against her chest and not her hands. She thanked him and tucked it into the saddlebag.

The man eased his way back down the rock pile. She watched as the top of the pile slid further. Her body shook. She didn't want to think of being buried under those rocks if they gave way. She'd rather brave the storm than be buried alive and suffocate to death. With hands and legs that were not getting any steadier, she managed to remount. She shivered as the rain soaked her through to her skin. Without the tarp, it hadn't taken long. Her backpack was waterproof. Her best bet was to get back to Matt on the double, get a fire going under the overhang, and then change.

Thunder rolled over the land, and she watched as lightning struck closer than she liked. The horse was nervous but wasn't balking.  Hope prayed the horse stayed on course and underneath her.  The last thing she needed was a runaway horse.  But the mare remained calm.  A couple of hours into the return trip, Hope had to stop and rest the horse, and she shivered in her wet clothes.  Her ribs were throbbing. She looked into the saddlebag for the first-aid kit. She could have wept when she found at least thirty tablets.  She grabbed a couple and swallowed them with mouthfuls of water from her canteen.  She found a clean spot and refilled it.  The water was running rough as the storm continued and the rain ran from the higher elevations.  As the ground turned to mud, she climbed back on the mare.

It was slow going the rest of the afternoon.  Her attention was divided between keeping herself and the mare upright and keeping her eyes on the lightning strikes.  Every time the sky lit up, she was glad to see it in the distance.  She was also glad the ache in her ribs eased some, as did the headache.  She had a knot on the back of her head where her head struck the ground, but she hadn't broken skin, and she hadn't passed out the way Matt had.

It was another hour before she was at the spot where she and Meggie had crossed the river.  Earlier she had been able to see the bottom, but now the muddy water was higher.  She saw reeds that were still above the water a few yards up. Knowing she had to get across, this was her best option.

The mare was strong, but the speed of the water

was too much for Hope; she'd only gotten a few steps before the water was up to her knees and threatened to knock her over. She had wanted to lead the horse across, but she wasn't going to be able to walk it on her own. Cursing the weather and the two boys who were the root of all this, she mounted. The horse stubbornly ignored the kick of her heels. She pulled up on the reins and kicked a little harder. The horse obeyed. When they were safely across, Hope let out the breath she'd been holding. The horse had wobbled in a few places, but she'd managed.

Hope dismounted and had to sit to ease the trembling in her limbs. She watched, shaking her head, as the mare went back to grazing. She ate the protein bar in her pocket and drank some more water. She hated giving into fear. But with the rain pouring down, lightning striking closer and closer, fear for Matt overrode fear for herself.

It was dark when she made it back to where they had camped. She had long since stopped shivering, and her hands weren't cooperating at all. She had to get warmed up before she got to Matt. She prayed he wasn't soaked through the way she was.

"What the hell are you doing back here?" Matt's voice came from the darkened overhang. She squinted against the light of the LED lantern when he flicked it on.

She was afraid her teeth would chatter if she spoke. She simply shook her head. The other horse was under the overhang, nickering at the mare. Her mare turned and walked over. Legs numb, Hope swung her left leg over the saddle. She started to ease down, but her hands slipped, and she landed in a heap on the ground. She cried out when she hit, her ribs jarring as her knees hit the dirt.

Matt was cursing from the overhang. He started to toss the survival blanket to the side.

Hope rolled to her knees. "Don't you dare get out of that bed. I can take care of myself."

"Somehow I doubt it, sweetheart."

Hope ignored him. She managed to get to her feet, untie her bag, get out the first aid kit, and untie her sleeping bag from under the waterproof cover. She needed to get warm. Fast. It would be a tight squeeze under the overhang, with two adults and two horses, but she was grateful.

"You need to get those clothes off." Matt pulled the survival blanket off and managed to lay his sleeping bag flat.

Hope tossed her things to Matt to keep them dry.

Matt unrolled her sleeping bag and unzipped it. He spread it out so that they would be sharing the two bags. "Take them off, Hope."

Her fingers were shaking as she tried to unfasten the stubborn buttons of her flannel. She had a hard time with them when they were dry, and she wasn't exhausted. Frustrated, she yanked the fabric off and over her head. She glanced at Matt, who was kindly closing his eyes. She fumbled with the button and zipper of her jeans and wanted to cry when they proved just as difficult to remove. She let out the frustrated breath she had been holding as she managed to strip them off. She pulled off her clammy bra and underwear.

She climbed under the blanket, her skin chilled, her hair soaking wet, and she began shaking in earnest.

Matt flipped the survival blanket back over the top of the sleeping bag. He pulled her half-frozen body to him. "You're like ice."

Hope didn't think the statement needed a response. She curled up under the blanket, trying to keep what little heat she had in. She heard Matt curse and pulled her even closer to him.

"I can't get this damn shirt off. Bare skin would be better, but this will have to do."

Bare or not, his body was a lot warmer than hers. She didn't protest when he pulled her chilled fingers into his armpits as he pulled her higher up against his chest. His good arm briskly rubbed her back, trying to warm her up.

"Did you get Meggie to safety?" Matt's voice rumbled under her ear.

"Rockslide. Got her over. Taking her back to her mom."

"And why are you here, Hope? You should've gone back."

"Rocks. Couldn't breathe. I couldn't leave you here."

"Couldn't breathe?"

Hope felt tears leaking from the corners of her eyes. She started to pull her hands away, but he held her in place.

"A few tears won't hurt, Hope. You'll feel better."

Hope didn't want to cry. But she had been so scared: scared the storm would keep her from getting back to Matt, scared she'd be hit by lightning, scared the water would sweep her and the mare away, and scared she'd succumb to hypothermia. She gave herself permission to indulge in a few tears.

Hope held Matt until her shivering subsided and her tears were spent. She smiled against his chest when she realized he was crooning to her very much like she had done to Meggie. It felt good to be held, to be cared for. She laid her cheek on his chest and dozed off.

She wasn't sure how long she'd lain there and slept when she felt Matt shifting beneath her.

"Let's get a shirt on you, at least."

Hope stared at her pack but was too tired to move. She felt Matt's hands on her bare back as he draped fabric over her.

"Sit up, get your arms in the sleeves, and I'll button it. It will help keep you warm tonight."

Hope slid off his chest and sat up. She fumbled to get her arms in the oversized sleeves, realizing it was his shirt. She blushed when his hands pulled the flannel shirt shut and fastened the buttons. Embarrassment at him seeing her completely naked was the least of her worries.

Matt tugged her back down and covered them. Hope yawned against his chest as she spoke. "How did you get back here?"

Matt wrapped her against his side. "Allie will tell you sheer stubbornness. And your markers made it a lot easier. But let's just say I'm glad I didn't have to go any further. My head is killing me."

Hope stirred, remembering the first aid kit. "I can help fix that. We should eat something too."

Matt just watched. He took the pills she handed to him and let her prop up his head so he could drink the water she held to his lips. "This hotel sucks, I might add. But the service is great."

Hope smiled and laughed a little. "Glad to see the knock to your head didn't dim your sense of humor. Though I can't attest to your having one. How is your back?"

"After you've eaten, I'll let you take a look."

She didn't like the way he said that, but she dug into her pack and pulled a couple of containers out instead of insisting he roll over. "You want field ration container one or two?"

"What's the difference?"

Hope smiled at him. "Nothing."

Hope opened it and handed it to him.

He grimaced. "Food sucks too."

Since she agreed, she just nodded and ate hers as quickly as she could swallow it down. She realized he was making a bit of a mess. "Let me."

She helped him finish his meal. She then went

around to his other side so she could roll him onto his good arm. She unbuttoned his shirt, trying but failing to ignore the muscles of his chest, so she could lift it off his back. She gasped at the condition of his back. The bandages were off, and some of the cuts were oozing. She peeled off the ruined bandages. "What did you do? Drag yourself here?"

Matt groaned. "You're making it hard to be all tough and macho over here. But damn, that hurts."

"One of these is infected. You did, didn't you?"

Matt ignored her question. "I've no doubt you can patch me up."

Hope was quiet as she worked on his back, the muscles there as impressive as the ones on his chest. Thankfully there was antibiotic ointment, fresh bandages, and a new roll of tape in the first aid kit. She pulled his shirt down, and he rolled onto his back so she could button his shirt back up. She looked over at her soaking wet clothes.

"Leave them. There is nowhere to hang them to dry anyway."

She bit her bottom lip. "I'm out of socks. I used the pair I packed on Meggie's splint."

"I've got an extra pair. Just relax. You pushed your body too hard today."

Hope winced as she lay back down. Once she was stretched out, her ribs stopped aching so much.

Hope listened to the rain as the downpour slowed and the thunder moved further away. She let Matt pull her back to his side. She rolled against him, careful not to hurt his arm.

Matt rubbed her back. "Hope?"

Her eyes were closed, and she could feel herself starting to drift.

"Thank you for coming back for me. I owe you for that."

"Mmm," was Hope's only response as she fell into a deep sleep.

Chapter Seven

It was still raining when Matt woke, though it was now a mere spattering of drops. He tried to stay still as his world spun. He had overdone it yesterday, but he hadn't had a choice. It was either stay where he was and end up soaked to the bone like Hope had or drag his sorry hide back to the only shelter he'd seen. Hope was wrapped against him, and she was snoring just a little.

She was such a tiny thing, but she had curves everywhere a man could want them. Her firm breasts were currently pressed against his side. He'd gotten a glimpse of them yesterday, and this morning the memory was enough to make him ache. Her waist flared into hips a man could hold onto. Her hands were soft, despite the physical labor of taking care of the farm animals these past weeks. Her legs were tangled with his, and her small feet were tucked under his calves. She fit him everywhere a woman should fit.

He groaned and got his unruly thoughts under control. She lay trustingly against him, and he wouldn't do anything to damage that trust. He had a feeling she didn't trust many people. She avoided almost everyone she worked with unless she had to interact with them. But she had thanked him, shared a meal with him, and frankly, she'd likely saved his life. Rescue wasn't coming in this rain. The terrain was too treacherous when wet.

He did let himself kiss the skin next to her ear. She mumbled. "Hope?"

Her hand lifted to the spot where he'd kissed her. "Was nice."

He looked down at her, but her eyes were still closed. He couldn't help smiling at her. He kissed her fingers. "Hope, I promise you can go back to sleep, but I need some help."

She mumbled as she sat up. He saw her wince, and she grabbed her side.

He brushed her hair from her cheeks. "What hurts, Hope? You said you weren't hurt."

Hope's eyes finally opened. She was clutching her side. "My ribs hurt, that's all. A very large man landed on me, along with a ten-year-old girl."

Matt didn't remember the fall. "I landed on you?"

Hope tucked her knees under her and pulled his flannel over her bare legs. "I had some dumb idea that I could break your fall."

Matt's eyes darkened as his hands went to her ribs. He gently prodded them and could tell when he'd hit the spot. "I can't tell if you have a broken rib or not. But you probably did break my fall. Don't you ever do that again."

Hope moved away from his hands. "I don't plan to. Just do me a favor, and don't fall off any more cliffs. You saved Meggie's life. She'd have gone over headfirst if you hadn't gotten a hold of her and twisted so you took the brunt of the fall. Those rocks sliced up your back instead of hers."

"I don't remember."

Hope unfortunately did. "People often don't after a head injury. It's for the best, in my opinion. Who wants to remember that?"

It sounded to Matt like she was speaking from personal experience. But her face was closed off; she wasn't looking at him, and her lips were pinched. Later he would push, but not today.

Hope dug into her bag and found a pair of underwear and her sweatpants. "Eyes, Matt. Then I'll help you. What do you need?"

He obediently closed his eyes as she got dressed. He opened them when she said okay. She was still in his flannel. It dwarfed her, but it made him feel better that she was wrapped up and warm.

"Well?" Hope tucked one of the edges of the flannel into her sweatpants.

"Bathroom."

Her eyes widened for a moment. "I can't believe I didn't think of that last night."

Matt wasn't going to make her get up after her trek in the rain, but he couldn't wait any longer.

It took some doing, but Hope got him to his feet. He had to hold onto her until the world stopped spinning. She helped him around the corner of the outcropping. "Do you need me to stay?"

Matt gave her a pained look. "No."

She retreated and went around the other corner. Matt used the rocks to keep himself on his feet. He knew he was having an easier time of it than she was.

He was halfway around the rock when she came to him. She helped him back to the sleeping bags, but he sat instead of lying down.

Hope dug into her bag and handed him a couple of wet wipes. "Not a bath, but you'll feel better for it."

"What else do you have in that bag?"

Hope wiped her face, hands, and feet. She caught him staring at her feet. "They're just feet, Matt."

Matt opened the wipe. "Yeah, but they're attached to a woman."

Hope opened her mouth, then apparently thought better of it and closed it. She wiped under her arms and pulled a roll-on deodorant out of her bag. After she used it, she tossed it to him. "You're not smelling so good either. Here."

"Gotta love the smell of roses in the morning." Matt wasn't going to be picky. If she wanted him to use it, he would.

Hope came back to the sleeping bag and sat next to Matt. "We're not going anywhere today."

Matt would have nodded in agreement, but he didn't want to move his head. "Not today."

Hope glanced at him. "Want to lie down?"

Matt looked up at the sky that was lightening up through the clouds. "Soon."

Hope nudged him so she could take a look at his back. "Much better. Let me redress the bad one. It's still oozing."

Matt stayed still while she fussed. It needed stitches, and he'd pulled the wound open when he moved his shoulder. It was stiffening up on him, and it still hurt. "Any more pain pills in there?"

Hope grabbed the first aid kit. "Aren't you supposed to be all manly and live with the pain?"

Matt stayed her hand. "Personally, letting myself or anyone else suffer, manly or not, never seemed right. Not when there is something I can do about it."

Hope leaned up and kissed his whiskered cheek. "I like you, Matt."

Matt saw her eyes drop as she sat back. He tucked a finger under her chin and raised her face back to his. "I like you, Hope. And when I don't feel so crappy, maybe we can go out again."

Hope's eyes held his. "Matt?"

Matt leaned forward. Her eyes held his, but she didn't pull back. His mouth settled on hers. He felt her hand grab a fistful of his shirt. She tentatively kissed him back, as if she wasn't sure she wanted to be doing this. He leaned forward, intent on deepening the kiss, when his world went dizzy, and he had to grab her shoulder for balance.

"Lay back down, Matt. You're not up to kissing."

Matt let her help him lie down flat on his back. "It's a sad day when a man is not up to kissing a beautiful woman."

Hope blushed. "I think you took a much harder hit on the head than I thought."

He took her hand in his. "Don't think you're beautiful, Hope?"

"Beauty is in the eye of the beholder."

Matt kept her hand in his. "Exactly. And I say you're beautiful."

Hope squeezed his hand and then gently pulled away. "Thank you, I guess. Beauty never seemed too important, though you're not so bad yourself."

Hope shook out a couple of capsules and helped Matt hold his head up as he swallowed them.

Matt pulled her so she was lying with him. "I've got the tall and handsome part. I lament that I have blond hair."

She touched the gold strands that went past his shoulders. "Tall, blond, and handsome works just as well."

Matt felt his eyes close. "Yeah?"

She kissed his cheek again. "Yeah. Go to sleep. I won't go anywhere."

* * *

Hope told herself to breathe as she watched Matt sleep. He'd been flirting with her last night. When was the last time a man had flirted with her? When was the last time she'd flirted back? She couldn't remember. And he'd kissed her. She hadn't kissed anyone in two years. Maybe longer, but her memories were hazy. She did remember that she no longer liked kissing Marlon. His lips were dry, and his eyes stayed open and watch her. It had gotten to the point where being in the same room as him disgusted her.

Hope went back to emptying her backpack. She didn't want to think about Marlon. She wanted to think about Matt. He was kind. He was handsome. He wasn't full of himself. He wasn't afraid to show weakness or to be vulnerable. It was no wonder she was attracted to him. He couldn't be more different from the men she had known in her past.

And he was a great kisser. Had he not gotten dizzy, she'd have let him keep kissing her. They both needed to brush their teeth. They both weren't smelling so good, but his mouth had been so sweet on hers. He didn't force the kiss but asked her to participate and kiss him back. And she had.

The rain was easing up. More storm clouds were heading their way, but she'd take the reprieve. She needed to see if she could find some dry wood. They had very little left. She had passed some other overhangs when she'd gone wandering and found Meggie. None of them were big enough to camp under, but perhaps she'd find some dry twigs and sticks.

She grabbed a pair of Matt's socks from his bag. He didn't move as she leaned over him. Rest was the best thing for him. She'd rest soon, but as the only able-bodied person, she needed to make sure they stayed warm and dry until they could get out of here.

She replaced her sweats with her wet jeans and

pulled on Matt's socks. She had to tug hard to get her boots over the thick socks, and the stiff laces gave her trouble. But they were mostly dry, unlike her clothes. She was going to get wet; there was nothing she could do. Meggie had her spare tarp, and she wasn't going to take the survival blanket.

She took off Matt's flannel and exchanged it for the t-shirt she slept in. She'd put his back on when she got back. She pulled her wet shirt over the dry t-shirt, and thankfully it wasn't as wet as her jeans. She took a moment to get the horses watered and fed. She promised both of them a good brushing and a fresh apple when they got home.

Hope set out, hoping Matt would stay asleep. He'd been sound asleep for almost an hour, and she hoped he would stay that way a bit longer. She set her hat on her head, the hat Matt had given her, and set off. She didn't find much more than twigs and some small sticks, but she kept filling her bag. In the daylight, she could see much further. There were some larger outcroppings that she hadn't seen in the dark.

Hope was careful to mark her path as she went. She found some larger branches under the overhangs in the distance. Her pack was full, and the rain was starting to roll in again. She turned, and under another overhang was a large branch that had broken off a tree. That one, she thought, would keep them going for the afternoon.

Mindful of the mud, she carefully made her way over. There was a ravine, and to get over the branch, she had to walk over an open area. But she could easily step over, so she set her backpack down. She was careful to keep her eyes on the ground.

She bent to grab the base of the branch when something red caught her eye. She gasped and scrambled back. Heart racing, she went to her knees and looked down. Open eyes were staring up at her. The eyes were blue and glazed over; short brunette hair was matted to a pale face. The woman lying on the rocks below was beyond help; Hope could see the lividity in her body. She gagged but managed to keep from getting sick. The woman's body was mostly protected from the elements; with the rain coming, she'd be there a while longer. At least where she was lying, it wasn't easy for animals to get to her.

Hope wretched again, her protein bar from earlier trying to come back up, but she swallowed the lump in her throat and took some deep breaths. She slipped as she tried to stand, her pants now fully coated in mud from the knees down, but she managed to get to her feet. She wiped her muddy hands on her thighs and dug out a few sticks from her pack and marked the location. Then she grabbed the base of the large branch and dragged it with her. She stopped and slung her backpack over both her shoulders as she went, and tears fell for the woman she found. She only hoped that by finding her here, there would be some closure for whoever cared about her.

It took another hour for her to drag the branch back to where Matt was. The muscles in her arms were burning, and her ribs were hurting.

Matt's eyes opened as he heard her coming toward him, the oversized branch dragging behind her. "I'm glad you had enough sense to come back before the next storm hit."

Hope glared at him but ignored the comment. She took the knife out of her pile of things and started shearing off the leaves and smaller branches. Her hands were shaking, so she was being extra careful not to cut her hand.

Matt groaned. "I was worried."

Hope looked up at the sky. Dark clouds were coming fast. She closed her eyes. The face of the dead woman flashed behind her lids. "You need to make a call."

Matt carefully sat up. "Hope?"

Hope dropped the branch and the knife. She covered her tears with her hands. "I found a body. A woman. She must have fallen or something. I was looking for dry wood to burn. She's down a ravine, lying on a rock ledge."

Matt held his arms out to her, and she went to them. She was careful to stay off the sleeping bag as she knelt beside him. She wrapped her arms around him, absorbing some of his strength. "God, Matt. She's just lying there. No one would have known."

She held him for a few more moments. "She's about a half-hour hike north, past where we found Meggie. I marked the path."

Matt grabbed and turned on the satellite phone.

"Mike, it's Matt."

Hope tuned him out. She went back to the branch; her hands numb as she worked.

"Hope, let me. I can do that lying down."

Hope handed Matt the knife and dragged the branch over. He dug a small hatchet out of his pack. He cut the pieces into more manageable sizes while Hope built a fire. She boiled some water for coffee after tending to the horses. If anything, the caffeine should help Matt's headache. Hers too. She stripped off her wet boots and Matt's socks. She laid them near the fire to dry.

She and Matt sat side by side, sipping the coffee. "It was Meggie's mom who told Jeremy where to look for Meggie, right?"

Matt put his arm around her. "Meggie's mom is safe. Meggie is too. The boys are still missing. Trixie is with Mike. Mike says he's spoiling her."

Hope relaxed against Matt. She finished her coffee and set the cup to the side. "She has that effect on people."

Matt tucked her head against his shoulder. "I tried to find you after Jeremy, well, after Jeremy. You weren't at the address in your personnel files. Where are you staying?"

Hope felt her heart lurch in her chest. "You looked for me? Why?"

Matt stroked her hair. "Those boys attacked Jessie, Hope. She saw them harassing you, though she didn't know it was you. Jeremy put two and two together after he remembered you'd been near the main office that morning. It's Jessie's word against theirs, but corroborating her story with yours will make the case against them stronger."

Hope closed her eyes. In her attempt to avoid the police, she had left another woman vulnerable. "How can two boys that age do something like that?"

Matt didn't answer. He just kept stroking her hair.

Hope opened her eyes and looked up at him. "I don't want to tell you where I was. But it wasn't far."

"Maybe one day you'll trust me."

Hope pulled away. "It's not about trust, Matt."

"More like secrets. You have a lot of them. I can see them in your eyes."

Hope pulled her knees to her chest and wrapped her arms around them.

Matt lay back down. "Not going to argue?"

Hope tossed a few more branches on the fire. "Nothing to argue about. But my secrets are mine. I'm sure you have a few."

Matt yawned. "Not as many as you might think. I'm a straightforward man."

Hope turned her head to look at him. "How are Allie and the baby?"

Matt patted the spot next to him on the sleeping bag. "No baby yet. Jeremy Junior is taking his time. Come lay down. I won't ask any more questions tonight."

Despite the fire, she was chilled. Her throat was getting scratchy, and fatigue was dragging at her. Not caring at the moment if he watched, she removed the muddy jeans, replaced her damp shirts with Matt's, and climbed under the sleeping bag.

Without a second thought, she scooted next to him. She relaxed when his arm came around her. "For Allie's sake, I hope the baby comes soon. Is she why you bought into the business?"

"Both of them, I suppose, though it was Allie's inheritance. When she told me she was pregnant, I did step it up a little. I had to take a loan out to cover the rest, though I didn't tell her or Jeremy that. They're family."

"What were you doing when you weren't here?"

Matt tucked her head to his chest. Hope knew she shouldn't get so comfortable with him, but the lure of his large, warm body was too much to resist.

"I drove fuel trucks up in North Dakota. Did a lot of the same in Alaska. Saved all my money living out of my truck. Money's good if you can hustle. I drifted a lot after the military. I toyed with going to medical school, but I never really enjoyed school. Probably because I skipped it at every opportunity."

Hope propped her chin on his arm. "Were you a troublemaker?"

"Rebellious. So probably."

"You said you grew up with Jeremy. He doesn't strike me as the troublemaker type. He's too rigid. Guessing he wasn't a rule breaker."

Matt laughed, his chest rumbling beneath her cheek. "He was the rule follower. He probably kept me out of jail. We grew up in foster homes. We ended up in the same one when we were twelve. I was quite the hoyden by then. I called him names, he decked me, and we became fast friends. We were there for three years. Then when our foster parents had to give us up, we went to the same facility. We lived there until we were eighteen. Jeremy got good grades and went to college on a scholarship program. I joined the army. Allie was two years older than me and already a medic. I trained under her."

Hope filed away that tidbit about Matt. She didn't remember her childhood, but she couldn't imagine growing up in foster care and temporary homes. "You said you introduced them?"

"I did. Love at first sight. They both deny it, well, Allie does. She thinks she's too practical to believe in love at first sight. It's true just the same. Allie grew up with just her father. He's a good man. Allie had high expectations in a mate. Thankfully for Jeremy, he met them."

Hope felt bad. But she didn't have anything she was willing to share about her past with him. And given that she did have secrets, a lot of them, she should keep her distance, but he found it impossible. She tried to think of something to say. She was looking at the horses. She smiled to herself.

"I've always liked animals. I learned to ride when I was Meggie's age. I had a beautiful mare. Now that I think about it, her coloring was a lot like Trixie's. Golden body with a black mane and tail. I named her

Butterscotch. She passed at the ripe old age of twenty-nine."

Matt's voice was drowsy when he spoke. "Trixie's almost the size of a horse. Allie's dad taught me to ride. He said I was a natural cowboy. I worked a couple of winters on his ranch right out of the army. He'll be visiting soon to meet his grandson."

Hope got up long enough to douse the fire and take a quick trip to the bathroom. "Good night, Matt."

He was already asleep.

## Chapter Eight

The storm was over.  Matt could tell in the air.  He was still having dizzy spells, but he had to get Hope out of the canyon.  And it was a sure bet she wasn't going to leave without him.  She'd hovered over him like a mother hen for three days.  When she'd woken in the middle of the night in the throes of a nightmare, he decided then and there they were leaving.  She admitted she had dreamed of the woman she found.  Matt knew these canyons were dangerous. What was a woman, all alone, doing up here?  No one had called in a missing woman, other than the Edgerton woman and her family.

Hope was still asleep when he rang Mike and told him to be on the lookout for them.  Mike had advised the best trail to take down the mountain.  The best news was that Allie had finally delivered her baby.  He was grinning from ear to ear when Hope woke up.

"What?"  Hope pushed her curls out of her face as she sat up.

"Boy.  Eight pounds even.  Twenty-one inches. Mom and baby are doing fine."

Hope smiled at Matt.  "A nice, healthy baby.  A bit big for a woman Allie's size, but Jeremy isn't a lightweight."

Matt tried to keep his head as still as he could as he

changed into warmer clothes. "We're going to get out of here. Mike said he thinks the western pass should be open. We won't have to cross the river until we're at a lower elevation. He's going to send some men to try to meet up with us. We both need a hot meal, see a doctor, and get some fluids. Hopefully in that order."

Hope pulled on her sweatpants under Matt's shirt. She then helped break camp. She tried to get Matt to relax while she got things together, but he refused. A short while later, she helped him mount his horse. Matt had swallowed a couple of pills, and hopefully, the pounding headache would be kept at bay.

The trip down the mountain was thankfully uneventful. He kept the horses to a slow pace. They were taking a longer route, but he hoped they'd make it to flat land by nightfall. They stopped for lunch later in the day. Hope had been quiet. She didn't seem quite steady when she slid from the horse. He wasn't much better, but he didn't like the pallor of her skin.

He pressed his wrist to her forehead. "You're running a fever."

Hope coughed into her elbow. "We just need to keep going."

She was right about that. She'd smeared more medicine on the cuts on his back. One of them was getting infected. He could feel it. He was sure there was some rock debris deep in the cut, but there was only so much Hope could do with a canteen and a piece of his torn shirt. Matt spread out her tarp, and they sat and ate. He made her finish the canteen of water.

It was dusk when they heard shouting. Two men on horseback and one in a truck were heading their way. Matt dismounted and let them come to them. Hope's eyes were half closed. She wasn't sleeping, but she was close.

Ignoring the pain in his head and shoulder, he eased Hope out of the saddle and onto the ground.

Mike smiled at him. "You had us worried. Glad to see you standing. You too, Miss Whitfield."

Hope opened her eyes as Matt helped her down, but all she managed was a nod.

Matt led her to the waiting truck. Two men took their horses, along with their meager supplies. Matt stopped them and grabbed their backpacks. He had a clean shirt left but wasn't sure what might be in Hope's.

Matt pulled Hope to his side, and she dozed against him. Now that they were in a warm truck, his tension started to fade. "Are the police headed up the mountain to retrieve the woman's body?"

Mike concentrated on the road. Darkness had fallen. "Tomorrow they should be. Now that the storm has subsided, the state will likely send up a chopper. The odd thing is no one has been reported missing. If the woman was dead when Hope found her, she's been there longer than the three days you've been up there."

Hope stirred. "It's sad. No one is looking for her."

Mike finally hit a main road and floored it. "It will take about an hour to get to the hospital. It's small, but they'll get the two of you patched up."

The ride was mostly a blur. Matt and Hope dozed most of the way. It wasn't until they pulled into a brightly lit parking lot that Matt stirred. He nudged Hope. "Wake up, sweetheart. I can't carry you in."

Matt and Hope trailed behind Mike. Jeremy came from behind the double doors.

Matt saw Jeremy first. "I have never been so glad to see your ugly mug."

Jeremy hugged him. "That's my line. You look like hell."

Matt let him go. "Thanks. Glad to know I look as bad as I feel."

Jeremy briefly hugged Hope. "I'm glad you're okay. Meggie told us you're the one who found her."

"Matt's the one who got her off the cliff."

Jeremy turned to Matt. "Her damn brothers chased her up there. She claims they laughed the whole time. Some people off the highway think they saw a couple of boys hitchhiking. They might have backtracked and gotten off the mountain before their mother."

"Allie in a room?" Matt was the first at the triage desk, and he handed over his driver's license and insurance card.

"She's exhausted. Sawyer took his time being born. Once the baby came, she started to worry about you two.  As soon as she can, she's going to want to see you."

The nurse finished taking Matt's vitals.  She then gestured for Hope.  She shook her head.

Matt took her arm.  "Hope, you need to be seen."

Hope turned away from Jeremy and looked at Matt.  "I can't afford to be seen."

Jeremy came around.  "The ranch will cover it."

Hope glared at him.  "You fired me, remember?  I don't have insurance, and I'll be damned if you pay my bills."

Matt cupped her cheek, turning her eyes back to his.  "Hope, please.  You're running a fever.  You were hypothermic.  You can pay me back if it makes you feel better, but I'll cover the bill."

Hope took a seat in the chair.  She dug out her driver's license and handed it to the nurse.  "Remember when I said I liked you?"

Matt smiled at her.  "Yeah."

She looked up at him through her lashes.  "I take it back."

"Just as long as you get checked out."

Matt's name was called.  He waited for Hope to respond to his silent question.

Hope gave in.  "Go.  I promise I'll get seen."

Jeremy walked back with Matt.  "You two seem cozy."

Matt sat on the edge of the hospital bed as the nurse handed him a gown to change into.  His eyes were serious as he tried to strip off his shirt.  "She came back for me.  She should have gotten off the mountain with Meggie.  I'm in a lot better shape than I would have been if she hadn't.  I'd still be up on that mountain.  She's a damn good rider.  I think you can find her a job leading groups on horseback.  If you don't hire her back, I will."

Jeremy helped Matt get the rest of the way changed into the gown.  "Hell, she can do whatever she wants.  She can go back to being the world's lousiest housekeeper if that's what she wants.  Allie has already yelled and threatened me.  I'm much more afraid of her than you, pal."

"Aren't we both?"

Matt explained to the nurse, then the doctor, what had happened.  He had Jeremy go check on Hope while he was sent up for an MRI.  When he got back, he was hooked up to antibiotics in his IV, his back was thoroughly cleaned and stitched, and his arm was in a sling.  The pain medication they gave him made him drowsy. When Jeremy came back and said that Hope was cooperating, Matt drifted off to sleep.

* * *


Hope refused to be admitted.  She was signing the waiver when a police officer came into the room.

"Hope Whitfield?"

Her throat constricted at the sight of his uniform, and she could only nod.

"I'm Officer James Callahan.  I wanted to get your

statement."

Hope was tempted to ask which one. The two boys or the dead woman? She kept silent. The easiest way to not say too much was to only answer direct questions.

"I spoke with Jessica at the ranch about the two boys who attacked her. She said she witnessed them attacking you. I need your statement."

Hope gave him a brief rundown of what happened.

"None of the injuries you're getting treated for were from the altercation with the boys?"

Hope thanked the nurse and accepted her discharge papers. "No. I was part of the team that went looking for Meggie Edgerton. I got hurt on the mountain, along with Matt Henney."

The man jotted down a few notes. "All right. The boys are on the run. We'll need you to come in and sign a statement, but it can hold until you're feeling better. Sooner if we get those boys in custody before then."

Hope took the card from the officer. The address to the police station was on it. She tucked it into her backpack. She was relieved when he left. The only clean clothes she had left were a thermal undershirt. She pulled her bra back on, yanked on the now dirty sweats she'd worn down the mountain, and the clean shirt. The nurse had given her a pair of socks with rubber on the bottom. She picked up her boots, not willing to put them on until it was time to leave.

She inquired which room was Matt's. She poked

her head in. "Hi."

Matt's eyes were closed, but he gestured her inside. "Why are you not in a bed?"

She set her things down and came to stand beside him. "I got lots of fluids, ate a sandwich, and got a prescription.    Diagnosis    is    dehydration    and exhaustion. I'm not going to be admitted because I'm tired."

"And your ribs?" Matt blindly held out his hand.

She took it. "Cracked not broken. I have pills for the pain. Antibiotics as a precaution. Happy?"

"I will be. Doc is making me stay. Fluids and antibiotics for the night. And a pain pill for my concussion and shoulder."

Hope had a slight concussion, but she didn't tell Matt that. She leaned over and kissed his cheek. "Just sleep. Mike left but said he'd be back when you're ready to leave."

Hope had thought of having Mike drive her back, but the thought of going back to her tent held no appeal right now. Not to mention the rest of her stuff went with the horses. The hospital was warm. Mike assured her Trixie was okay, so she was going to stay with Matt until he was discharged. She'd worry about the next steps then.

Matt briefly opened his eyes. He tapped his mouth. "How about right there?"

Hope leaned over and kissed him on his lips. He didn't kiss her back, just sighed and dropped off to sleep.

Jeremy knocked. Hope jumped. She blushed and took a seat.

"Allie is out like a light."

Hope yawned and leaned back. The chair was extremely uncomfortable, but she was too tired to care. "Allie is okay?"

Jeremy took the seat next to her. "She's fine."

Hope glanced at Jeremy. "Baby too?"

Jeremy rubbed his tired eyes. "We named him Sawyer. After Allie's grandpa. He passed a couple of winters ago. He's doing fine. All ten fingers and toes, and a great set of lungs."

Hope smiled. "I hope I get to see him."

Jeremy leaned forward, exhaustion in every line of his body. "Allie and I can't thank you enough for what you did for Matt. It couldn't have been easy."

Hope stiffened in her seat. "You mean for Helpless Hope? Don't lose sleep over it."

Jeremy's lips tightened. "I mean it, Hope. He, Allie, and now Sawyer are the only family I have. I couldn't be there. I'm glad you were."

Hope relented. "I'm glad I was there too."

They were quiet for a while. Eventually, transport came to wheel Matt upstairs. Hope grabbed her things, and Jeremy grabbed Matt's. They stood to the side while the nurse got his IV hooked up, took his vitals, and slipped out of the room.

"I'm going back to Allie's room. Matt has his cell. Text me if you or Matt need anything. Otherwise, get some rest. You look as bad as he does."

Hope gazed at the bathroom. She wanted a shower. She glanced down at herself. Reluctantly, she pulled some money out of her wallet and went to the gift shop. She grabbed the cheapest bottle of shampoo and a bar of soap. She cringed at the price tags but grabbed a sweatshirt to wear over her thermal sweatpants and a pair of socks. She then grabbed a couple of candy bars and a bottle of tea. She never wanted to eat a protein bar again.

Matt was still sleeping when she got back to his room. The lights were off. She slipped her toothbrush and toothpaste from her backpack, thankful she'd packed it. She took a hot shower but didn't linger like she wanted to. Matt was right; she had a fever. She needed to lie down and sleep. But she was clean, had on fresh clothes, and felt human again. There was no bed, but the chair reclined. She grabbed a pillow and blanket from the cabinet and settled into the chair. She nibbled at her candy bar despite just having brushed her teeth and watched Matt sleep. Her body was exhausted, but her mind wasn't ready to sleep.

When she closed her eyes, visions of that poor woman lying on the ledge were all she could see. The woman's eyes had been open, and they haunted her. The attack from those two boys seemed so long ago, overshadowed by the search for Meggie, Matt being hurt, and finding that woman. But she would do her duty, go to the police station, and sign a statement. She shuddered at the thought of having to testify in court. If the boys had any sense, they'd plead guilty and try to get a lighter sentence. Even Meggie had told the police that her brothers had chased her up that cliff.

*You can't remember, Mrs. Turner? You testified that you witnessed an argument between the victim and the defendant. And now you can't remember? Or did you lie? You lied to protect yourself. To push suspicion onto my client to cover up your guilt.*

Hope rolled onto her side, trying to still the memories in her head. She hated it when they snuck up on her. Sometimes they were like a film reel. They didn't seem real. Yet she knew they were. She watched Matt until her eyes drifted closed again.

The sun was shining when she woke. She woke with a start when a nurse came. Her body ached and she'd stiffened up. But her head didn't hurt as badly as it had, though she thought she might still have a fever. Her ribs protested the sudden movement. She brought the leg rest down and rubbed the sleep from her eyes.

"You look a lot better." Matt looked her over. "I'd kill for a shower."

Hope felt momentary guilt at having snuck one, then brushed it aside. "You'll have to settle for a hot breakfast."

Matt grinned at her. "Don't want to join me in the shower and help wash my back?"

Hope wasn't about to admit that she did. She dug into her pack for some money. "You've gotten awfully familiar."

"Perhaps. But you did kiss me."

Hope tucked the money in her pocket. "I'm going to get some coffee. You should order breakfast."

"Eat something, Hope."

She ignored his comment. "I'll be back."

She felt Matt's eyes on her as she left. She almost bumped into Jeremy.

"Sorry. Hi."

"Hi. We're getting out of here around noon. How's Matt?"

Hope thought about it for a second. "Feeling frisky, I think. And he wants a shower."

Jeremy glanced at Matt's door. "Don't hurt him."

Hope stammered over her words. "Excuse me?"

Jeremy turned back to her. "You heard me."

Hope's heart raced a little at what might be a threat. She turned her back on him and left. She didn't like Jeremy. She didn't like the way he looked at her; looked through her.

She bought a breakfast sandwich, downed two cups of coffee, and grabbed a third. She then snagged a donut for Matt. When she got back to his room, she knocked before entering.

Matt was in bed, but he'd clearly gotten the shower he wanted. His hair hung in damp, golden waves over his shoulders. She set the donut on the tray by him. "Thought you might like some sugar."

Matt glanced at her hand. "I'd rather have that coffee."

Hope set it down. "It's black."

"Good."

Jeremy was sitting in a chair nearby. "I was telling Matt there's still no word on the teenagers. Half the state is looking for them. They robbed a gas station about thirty miles from here."

Hope sat on the bed next to Matt. "That isn't very far."

Jeremy yawned. "No. Police figure they stole a car but are lying low. Those two are landing themselves in a heap of trouble. The woman you found was retrieved this morning. She's on her way to the state coroner. I know the pilot. She said the woman was strangled."

Hope felt every ounce of blood drain from her head. "What did you say?"

Matt took her hand and squeezed it. "Breathe, Hope."

She took a huge gulp of air and started coughing. She quickly excused herself and closed herself in the bathroom.

*You're lucky to be alive. If you hadn't been found by someone who knows CPR, we wouldn't be talking right now. I know this is a lot to absorb. And I know you must be frightened. But you're alive. You need to focus on that.*

Hope turned on the exhaust fan and faucet to drown out the sound of her losing her breakfast. She heaved until there was nothing left. She made herself get up off the floor and rinse her mouth. Her eyes were hollow, and they were red with unshed tears. Her heart was pounding so hard in her chest that she thought she might faint.

But she stayed upright, took deep breaths until her heart slowed, and looked at the closed door. She could only imagine what they were thinking.

Two pairs of male eyes watched her when she came out of the bathroom.

Chapter Nine

"I'm so glad to be home."  Matt threw his bag on the floor and dropped down on the couch.  Well, he eased himself down.  His head was throbbing from the drive home, but he didn't care.

Hope closed the door behind them.  She set her pack down by the door.  "It's getting late.  Are you hungry?"

Matt leaned his head back.  "I think there's a frozen pizza in the freezer."

Hope went to his kitchen.  Matt watched her putter around, finding plates and napkins, and figuring out how to work his oven. When she put the pizza in and set the timer, he patted the cushions next to him.  He could see the hesitancy on Hope's face, but she came and sat beside him.

He took her hand and rubbed the back of her fingers. "You were pretty upset earlier."

Hope glanced at him.  "I learned that the woman I found was murdered.  Seems like a normal response to me."

Matt continued to rub her fingers.  "Didn't say it wasn't."

She looked at their joined hands.  "I guess you would have seen a lot of bad stuff as an army medic."

"I did, but that doesn't mean it stops affecting you.

I hope they find the bastard that did that to her. No matter where I was, no matter who we were helping, it never made sense to me. I can't suffer people hurting others. Her death had no purpose, outside of whatever sick motive was inside his head."

Hope whispered. "What if she was married? Had children? How can no one be looking for her?"

Matt had similar thoughts. "Maybe she's not from around here. She could have been vacationing and no one is looking yet. All we can do is hope."

Hope smiled tiredly. "Sometimes hope is in short supply. But I'll second that."

They sat quietly for a time until the timer dinged. Hope slowly got to her feet and divided the pizza between them.

Matt thanked her and took a huge bite. "Man, that's good."

Hope chewed her equally large bite. "Almost as good as the candy bar I ate last night. I swore no more protein bars."

When they were done eating, Matt cleaned up. Hope started heading for the door. "Where are you going?"

Hope stopped as she was reaching for her bag. "It's late. I should go."

Matt came and took her hands in his. He looked down into her eyes. "Stay."

Hope shook her head. "It's late. We both need more sleep."

Matt walked backward with her hands in his, and

she followed. "Sleep was what I had in mind. We've been sharing a sleeping bag for days. One more night. I know you're not feeling well, and I don't want you driving home in the dark. I've got clothes you can sleep in."

Hope leaned into him. "Matt?"

"Just sleep."

He knew she was going to stay when she wrapped her arms around his waist. He led her back to his bedroom where he rummaged through his dresser for something for her to wear. He let her use the bathroom first. He had the overhead light off and just a lamp on when she joined him.

Wearing just his t-shirt and her underwear, Hope slid under the sheet and moaned. "It's been too long since I've slept in a bed."

Matt turned the lamp off. "Sure feels that way, doesn't it? The hospital bed doesn't count."

Hope rolled to her side, tucking her arm under the pillow. "Night, Matt."

Matt kissed the top of her hair. "Good night."

* * *

It was still dark when Hope woke, remnants of a nightmare fading. She couldn't quite remember what it was about, but it didn't matter. The fear was there. She rolled so she was facing Matt. His head was propped on his hand, and he was looking down at her. She could see heat in his eyes. It triggered a matching heat in her.

"Hope?"

Without another thought, Hope wrapped her arms around his neck and brought her lips to his. She moaned in the back of her throat as his weight settled on top of her. His lips were mobile on hers, relearning their shape. When his tongue traced the seam of her lips, she opened for him.

For a time, Matt seemed content to kiss her. She slid one of her legs between his, her hands roaming his chest under the t-shirt he'd worn to bed. Matt kept himself braced on his good arm as his mouth left hers to kiss a path to her ear, her neck, her collarbone. His tongue traced a damp path over the skin where the t-shirt she wore was loose.

Matt sat up. "Help me."

Hope sat up, and between the two of them, they got his shirt off. She yanked hers off, baring herself to his gaze. Matt bent to kiss the tip of one breast, then the other, his fingers painting random patterns on the skin of her back.

Matt cursed his shoulder as he tried to ease her down. "This might take a little work."

Hope pushed him down on the bed, settling her body against his. They both lay on their sides, learning the textures, curves, and hollows of each other's bodies. Matt managed to slip off her underwear. She curled one thigh over his hip as she brought her lips back to his.

Open as she was to him, his fingers delved

between her thighs, and she gasped into his mouth as he found her slick flesh. She stopped her exploration and savored the feeling. Had anyone touched her like this? Had she wanted them to? Hope didn't care. No one else in her past mattered. Only Matt mattered.

When Matt's fingers left her, she unwrapped herself so she could get his pajama pants off. He lifted his hips for her. Her fingers traced a path up his inner thigh, just as he had. She curled her fingers around him, learning him the way he had her.

"Condom. Damn things are in the bathroom somewhere."

Hope pressed a hand to his chest when he went to sit up. "I'll get it."

She was self-conscious as she walked naked to the bathroom. Her hands were trembling, but it was a good trembling. She didn't find them in the medicine cabinet, where she thought a man might stash them. Under the cabinet, there was a cardboard box. She found an unopened box at the bottom of it. She brought the box back in with her. Her fingers weren't cooperating, so she handed it to him.

Matt ripped open the box, several of them scattering. He grabbed the nearest one, opened it with his teeth, and rolled it on.

Hope climbed back into bed. She straddled his hips, but he rolled them so that she was lying on her back. He braced himself over her with his good arm. His eyes held hers. She nodded to him. Her back arched and her body clenched around him as his body invaded hers. Her feminine muscles pulsed around his, her body overly sensitized. She locked her legs around him and pulled his mouth back to hers. She reveled in the feel of his naked body against hers as he settled his weight on top of her, his stomach pressed to hers.

Matt didn't need any more urging. His bum shoulder didn't hinder him; the sleek muscles of his back bunched under her palms. She gasped and moaned under him, her breath coming in deep inhalations and exhalations. She could already feel her body tightening around him as he quickened his pace; could feel him as he slid just that little bit deeper. She cried out and convulsed around him. He kept his rhythm, his fingers sliding between their bodies, and she once again tightened around him. She felt his climax deep inside, and she climaxed again with him.

Neither of them moved. Hope could feel Matt's warm breath in her ear. She felt the perspiration slick between their bodies. She pressed kisses to his chest and shoulder where her mouth could reach.

Matt eventually pulled out and rolled onto his back. "Damn, woman."

Hope slid her palms over the muscles of his abdomen, her arm brushing his now softened flesh. She wrapped her arm around him and settled her head and chest against his chest.

Matt stripped off the condom and tossed it in the nearby trash can. His arms came around her.

Hope didn't feel like talking, and apparently, he didn't either. She listened to his heart as it slowed under her ear. His hand swept up and down her bare back, from shoulder to hip. She pressed herself closer, enjoying the feel of his chest hair against her sensitized breasts.

Hope yawned and closed her eyes. Matt's hand eventually stilled. She once again fell asleep.

* * *

When the sun was fully up, Hope was the first to wake. Matt barely stirred as she peeled herself off him. She gazed down at him. She knew last night was special. She wanted to remember this night with him forever. Her legs were rubbery, but it was a good feeling. She picked up her underwear and went to the bathroom where she'd left the rest of her clothes folded up. She hopped in the shower, using his shampoo and soap. She remained under the hot spray until the water started to cool. When she stepped out of the tub, she smelled a little more masculine than she was used to, but it didn't bother her.

Hair combed and her sweat clothes back on, Hope went to the kitchen to fix coffee. She glanced at the clock. It was almost ten. She couldn't remember the last time she'd slept so late. Coffee was almost done when the front door opened.

Allie's voice chimed through the space. "Matt, come meet your godson."

Jeremy came in behind her, carrying the tiny baby. Both stopped in their tracks when they spotted Hope in the kitchen.

Allie was the first to speak. "Hi."

Hope replied, heat crawling up her neck and face. "Hi."

Jeremy shook his head as he handed Sawyer to Allie. "I'll go get Matt. That guy sleeps like a log."

Hope had noticed but didn't say so. "Coffee?"

"Not for me. I'm breastfeeding. Or trying to, anyway. But Jeremy will have one. Black. I'll take a bottle of water. There's some in the fridge."

Hope pulled down three mugs after opening a couple of cabinets to find them and poured each of them a cup. "Does Matt use sugar or milk?"

Allie took a seat at the small kitchen table she had picked out. "Just milk. Light."

Hope opened the water bottle and set it down, then set down the coffee. She stayed standing and sipped hers.

Allie's serious face then smiled. "Want to hold him?"

Hope glanced at the baby. He had a wash of dark hair; his perfect little mouth was moving in his sleep.

Allie got up and shifted the baby into Hope's arms. "Took me a minute to get the hang of it."

Hope kept her arms steady under the baby. "He's so tiny. Looks like Jeremy."

Allie laughed. "That's what I said. I hope he gets a few of my features when he grows up. But Jeremy is a hottie, so it's not a bad thing for Sawyer when he's older."

Hope touched a finger to his small mouth. "Much older."

Hope rocked him a little. He was tiny and cute as a button. She felt a wave of longing flood her. Then she tensed.

*Pregnant? You did this on purpose. Get rid of it, Jaclyn. Or I swear I will. I'll be damned if you use your baby as an excuse to milk every dime out of me for the next eighteen years.*

Allie shot to her feet. "Are you okay? You turned white as a sheet."

Hope choked back tears she hadn't shed in over two years. Or couldn't remember shedding. "Sorry. Just got a little dizzy. I'm still not a hundred percent."

Allie took Sawyer from her. "Sit. Jeremy makes a mean omelet. We'll put him on kitchen duty when he and Matt finally get out here. Likely they're having a man talk."

Hope had no doubt she was the topic of conversation. In the quiet of the trailer, she could hear the murmuring of male voices. She knew she didn't belong here. When Matt asked her to stay, she had no willpower. And she hadn't wanted to go back to her cold, lonely tent. When she'd woken and Matt had been looking at her, she made the only decision she wanted to make. She wanted him. Even if only for a night. If only a brief moment. He had been everything she could have wanted in a lover, but he was so much more than that. She hoped whatever woman he ended up with, she would appreciate him for the man he was and the many facets of his personality that she'd come to love.

"I swear you're paler than you were a minute ago. You must still be wiped out. Maybe you should go back to bed."

She didn't love Matt. She barely knew him. Hope tore herself away from her thoughts. "Stress of it."

"I can't believe that poor woman was strangled. What are the chances that anyone would have found her?"

Hope didn't have an answer. She thought the odds were even worse that it would be her. "I'm just glad I did. I almost didn't. If I hadn't had to go further to find dry wood for the fire, she wouldn't have been found."

Matt came out of the bedroom, a smile on his face as he saw her at his table. He leaned down and kissed her as he grabbed the cup of coffee. "Morning."

Hope knew she was blushing from hairline to toe. "Morning."

Allie kissed Matt on the cheek when he bent down to her. "Your godson finally arrived."

Setting down his coffee, Matt slipped the baby from her arms. "Hey, little man. Spitting image of his father. Such a pity."

Jeremy sat next to his wife and grabbed the coffee she pushed over to him. "Next time we'll try for a girl who looks like Allie."

Matt yawned and took a seat, cuddling the baby to his chest. "Better get to it. You're not getting any younger."

Allie shushed him. "Neither am I. We figure we'll try again when little man here is a year old or so. But it took so long to conceive him. If he's all we'll have, I'll consider myself a blessed woman. And you're one to talk. You're as old as Jeremy."

Hope recalled telling Matt she was turning thirty-two. She had, the day he'd signed the papers for the ranch, and she'd paid the property taxes. "You never did say how old you were."

Matt's eyes didn't leave the baby. "Not a state secret. I'm thirty-seven."

Allie chimed in. "And I'm the oldest of the group at thirty-nine. Time is ticking in the baby department."

Hope's gaze turned to Matt and the baby he was holding. "You look like you know what you're doing."

Matt kissed the top of the baby's head before handing him back to Allie when he started fussing. "I took care of my share of kids in the field. If I had gone to medical school, I'd have studied pediatrics. But by the time I got out, I was just too burnt out to go back to school."

Allie nudged Jeremy. "We're putting you on breakfast detail. I'm going to go change and feed him. Matt, I'm borrowing your bedroom. If I don't come back, I fell asleep. Just come get me when breakfast is done."

Matt saluted Allie before turning to Jeremy. "You're a lucky man."

Jeremy went about fixing breakfast. "Luckiest man alive. How are the two of you faring, outside of the obvious? Your head must be feeling better."

Matt took one of her hands as the other slid around Hope's rib cage and gently prodded where she had been hurt. "How are your ribs?"

Hope was starting to need this physical connection between the two of them. She gently eased her hand from his, knowing she needed to leave and put some distance between the two of them. "They're fine. No doubt they'll ache for a while."

Matt dropped silent as he released her and just watched her. Hope tried not to squirm under his gaze.

Allie did come back, just in time to eat. "Sawyer fell back asleep. Figure he'll be okay in there while we eat."

Matt kept his eyes on Hope. "My home is his home."

Hope tore her gaze away and focused on breakfast. When they were done eating, Hope glanced back at Matt. "I do need to go."

Jeremy cleared his throat. "I wanted to talk to you. About before."

Hope sat completely still. "Before what?"

"About firing you. Given the circumstances, I can see how it happened. And I was in a foul mood. I'd like to offer you your job back. Like I said, Matt told me you're excellent on a horse. We're always looking for people to exercise them and take groups up the trails. We usually send two people with the groups, so you wouldn't be by yourself with them."

Hope got to her feet. "I don't think that's a good idea."

Matt disagreed. "I think it's a great idea."

Hope shot him a dirty look. "Before or after last night?"

Matt took her arm, ignored the looks Allie and Jeremy were giving them, and led her outside. "That doesn't even deserve an answer."

Hope knew it didn't. It had been a knee-jerk reaction. "Jeremy doesn't like me. He'd been looking for an excuse to fire me. He found one."

Hope didn't resist when Matt pulled her against his chest. "He doesn't not like you. He just doesn't like people all that much. But he meant it in there; he wants to hire you back on. He wouldn't have said it if he didn't mean it. And I want you hired back on before last night."

Hope let him wind her arms around his neck. She leaned her weight against him. It was hard to fight a man who turned your insides to mush. And the reality was, she didn't have a lot of options. She had very little money left after paying the property taxes. She had Trixie to feed. Now she had a hospital bill. It was her bill to pay, and she'd pay it.

But she needed to be realistic about her

relationship with Matt. She reluctantly pulled away. "All right. But I'll keep the job I had. I like taking care of the animals. And after this last week, I'd rather not go back up into the canyon. Not yet. And I am going home. I need my dog and my stuff."

Matt stepped back. "All right. I'll concede. For now. But don't mistake me, Hope; I don't plan to stay away from you."

Hope doubted she would be able to keep away. "How about we try that date you suggested?"

Matt took her hand and led her back to the trailer. "Lets."

Chapter Ten

Matt wiped the sweat from his forehead. Jeremy had declared both he and Hope had to take the rest of the week off. Matt had only taken a day, but he'd been glad Hope had agreed. They both needed rest. But Hope didn't have a phone, and he didn't know where she lived, and he hadn't been able to talk to her. Perhaps they both needed some space. However, when she did turn up, he was going to demand her address. He didn't like not knowing where she was.

Jeremy joined him in the west barn. There were two mares ready to give birth any day. He had people taking turns watching them, and Matt had volunteered to take tonight. "How are our mamas doing?"

Matt finished brushing the appaloosa. "This one will be soon. Today or tomorrow, I'd wager."

Jeremy brushed the other one. "I took a message for you. State police called about that woman. They had some questions and wanted you to go to the station."

Matt set the brush aside. "Why? I'm not the one who found her. I didn't even see her body. Only Hope did."

Jeremy continued. "Hope is on her way there, according to the officer who called. They want to question her as well. I'd chalk it up to the fact that it's a murder investigation, but I can't think of what you or Hope could contribute. Hope didn't even know she'd been murdered until I told her."

Matt grabbed his things. "If Hope is on her way, then I'll head over there now."

Jeremy followed him out of the barn. "I had a feeling you'd say that. You got it bad, my friend."

Matt turned to Jeremy. "There's something about her. I don't know. Something about her pulls at me."

"Sad eyes. You always were a sucker for a damsel."

Matt's brow rose at that. "Name one."

Jeremy held up a hand and ticked off his fingers. "Tiffany, Rose Marie, Gretchen, what's her name, Amber…"

Matt threw up his hands. "All right. I get it. But Hope is stronger than any of those women. If you'll recall, she's the one who rescued me. What is the male equivalent of a damsel?"

Jeremy shook his head. "I have no idea. I don't think I want to find out. Go on. I'll have Mike watch the mare until you get back."

"You got it, boss."

Matt took time to take a quick shower and change into clean clothes. He smelled like the inside of a barn. It was after five when he got there. He looked around and saw Hope's car. Satisfied, he headed inside.

Hope was sitting at a desk, her back to him when he came in. The officer at the front desk directed him to where Hope was sitting.

"Officer. I'm Matt Henney."

The man rose. "Detective Parks. I'm glad you could make it. I've been talking to Mrs. Turner here, and she says she was with you when the murder of the woman occurred."

Hope turned her eyes to his for a brief moment. There was nothing in them. She turned back to the detective. "It's Whitfield, Detective."

"So you said. Changed your legal name back to your maiden name last year."

Matt's fists clenched at his sides. "Mrs.?"

Hope kept her back to his. "Mrs. My husband's name is Turner."

The detective gestured for Matt to sit. "Ms. Whitfield says that on the twentieth of May, she was with you and a few other men looking for Meggie Edgerton. The coroner estimates the time of death of my victim sometime between the twentieth and the twenty-first. It's hard to be completely sure. It could have been earlier. Ms. Whitfield says no one can vouch for her whereabouts on the nineteenth, but that you could for the other two days."

Matt felt anger burning under his skin, but he didn't let it show. "I can vouch for her from the late afternoon of the twentieth until the morning three days ago."

"And you didn't see the body? Ms. Whitfield is the one who found it?"

"I was concussed and had a dislocated shoulder. I

was too dizzy to walk. She was out gathering wood when she came back and told me she'd found a woman's body on a ledge in the ravine north of our camp. I called it in on our satellite phone. One of our employees, Mike Ridley, took the call."

"I spoke to him briefly on the phone. He confirmed the time you called."

Matt loosened his fist. "Why are you asking me to provide an alibi?"

The detective shut his notebook with a quick snap of his hand. "Mrs. Turner has a criminal history that ties to this case. And the body she found was in a remote location. Not exactly out in the open where one would stumble upon it."

Hope gave the first sign of life since Matt sat down. "I do not have a criminal history."

The detective crossed his ankle over his knee. "Not an official one. But I think you would agree that the details surrounding you and your husband could be pertinent to this case. And like I said, that body wasn't exactly out in the open."

"No, I would not agree. I've answered all your ridiculous questions. If you are not going to charge me, I'm leaving."

"Don't leave town, Mrs. Turner; I will be calling again."

Matt grabbed Hope's wrist. "Anything else, detective?"

"Not right now, Mr. Henney. I'll be in touch if I have further questions."

Hope jerked her arm, but Matt held firm. He walked her outside. When they got to her car, he released her. "Mrs. Turner, Hope? You're married?"

Hope nervously swallowed. "Yes."

"Today. Right now. You're married?"

Hope gave him the same single-word answer. "Yes."

Matt cursed. "Who is he? Where is he?"

Hope dug her keys out of her pocket. "His name is Marlon Turner. I don't know where he is."

Matt cursed again, this time causing her to jump. Matt turned to go to his truck. Then he spun back. "Don't you think that's something you should tell the guy you're screwing?"

Hope flinched. "No."

Matt opened her car door himself. He slammed it when she slid inside.

Anger overtook him as he stormed to his truck. He climbed in and slammed his door. Red hot fury burned in him. She had lied. They had set fire to his sheets, and she was married.

He slammed his palms on his steering wheel, then jammed the key in the ignition. But he didn't drive off until his temper was under control. Hope's sweet face was all he could see. And she had lied through her pretty little teeth.

When Matt got back to the ranch, he knew he needed to work off his pent-up anger. Mucking stalls out was as good as anything. He nodded at Mike but kept going. For the next two hours, he worked until his muscles hurt.

Jeremy found him sitting on the ground outside the stables three hours later. "Mike said you were in a rage. You okay?"

Matt took a swallow of his warm beer. It had been cold when he opened it, but he didn't want it. Alcohol never solved one's problems. One of the only lessons he'd learned from his deadbeat father before the state had taken him from him.

"Matt?" Jeremy sat on the dirt beside him.

"She's married."

Jeremy jerked his head. "What?"

"Married. The woman is married. Admitted it right to my face. Not an excuse, not an apology. Just yes, she's married."

Jeremy took the beer from him and finished it. "Not sure what to say to that."

Matt glanced at his friend. He could see anger on his friend's face. Not as angry as he was, but it was there. "Nothing to say. Married is married."

"And off-limits."

Matt got up and pulled a couple of fresh beers from the fridge where he'd stashed them. "I've never messed with other men's wives or girlfriends. The way I figure it, a man or woman who cheats once will keep doing it. Never fancied myself the other man. It never occurred to me to ask her. She seemed so alone. Isolated."

Jeremy popped the tops on their beers. "She kept to herself. We know she lied about where she was staying. She's been secretive. Now we know why."

"She said his name is Marlon Turner. Why does that sound familiar?"

"You and Allie both said you felt like you knew her from somewhere."

Matt took two pulls of his beer. "I need my computer."

"Want me to come with you? We can get drunk."

Matt just shook his head. "No. You have a wife and a new baby who needs you. I'm just pissed."

Jeremy gave him a knowing look. "And hurt. You like her a lot. I knew it before I realized you'd slept with her."

Matt swore. "And hurt. I'll get over it. But never mind. I'll still sit with the horses tonight. The fresh air will do me good."

Jeremy finished his beer. "Call me if you need me."

Matt didn't respond, just sat and finished his beer. Two hours later, the Appaloosa went into labor. She didn't need his help, but he was there just the same. It wasn't quite dawn when the foal was born. He watched the little filly get to her legs. Mama took to her baby right away. He waited a little while before he moved mama and her baby to a clean stall and cleaned up the mess. Since Jeremy would want to know, he sent him a quick text. The return text wasn't quite coherent, but Matt got the idea. Jeremy and Allie were still adjusting to a new baby of their own.

Matt stayed with the horses until he was relieved

in the morning. Tired, hungry, and still angry, he went home. He took a long, hot shower, letting the water pound on his sore muscles. His head ached, but he ignored it.

He made a quick breakfast before grabbing his laptop. He punched in the name Marlon Turner. A high-profile name came up. Defense attorney in Los Angeles. Age fifty-two. Matt kept reading. Now he knew where he knew the name. He'd defended some dirtbag Hollywood producer who had killed a kid while driving drunk. Got the charges down to involuntary manslaughter. Guy was sentenced to eighteen months and paid a fine. That's all that boy's life had been worth. Because it had been a child, it had made the national press.

Guy was slick-looking. His hair was salt and pepper. The suit he wore probably cost a few thousand. He was smiling for the camera, his straight white teeth exposed. If this was the guy Hope was married to, what in the hell did she see in him? A quick bio said he was the son of a retired defense attorney who also tried several high-profile cases. It said he was twice married, but there was no mention of either of his wives' names.

There was a quick tap at his door. Allie popped her head in. "Can I come in?"

"Come to console me?"

Allie looked over his shoulder. "Yes. Who is that?"

Matt closed the laptop. "That may or may not be Hope's husband. I'm sure he's not the only Marlon

Turner in the world."

"The Mercedes."

He rubbed his tired eyes. "It's older, but yeah."

"She didn't say anything?"

Matt leaned back in his chair. "No. Though we didn't exactly have a lengthy conversation. I asked her if she was married. She said yes. She left. I left."

Allie bit her lip. "You know I hate to stick my nose in, but I feel like I should."

Matt didn't say anything. Allie wasn't one to meddle.

"What if she's running from him? When I hired her, I got this feeling of desperation. You can't fake that."

"It isn't a good excuse for not telling me."

Allie leaned her elbows on the table. "Maybe it is for her. Or maybe I'm just seeing what I want to see. I liked her when I met her. I had this crazy feeling I knew her."

"Yeah, so did I. I can't put my finger on it."

Allie got up and poured Matt a fresh cup of coffee. "So now what?"

"So now what, what? She's married, Allie. It's done."

"I don't believe that. And neither do you."

Matt kept silent. It had to be done. He didn't sleep with married women. He didn't have a lot of personal codes, but that was one of them. You don't hit women or children; you help others when they need help, you defend your country, and you don't sleep with married women.

"Just think about it, Matt.  Maybe she had a good reason for not telling you.  Put yourself in her shoes."

Matt took the coffee from her.  "I'll think about it.  Good enough?"

Allie kissed his cheek before heading for the door.  "Good enough."

* * *

But it wasn't good enough.  Matt couldn't stop thinking about Hope.  About the way she'd sat in the police station, her eyes void of any emotion.  About the way she'd corrected the detective when he called her Mrs. Turner.  The way her eyes lit with fury at the insinuation that she was a criminal.  And what of the comment that she and her husband's past was not relevant to the case?  Matt should have dug deeper into Marlon Turner, but he couldn't be sure it was the same man.  If the case hadn't involved a child, Matt wouldn't even have remembered his name.

So Matt did what he did best.  He worked.  It took the rest of the week for his headaches to fully fade.  His shoulder felt much better, though it still ached after a day's work.  The tendons would have been stretched when it dislocated, so he did his best not to overtax them.  But while he worked, he thought of Hope.

His phone buzzed, and he pulled it from his pocket.  Jeremy wanted to see him.  Matt shot off a couple of orders to the men and walked to the main office. The air was warm, and the sun was shining. It was almost a perfect day.

Jeremy waved him into the office. "I got word from Jessie that the police found the teenagers who attacked her. They were found near the Canadian border. Dumb kids didn't know you needed a passport to cross. Got caught trying to cross illegally."

Matt dropped into the chair across from Jeremy. "Glad they were finally caught. It's hard to believe two teenagers assaulted two women and terrorized their sister."

Jeremy tossed the pen he was holding. "They found themselves a couple of victims on their way to the border. They crossed state lines. I'm guessing the Feds are involved. But I rang up the state police and they have Jessie's and Hope's victim statements. You're the only other local witness. They wanted to corroborate your story with Jessie's. They said you can just call."

Matt pinched the bridge of his nose. "I'll drive out there. I've got some errands I've been meaning to run, and I need to get groceries. And frankly, the drive will be good for me."

Jeremy walked Matt out. "You do your best thinking on the road. I figure that's why you drove a semi for so many years."

Matt had grown weary of the open road, but he had seen a lot of the country that way. The long days on the road had been worth it to now own a piece of this land. "I much prefer ranch life. And I'd rather be climbing a mountain than delivering fuel. I'll see you tomorrow."

The state police station was only an hour's drive. It didn't give him much time to think, but he'd been doing too much of it lately. He saw Detective Parks at his desk, but a different detective took his statement. Before he left, he decided to go talk to the detective.

The man looked up. "Mr. Henney, right?"

"Yeah. I was wondering if there was any news on the murder of that woman."

The detective leaned back in his seat. "Got a name. Does the name Natalie Gerber sound familiar?"

It did. "I know a Landon Gerber. He owns a big spread north of the Waters Ranch. I think he has a couple of daughters."

"Natalie and Rebecca."

"Damn. And they didn't report her missing?"

The detective gestured for him to sit. "Do you know Mr. Gerber personally?"

"I know him well, I guess. As well as anyone else around here. My business partners and I bought a couple of horses from him last year. He's a well-known breeder. Deals straight."

The detective nodded. "I heard he's a straight shooter from everyone I've spoken with. No one thinks he'd have hurt his daughter. His other daughter alibied him. They were delivering a horse a few hundred miles away around the time Natalie was killed."

"I know you're not supposed to talk about the case, but why would you think Hope Whitfield has anything to do with Natalie's murder?"

"For one, her name isn't Hope Whitfield. It's Jaclyn Turner. Hope is her middle name, and Whitfield is her maiden name. It's public record, but her husband was on trial for killing his girlfriend. He was accused of strangling her to death. But when his wife was attacked and strangled the same way his girlfriend was killed, and he had been in police custody, the D.A.'s office eventually dropped the charges. But it got ugly. Mrs. Turner was to be a witness for the prosecution. Then suddenly she claims she doesn't remember. Her husband's lawyer was all over the news saying how hurt Mr. Turner was that his wife would make up lies about him. And how he still loved her and that they needed to move past this bump in their relationship. As if accusing your husband of murder is an everyday occurrence."

Matt couldn't believe what he was hearing. "I assume there's more."

The detective continued. "Mrs. Turner moved back in with her husband, only to disappear a few days later. The press had a field day. Mr. Turner hired a private investigator. The investigator goes on television and says he has reason to believe Mrs. Turner murdered her husband's girlfriend. That her so-called assault was perpetrated by Mrs. Turner to lead investigators away from looking in her direction.

She hadn't done herself any favors with her disappearing act. I saw some of the news footage. You wouldn't know it's the same woman. But either way, Jaclyn Turner or Hope Whitfield, she is now in our state, and she just happens upon a woman who was strangled and dumped? I'm not a firm believer in coincidences. But I don't have evidence, and I don't have a motive."

Matt couldn't reconcile what the detective was telling him with the woman he knew as Hope Whitfield. "Thanks. I appreciate your talking to me."

"You two seemed close. I wouldn't advise getting any closer."

Matt nodded and left the station. He took a few deep breaths of fresh air. When he climbed into his truck, he closed his eyes, absorbing what the detective told him. But no matter how he played it out in his mind, he couldn't believe Hope was a murderer.

Chapter Eleven

Hope closed the door of her car and leaned against it. She could see guests, some of them getting an early start on their day. She could smell the scents of the farm and barns in the distance. She rubbed her chilled arms and headed to the main office.

She figured it was part desperation and part masochism that had her showing up for work. The likelihood that she had a job was likely nonexistent. It had been one thing when Jeremy and Matt had offered Hope Whitfield her job back, another when it was Jaclyn Turner. When she pulled the door open, it was Matt she almost ran into.

Matt steadied her but abruptly dropped his hand. "I wasn't sure you would show up today."

Hope did her best not to fidget. Or stare. He was the only man in her memory that she'd been intimate with, and he seemed none too pleased to see her. Of course, for him, she was just one of many.

Jeremy came out of the office while she and Matt stared at each other. He cleared his throat. "If it were up to me, I'd boot you out. But I'll let Matt decide."

Hope's hand tightened on her bag, but her eyes never left Matt's.

Matt waved a hand at Jeremy. "I owe her, if nothing else. She already thinks the only reason we offered her the job back was because we slept together. Might as well make it official. I'll meet you in the barn once you're done renewing your paperwork."

Hope flinched at his insinuation. Definitely desperate and masochistic.

Jeremy waved at the young woman at the desk. "Please get Hope's paperwork back in the system. We'll consider the past few days a vacation. There won't be any more."

Hope ignored the threat. She took a seat and answered all of the woman's questions. She then pulled her work gloves out of her bag, along with Matt's hat. She'd been tempted to burn it but knew he had every right to his anger. But it hurt. And for Hope, who had lived through so much hurt the past two years, she felt like she was being perpetually punished simply for being alive.

She received a few nods from the other workers, and she responded in kind. The men and women who worked with the animals were nicer than the women she had worked with on the cleaning staff. The ranch hands were more discreet, keeping their feelings to themselves.

She went back to the same chores Matt had given to her before. The deal was she got her old job back, and she was determined to do it. She worked the morning, feeling each time Matt's eyes drifted to her. She purposely kept her back to him, not wanting to draw any attention her way.

When it was time for lunch, she slipped out the back of the barn and headed to her car where she'd left the lunch she'd packed. She couldn't bear to go to the mess hall with all of the curious eyes on her. She'd already had enough of that today. They all knew she'd been fired, and she would bet they all knew the reason she'd been rehired. Though she supposed saving the boss's life was a pretty darn good reason to give someone their job back.

She'd only gotten halfway back to her car when Matt caught up to her. He kept his stride to her pace, not saying a word. When they neared an outbuilding, he tugged her behind it. Hope would have refused if given the chance, but he pulled her in so fast and had her between the building and his body. He wasn't touching her, but he was crowding her, and she knew he wasn't going to let her leave.

For a moment, they just stood there looking at each other. It would have been funny if it didn't hurt so much to see anger in his eyes directed at her.

She let her legs slide out from under her until she was sitting on the ground. Matt joined her.

Matt broke the silence. "Is your husband that lawyer from L.A.?"

Hope pulled her knees to her chest, not at all surprised that he knew who her husband was. "Yes."

Matt's jaw clenched. "You told me once you're not from L.A.? That true?"

Hope glanced at him. "Not originally."

Matt's frustration was palpable. "Where

originally?"

"Boston.  My father was born there.  My mother was born in Virginia, but she hated it, so when they married, they remained in Boston."

"Allie's dad is from Virginia.  Still lives there.  He owns a farm that's been in the family for a century."

Hope glanced to see if he was fishing for information, but he looked more like he wanted to shout at her and was trying not to.  "What about Allie's mom?"

"Left when she was a kid.  Why didn't you tell me, Hope?"

Hope knew she was only going to make him angrier, but she felt compelled to tell him the truth. "Because it doesn't matter."

Matt got to his feet.  "It matters to me."

Hope's throat constricted, but she held firm. "That's your problem, not mine.  One night doesn't make a relationship.  If we had gotten beyond boss and employee and pure survival, maybe I would have told you.  We're not friends, Matt.  He's none of your business."

Matt started to leave but then turned back to her. "Why are you here?  And I don't mean the ranch."

Hope dropped her head to her knees.  "That would be the other secret."

Matt ran a frustrated hand through his hair.  "And we're not friends, so you won't tell me."

Hope turned her head to the side.  "You're catching on."

"You said you didn't know where he was.  Is that true?"

Hope stayed curled up on the ground.  "Right now, today, it's true.  I assume he's in L.A., but he's not taking my calls."

Matt leaned up against the building but didn't sit this time.  "How long has he not been taking your calls?"

Hope got up and dusted off the seat of her jeans. "Only recently.  Why does it matter to you?  You're obviously uncomfortable that you had sex with a married woman.  So we skip that date we talked about.  You go back to being the boss and I go back to being the employee.  I'm sure there are any number of women around here who would be willing and able to be exactly what you want."

Matt took her shoulder.  "And what do I want, Hope?"

"For starters, someone not married.  Someone who will spill their guts to you.  I'm not perfect, Matt.  I don't pretend to be.  But I will not, and won't ever, apologize to you for not telling you.  I don't owe you an explanation."

"Fine.  Have it your way."

Hope watched Matt walk away.  She felt tears sting her eyes, and they seeped between her closed lashes. Pain shimmered through her, but it was done.  They were done. When she'd come here, all she wanted to do was take possession of the land left to her by an aunt she had never met and meet the half-sister she'd never met.  She wanted to work until she had enough money to pay off her debts and figure out what she was going to do with the rest of her life.

So far, she had taken possession of a property that was uninhabitable, at least the house.  She had not connected with her half-sister.  And given how things were going, she would likely not have enough money to cover her debts, much less plan a future anytime soon.  She had been relieved when Jeremy let Matt decide whether to keep her on.  There was a lot of compassion in Matt, and no doubt he did feel he owed her.  But compassion and gratitude would only last so long in the face of a stubborn woman intent on keeping her secrets.

* * *

A week passed.  Then another.  And another.  Summer was in full swing.  She'd been in touch with the police, and the two boys had pleaded guilty to all charges.  According to Jessie, they had been proud of their crimes and bragged in court.  Hope couldn't bring herself to go to the hearing.  Part of their plea was a sentence to juvenile detention until they were eighteen.  So one would spend two years, and one would spend three.  And then they would be out to do it all over again.

She hadn't heard anything from Detective Parks about the murder of that poor woman.  Local newspapers reported her name was Natalie Gerber and that she was from the area.  Funeral services had been held last month.  Hope had attended, but had stood in the distance, so as not to be seen.  She wasn't sure what drove her to go, but the memory of the woman's body on that ledge haunted her still.

She was on her way to the stables when she heard her name called.  Matt was in the distance.  He hadn't been around much.  She knew he was busy taking groups out camping, hiking, and climbing.  When he wasn't doing that, he took groups up the trails on horseback.

Matt stopped a few feet away.  "I need you to come with me today.  Holly is out sick, Jackson banged up his knee pretty badly and can't ride.  Everyone else is booked.  I'm taking a group up the trails.  You'll bring up the rear."

Matt didn't wait for her to respond.  His long legs ate up the distance between him and the other stables where the trail horses were housed.  She had to run and then jog to keep up with him.

Jessie waved at her from where she was grooming one of the horses.  "Hi, Hope.  I hear you get to ride the trails today."

Hope watched as Matt saddled one of the smaller horses.  "You don't ride?"

Jessie shook her head.  "Back injury a few years ago.  I love horses, but I'm happy to stay on the ground. I'm terrified of falling."

Hope took the reins when Matt handed them to her.  "The mare I rode up the mountain was sure-footed. I bet you could handle her, but I get what you mean."

"Mount up." Matt patted the horse's rump as he went around the two women.

Jessie whispered. "He has a burr under his saddle if you know what I mean. I've known him for a couple of summers. He's usually laid-back, but not these days."

Hope glanced at his retreating back. "Maybe he's just tense. He is an owner now."

Jessie contemplated that. "Maybe. Some of the hands figure it's woman trouble, but no one has seen him with a woman. Well, other than you when you two found that poor girl in the canyon."

Hope tucked her head and mounted the horse. She was grateful when Jessie went back to work. She let the horse get used to her weight, and the horse relaxed. No doubt the mare was used to different riders all the time. She rode behind Matt to meet up with the group.

She stayed in the back and listened while Matt gave the group instructions. There were water and snacks in everyone's saddlebags. He encouraged everyone to take pictures, take in the view, and enjoy the next two hours on horseback.

Hope enjoyed her first ride up the trail with the group. There were lots of questions about the horses, the land they were riding through, and lots of giggles from the children when the animals did what animals do. But she found herself smiling along with them, listening to the timbre of Matt's voice as he answered questions, and enjoying the view along the way. It was very different in the daylight and when not searching for a missing child.

Hope found her shoulders relaxed for the first time in two years. She let the rhythm of the horse beneath her and the warm breeze on her skin lull her as she rode. The two-hour round trip went by fast. When they got back to the stables, there were lots of thank yous, last-minute questions, and excitement of heading on to the next activity. They took out a second group before lunch.

Hope forgot herself when Matt approached her. "That was fun. I should have taken you up on the offer to ride the trails."

Matt took her wrist until she was walking in step with him. They were halfway to the mess hall when Hope realized where they were headed.

She balked and yanked her wrist free. "I brought food."

Matt took her wrist again. "You need a solid meal in you. Riding the trails might not seem like hard work, but you'll be sore later."

Hope reluctantly followed. She saw a few people looking at her when she trailed behind Matt to get their meal. She saw the whispers and even heard a few comments. Angry that she was once again the object of gossip, she glared at them and then turned back to Matt.

Matt saw where she was looking. "There you go.

Give it right back to them."

Hope grabbed a pre-wrapped sandwich, a bowl of fruit slices, a carton of milk, and a couple of cookies. Matt grabbed a bag of chips and tossed it on her tray. She opted not to say a word as Matt led them to an empty table for two.

They were quiet as they ate. Hope wasn't sure what to say to him. Every time she saw him, she had an urge to give him the apology she swore she'd never give him. She wanted to tell him that Marlon wasn't important because they were separated and as soon as Marlon signed the papers, they'd be divorced. She wanted to explain that Marlon didn't feel like her husband, and she didn't think of him that way. He was an obstacle she needed to overcome before she'd be completely free of Jaclyn, and Hope could get the chance to figure out who Hope was. She didn't know how to articulate that to him. She could barely explain it satisfactorily to herself.

Matt finished every bite on his plate. "You are a good rider. You must have spent a lot of time on horseback over the years."

Hope knew she had because a friend from before her attack told her. And she'd seen the blue ribbons in an old keepsake box before she'd tossed the box in a dumpster. "I competed in cross-country riding in my teens and early twenties. Won a few ribbons, though I wasn't at top competitor levels."

Matt sat back. "That might be the first thing you've told me about yourself, other than you were born in Boston and are married. Your eyes lit up."

Hope swallowed the lump of food in her mouth. She had a fleeting memory of her in her riding clothes, her teeth in braces, and her long reddish-brown hair in braids. She remembered a beautiful golden mare, but like all her memories, this one faded as quickly as it had come.

Matt's mouth tightened. "And there is that look."

Hope didn't know what he meant. "What look?"

"The one that says butt out."

Hope was sorry for it. She rose from her seat and waited for him to join her. She tried to think of something else to say. Nothing came to her.

"We'll have two more groups to take out. You're free to go home after that. I have to meet up with Jeremy and tackle some paperwork that neither of us wants to do."

She kept in step with him as they headed back. "How's Allie and Sawyer doing?"

They were near the outbuilding they'd talked behind the day she had returned to work. Matt once again took her wrist and pulled her behind it. He looked down into her eyes as he pulled her with him. "Fine. I need to stay away from you, Hope."

Hope didn't understand what he meant until he pulled her body flush to his and his mouth took hers in a bruising kiss. She felt her back press up against the wall of the building as Matt's mouth devoured hers. She got up on her tiptoes, using what strength there was in her arms to bring her body closer. She moaned when his hands cupped a breast through her shirt. Her fingers fisted in his hair as she returned the kiss, as desperate as he was.

Then, abruptly, she was back on the ground, and Matt was stalking off toward the stables. She pressed trembling fingers to her mouth and her other hand to her chest, where her heart was pounding. Every part of her ached for him.

For the rest of the afternoon, he ignored her. The afternoon groups were as lively as the morning ones, but the relaxation of the morning was a distant memory. She was tense as they rode. She was torn between anger and frustration. If he had a problem with her being married, she could understand that. She even applauded him for it. Under other circumstances, she liked to think she'd be faithful. But the kiss had left want behind. She wanted to shake him. She wanted to tell him the truth. She wanted him to look at her like he had that night in his bed. She wanted him to kiss her like he did in front of his friends, a cross between satiated desire and possession.

When they got back to the stables, Matt told her she could go.

"Hope."

She stopped, but kept her back to him.

"I'll need you again tomorrow."

She could have laughed and cried at that statement. "Tomorrow."

The drive back to her "home" was a short one.

Trixie greeted her like always, but Trixie stayed on her heels as she went to her tent and tossed her things inside. The dog was sniffing the air and was alert to every sound.

Hope's heart raced a little. She glanced around, but the woods behind her were silent except for the normal sounds as dusk approached. Feeling unsettled at the dog's behavior, Hope looked around. Nothing seemed disturbed. Everything was where she'd left it. Hope walked the perimeter of her camp but didn't see anything.

She wandered closer to the house. The door was half on its hinges, which was normal. It creaked when she pushed it. There were dozens of critters inside, but they all scurried away at the presence of the woman and dog. Trixie sniffed around and Hope didn't like the sudden feeling of unease. There were decaying piles of leaves and dirt inside. As she took a few tentative steps beyond the door, it looked like some of those piles had been disturbed. There was more dirt in the air than normal, and Hope couldn't shake the feeling that something was off. She just couldn't pinpoint what.

Trixie just sniffed around. When Hope quickly exited the house, Trixie was once again at her heels. She squatted in front of the dog. "Was there an animal in there? Something you scared away?"

The dog licked her cheek and then rambled back to the tent. Hope kept her eyes and ears peeled, but nothing else seemed out of the ordinary.

She was uneasy the rest of the night.  She washed up inside the tent, which was not normally her habit, but tonight she felt very exposed.  As darkness fell, there was nothing out there that Trixie sensed.  Hope felt unease crawl over her skin.  She wanted to get into her car and leave.  But she wasn't about to let nerves and fear drive her away from what was hers. She doused the fire and went to bed early.  She didn't sleep well.

Chapter Twelve

Hope enjoyed another day on the trails. She got a kick out of the kids the most. It was nice to see families enjoying each other and nature. By the time the day was over, she was exhausted.

Sleep had eluded her last night. In the light of the morning, she realized she had overreacted. Likely it was animals that had been in the old house. Trixie would not have hesitated to chase something inside.

She was turning the horse over to the groom when she heard her name on the radio. Matt waved her over.

Jeremy was on the other side. "Hope. I need you to come to the main office. You have a visitor."

Hope's heart pounded in her chest. No one knew she was here, other than the police. But she couldn't imagine what else they might need from her. But she remembered the way Detective Parks had looked at her. He had sized her up to see if she fit his case. She knew she didn't, but knowing one was not guilty and proving it were very different things.

Matt was right behind her as she headed over. She didn't recognize the man standing next to the front door. He was taller than Matt, with black hair and a dark complexion. He was watching her as she came in.

"Mrs. Turner? I'm Agent Troy." The man pulled out a wallet and flashed an FBI badge.

Hope stared at the badge. "FBI?"

"I need to talk to you about your husband. Where can we talk in private?"

Hope didn't want to talk to him in private. Other than the agent, Matt was the only one here. And while she didn't want Matt involved with anything that involved Marlon, her dislike of law enforcement won out. "We can talk right here."

Matt went and opened the door to Jeremy's office. "In here."

Hope let out a relieved breath when Matt joined them.

The agent stayed standing while Hope dropped into a chair. Her legs were rubbery beneath her. "I can't imagine why the FBI wants to talk to me about Marlon."

"Are you sure you don't want to discuss this in private? This is not going to be a pleasant conversation."

Hope crossed her arms over her chest. "Since when is any conversation with law enforcement pleasant?"

The agent didn't react to her comment. He opened the leather briefcase he carried and pulled out a case file. He took out two photos and set them down.

Hope's first thought was that Marlon had lost weight. Her second registered what she was seeing. She gasped, shot to her feet, and backed away from the photos.  She felt Matt's hands close over her shoulders as her back hit his chest.  She felt the blood drain from her face, but she couldn't take her eyes off the photos.

Marlon's eyes were glazed in death.  His eyes looked bloodshot.  She could see a thin nylon rope wrapped around his neck.  Her hand instinctively went to her throat as she struggled to breathe.

Matt swore.  "For God's sake, pick them up."

The agent took his time.  "When was the last time you saw your husband, Mrs. Turner?"

Hope pressed herself into Matt.  "Two years ago. When I left him.  I haven't seen or talked to him since. We've only talked through lawyers."

The agent tapped the folder.  "When was the last time your lawyer talked to him?"

She let Matt guide her back to the chair.  She dropped onto it.  "Last year.  After that, I couldn't afford to pay the lawyer.  When did you find him?"

"That's the interesting question.  He was in a freezer for six months before we were able to identify him."

That made no sense.  "He was a lawyer.  A criminal one at that.  His prints are on record."

The agent contemplated her.  "His fingers were missing."

Horror filled her.  "I can't do this."

Hope slammed out of the office and ran outside. She went around the side of the building, her stomach retching as her lunch came back up.  She dropped to her knees, her heart pounding in her chest. Fear crashed through her. Ghosts of memories she wasn't sure were real assaulted her.

*You're lucky to be alive. The good Samaritan who found you was a nurse. She opened your airway and did CPR.*

The agent came around where Hope was on her knees. Matt brushed him out of the way as he helped her to her feet.

"I realize this is a shock. But there are about ten million reasons why I need to talk to you."

Hope's voice was a whisper. "Money."

"Yes, Mrs. Turner. Money. Often the biggest motivation for the things people do to one another."

Hope took a deep breath and tried to calm her racing heart. "Not me. His family. We have a prenuptial agreement. I'd get an allowance out of the estate in the event of his death."

The agent took out a notepad. "Who would inherit?"

She wrapped her arms around her waist. "I don't know. His son, I suppose. Maybe his dad. I don't have a copy of his will."

The agent gestured for her to come back inside. "I've got more questions. It would be better if you took a seat."

Matt took her arm. "Should I leave?"

Hope wanted to laugh at that. "I didn't kill him."

Matt took her hand and led her inside. "I know,

Hope."

Hope took a seat on the sofa that sat on the side wall instead of the chair. "What do you need to know? I haven't seen him. I called his office, but all they told me was that he was taking an extended vacation."

The agent took a seat on the edge of the desk. "That's the same story I got from his secretary. His son said he hadn't talked to him in a while. His father said much the same."

Hope struggled to remember something, anything, but it just wasn't there. "I'm not sure what you want from me."

"Why did you leave him?"

Another question she wasn't sure she truly knew the answer to. "I guess you could say I wasn't the same person I was before. We had a bad argument, and I decided I wanted out. He refused. I left and hired a lawyer."

"And it had nothing to do with the fact that you accused him of murdering his girlfriend?"

Hope paled. "Why do you ask questions when you already know the answers? I don't remember accusing him of murdering his girlfriend. But court documents state I did."

Agent Troy ignored the outburst. "Where have you lived since?"

"I left L.A. and I went to Oregon for a short while. I rented a house there on the southern coast. Then I started drifting east. I spent some time in Twin Falls,

Idaho. Then I guess you could say I roamed for a little while, with no legal address. Six months ago, I found out I was going to inherit a piece of property on my thirty-second birthday. So I came here. I've been working for the Waters most of that time."

Hope answered question after question, most of which she couldn't answer.

"And you don't own a cell?"

She shook her head. "No. I only have a P.O. Box. How did you find me?"

The agent tucked his papers back in his briefcase. "State police. You've been a busy woman. Attacked by two teenagers and found a dead woman. Coincidentally strangled. You don't mind submitting to a DNA swab, do you?"

Frustration and anger filled her, but all she did was nod. She let him swab the inside of her cheek. "I didn't kill her, and I didn't kill Marlon."

"Time will tell. I only have one more question for you. Can anyone provide you with an alibi six months ago?"

Her answer was an unsteady "no."

The agent handed her his card. "Call me if you think of anything else. I'll be in touch."

Matt spoke up. "Why is the FBI looking into the case of Mr. Turner's death?"

The agent tucked his briefcase under his arm. "A normal course of action when someone is killed. It really is most often the spouse or partner."

Matt opened the office door. "That doesn't explain

why the FBI is investigating it and not the local police."

The agent nodded. "No, it doesn't. Should an arrest be made, I'll discuss it with Mrs. Turner in an interrogation room. I'll be in touch, Mrs. Turner."

Hope dropped her head in her hands. Fear, anger, humiliation, and hopelessness consumed her. Unwanted tears fell and dripped onto her pants. Not tears for Marlon. But for herself. She wiped the tears away and jumped to her feet. "I have to go."

She bolted and started toward her car. She reached blindly into her bag for her keys.

Matt caught up to her and gently pulled her to a stop. "You shouldn't be driving. Let me take you home."

She yanked her arm from his grasp. "No."

Matt followed her to her car. He made one last effort. "Please, Hope. You're in no shape to drive."

She opened the door but hesitated. "I need to take time off. I don't even know where to start. I get bereavement time, yes?"

"I suppose that's how it works."

"I have to go." Hope climbed in and drove off, watching Matt in her rear view mirror.

When she got back to her camp, Trixie came bounding. She dropped to the ground, wrapped her arms around Trixie, and shed every tear she had been bottling up for so long.

* * *

Matt was rocking Sawyer as he finished telling Jeremy and Allie what had happened.

Allie was fixing lunch. "They think Hope killed him?"

Matt rubbed his hand soothingly on Sawyer's back as the baby drifted off to sleep. "I'm not sure. But it is a crazy coincidence that Hope finds out her husband was murdered, strangled no less, weeks after she found Natalie Gerber's body."

Jeremy handed Allie a pan. "There was another murder a town over. A young woman was strangled up near the Greater Pass. Her body was dumped in a wooded area not frequented by hikers. A local who was out fishing found her."

Matt got up and set the baby in the bassinet. "You're kidding? I didn't hear about it."

Allie shivered. "You don't suppose we have some crazy serial killer or something?"

Jeremy wrapped his arms around her. "Let's just say I don't want you going off by yourself until the police catch whoever killed those two women."

Allie laid her head on his chest as she gazed at her son. "It's just horrible."

Matt took over in the kitchen. "The agent wouldn't say why the FBI was investigating Hope's husband's murder. I think it's a bit of a stretch to think that his death is tied to the body Hope found. But I suppose they have to rule it out, and the cases cross state lines."

Allie kissed Jeremy's cheek and pulled away. "I wonder how Hope is feeling. From what we've gathered, they were not close. Two years is a long time to be estranged from one's husband and not seek a divorce. What's the next step?"

Matt kept his back to her and kept preparing dinner. "Next step is Hope's. She's going to take time off."

Jeremy joined him. "She's entitled to a week. But Allie was asking what you're going to do, and you know it. She's not a married woman anymore."

That hadn't gotten past Matt. But it didn't change the fact that she'd lied to him and that she believed herself married when she'd gone to bed with him. But the other part of him wanted to embrace the knowledge. Memories of Hope in his bed haunted his dreams. And despite knowing it was wrong, he still wanted her. That kiss yesterday told its own story.

Matt gave up the fight. "I need to find her. But I still don't know where she lives."

Jeremy set the table while Allie left to put Sawyer to bed. "You know she's stayed at that hotel in town. If she keeps to pattern, she'll be there tomorrow."

"There are so many questions I didn't ask her. She was distraught when she left. I shouldn't have let her drive."

Jeremy shook his head at that. "She's a grown woman, Matt. You can't make her do what you want. And maybe you weren't the best person to help her come to terms with the death of her husband."

Feeling a fresh burst of anger, Matt dished up dinner. "Every time I think about her being married, I get angry all over again."

"I give thanks every day that Allie wasn't married when I met her."

Matt raised his brow at his friend. "Do you think I would have introduced you? I knew you'd fall for her like a ton of bricks. And you did."

Allie came back. "I knew it was a conspiracy."

Matt pulled out a chair for her. "Love and loyalty are important. My father never understood that."

Jeremy cut that off. "Your father was a drunken loser. He didn't have an ounce of love in him. He drank all that out of himself. I doubt he ever knew what loyalty meant. No better than the piece of garbage that called himself my dad."

Allie leaned into him. "Sawyer will never know what you two experienced. His life will be full of love and laughter."

Jeremy kissed the top of her head. "That it will. So Matt, why don't you take the day off tomorrow? Go see if there is any chance of love or laughter in your immediate future."

"You don't even like her."

Jeremy shrugged. "You do. And if you do, then I do."

Allie seconded that. "Me too."

Matt was quiet for a time. "I think we need to let the staff and ranch hands know about what happened to that second woman. I don't like thinking about any of the women here wandering off alone. We can have the different managers speak to their teams."

Jeremy agreed. "I also think we'll increase security. I'll make a few calls in the morning. Guests are vulnerable as well. No one can imagine something terrible happening while on vacation."

Allie shivered. "I still can't believe it about Natalie. I didn't know her well, but we'd spoken some when I ran into her in town. Her father must be devastated."

Jeremy patted her hand. "I spoke with him shortly after we learned of her death. Offered him assistance if he needed it. He declined but said he'd let us know if he changed his mind. He's already gotten his other daughter out of town."

Matt didn't like the thought of Hope out there on her own. Tomorrow he'd do his best to find her.

* * *

Hope was torn between thinking of Matt and trying to decide what she should do. The agent hadn't been wrong. She was still Marlon's wife. She knew from the prenuptial contract that she was entitled to proceeds from his estate. She could take payments or a lump sum. But Hope didn't want Marlon's money. She had stopped being his wife two years ago, despite what the law said.

She knew she should call Marlon's son, Trey. He had given her his home number when she'd left his father. Trey had been at the house, and he was the one who helped her get out. His father had been swearing and throwing things; Trey had kept his father in check while she took the last of her belongings and left.

Hope spent her morning going through all of the papers she'd accumulated. She picked up the papers on top. If he had signed the divorce papers like she'd wanted, as his lawyer had advised him, she wouldn't be in this spot. She shuffled them and pulled out her marriage certificate. Hope didn't remember Jaclyn well. She was just as much a ghost to her as her husband. As much as her entire past was. Jaclyn Turner was gone, and Hope Whitfield now lived.

The next pile she wasn't interested in. She'd read through her medical records only once. Those she remembered. The days in the hospital and rehabilitation were Hope's first real memories. Not a great beginning, but full of potential. The third stack she supposed she could toss. That pile contained the court records and transcripts from Marlon's trial. Poor Miranda wouldn't get justice. And neither would her family.

Hope tucked them all back into the folder and pushed them under Trixie's bed. She was free. Free of Marlon. Free of all remnants of the past. Except for one. She still hadn't told her half-sister she existed. Her mother never once sought out the daughter she'd abandoned. Hope only knew of her because she found a copy of her half-sister's birth certificate in a pile with her own. That was how she learned she was to inherit this property and why she started making her way to Utah. That's also when she learned her sister had inherited the adjacent property and all of the buildings on it years before. The larger share had gone to the eldest daughter, with the smaller parcel going to the second. Hope had dug deep to make sure there weren't any more siblings.

Knowing she didn't have much choice, and that the longer she waited the harder it would be, Hope grabbed her things. The hotel had a phone. She could get her wash done, have a shower, and call Trey.

After Hope checked in and did her laundry, she locked herself in the room. Her heart pounding, she dialed.

"Trey Turner."

Hope had to clear her throat. "Hi, Trey. It's Hope. I mean, Jaclyn."

"Jaclyn. I'm so glad you called. I had no way to reach you. Dad's lawyers had no contact information. Your lawyer refused to talk to me. I take it you heard about Dad."

Hope closed her eyes as she took a seat. "An FBI agent found me. He told me what happened. He thinks I had something to do with it."

Trey scoffed over the line. "You wouldn't kill a fly or a mouse, much less a man. That whole mess with Miranda. I don't believe Dad killed her any more than I believe you did. But the FBI would have to investigate."

"Always a lawyer, Trey. Just like your dad and

granddad.  But you were always a lot nicer.  I appreciate the vote of confidence, but the agent did remind me about the prenuptial agreement your father and I signed.  I've got a copy of it.  I don't want anything.  I'd like to sign papers or whatever to that effect.  You should get your father's entire estate."

The line was silent for a moment.  Trey then cleared his throat.  "You're entitled to something.  I can only imagine what it was like to be married to him.  I did move into his house, though.  And I believe the prenup states I get the house."

Hope was glad of it.  "It's yours.  I don't think there is anything else there that is mine.  I was afraid to take anything that might belong to both of us."

The sound of Trey lighting a cigarette came through the line.  "There are a few things in the attic. I had the staff clean it out and bring it all down. There were some things that I think are your mother's, as well.  I'd like you to come get them.  That way you can decide if there is anything you'd like to keep."

Hope's stomach clenched at the thought of ever setting foot again in Marlon's house.  "If I give you an address, could you mail them?"

Trey inhaled and exhaled over the line.  "Jaclyn, I'd like for you to come get them.  I'd like to see you.  To see that you're okay.  And any papers you decide to sign, whether to take what you are more than owed or to sign it away, it would be best to do it under the eyes of an attorney.  Grandpa has been in a rage since word came of Dad's murder.  He's been harassing law enforcement.  Likely the FBI agent you talked to.  I don't want him to try to contest anything."

Hope pinched the bridge of her nose.  "I'd have to drive in.  I have a very large dog that will be coming with me."

"A dog?  Dad would be turning in his grave if he knew.  But drive, fly, whatever.  Just tell me when.  I can make sure your old bedroom is properly cleaned."

Hope didn't tell him what she thought of that idea.  "I'll get a hotel room."

Trey sounded apologetic.  "Of course.  I wasn't thinking.  I can bring your things to you at your hotel.  You can meet me at the office, sign the papers, and we'll catch up.  How does that sound?"

Like a nightmare, but she kept it to herself.  "I'll get back to you.  I have to take some time off work to come.  But thank you, Trey.  You were always nice to me."

"It was odd having a stepmother younger than me, but you never made it awkward.  I look forward to seeing you."

Hope hung up the line.  She glanced at her worn flip-flops, her cut-off shorts, and the t-shirt that was too big.  The money from Marlon's death would go very far indeed.  But she knew she couldn't.  Hope headed to the shower. One step at a time.

## Chapter Thirteen

Matt sat outside the rundown hotel on the outskirts of town. He'd been sitting in a parking lot across the street, parked in Allie's car instead of his truck. It was almost two, and he'd been sitting here for a while. In the past few hours, he'd seen some shady people coming and going, but no Hope. Not yet.

But this was the best plan he had to find her. He couldn't stake out the library or the grocery store until she showed up.

He was going to give it a couple more hours, then call it a day. But finally, at three, Hope pulled into the parking lot. Her curvy body was dressed in an oversized t-shirt and cutoff shorts. Cheap flip-flops and a pair of sunglasses completed the look. He stayed where he was. He didn't want to confront her here. He wanted to see where she went; confront her on her home turf.

She carried a laundry bag inside and didn't come back out for a couple of hours. She then went into her room. She came out an hour later, her hair wet and her laundry bag with her. He started the engine after she packed up her car and turned in the key at the front desk.

He kept his distance as he tailed her. He didn't

think she knew what Allie's car looked like, but he didn't want to take a chance that she'd notice him behind the wheel. She was headed back toward the ranch, but when she got to a fork in the road, she took the right turn instead of the left one that led to the ranch road.

He had to keep a longer distance. The GPS said they were on an unnamed road. But it was a dead end. There were properties that surrounded the Waters Ranch. If he wasn't mistaken, this road led to an abandoned house. He recalled Allie telling him she'd tried to locate the owner of the property. She had wanted to purchase it and build their home on this piece of land, but she hadn't had any luck. The only property records she had been able to find said the land was being held in a trust and that the owner had no desire to sell.

Matt parked the car and went the rest of the way on foot. Beyond a tree line, he could see the old house. It was condemned and probably had been for a decade. But that wouldn't stop a squatter. He didn't see Hope's car but could see tire tracks that went around to the back of the house.

Trixie came bounding out from behind the house, barking as she came toward him. The dog seemed more excited to see him than protective of her owner.

Hope came around the corner, hollering for Trixie. "What has gotten into you?"

Matt took off his sunglasses when Hope stopped in shock. "Me."

Hope glanced around as if she were looking for someone else. "How did you find me?"

Matt kept closing the distance between them. He wasn't sure, but she looked like she might run. "I followed you."

Hope wrapped her arms around herself in a protective stance and started walking backward. "Why?"

Matt stopped within a few feet of her. Two large strides, and he could touch her. "I was worried about you. And this seemed like the perfect opportunity to find out where you were living since you'd refused to tell me. What are you doing here?"

Hope's arms dropped to her side. "I live here."

Matt watched as Trixie bounded off behind the house. He brushed past Hope and followed the dog.

Hope dashed after him. "Matt, I don't want to talk to you right now. Things are complicated. We can talk when I come back to work."

Matt kept going. "I'm not inclined to wait."

He came around the corner. He wasn't sure what he expected to find, but a tent and a campfire weren't it. "You are living here."

Hope circled him. "That's what I said."

Her car was parked next to the house. Anyone approaching from the road wouldn't know anyone was here. He walked to the tent and flipped it open. There was a lantern, a pile of folded clothes, a makeshift bed, and a place for Trixie to sleep. That answered the question of whether she was here alone.

Matt dropped the flap and looked at her. Really looked at her. She had bruises under her eyes and her skin was pale. There was no smile there. No anger. Just nothing. "How long have you been living here?"

Hope dropped down onto a cushion she had on a tarp near the fire pit. "Since February, so over five months. Almost six."

Matt couldn't believe what she said. "In a tent? In February?"

Hope's words were monotone. "It was cold, but I survived. When it got really bad, I slept in my car."

Matt came over to her. She looked sick. He pressed his wrist against her forehead, but her skin was cool to his touch.

She pushed his hand away. Her voice broke when she spoke. "Why are you here?"

He dropped down so he was eye to eye with her. "Tell me about your husband. Why were you not in Los Angeles with him?"

Hope got on her knees and crawled into the tent. She came out with a thick manila envelope stuffed with papers. She pulled out a document and handed it to him. It was dated January two years ago. They were unsigned divorce papers. "I think this should answer a couple of your questions."

Matt took them and realized what they were. "One of them."

Hope set the folder down at her side. "I didn't know where Marlon was. I don't know if he was in Los Angeles. When I finally got the nerve to call his office and demand he sign them, the receptionist told me he was on sabbatical. I've been searching for him; I even hired a private investigator right after I started working at the ranch. It was like he dropped off the face of the Earth. I talked with his son today, but he didn't mention Marlon had been missing, and I didn't ask. All he said was that he hoped I would call. And was glad I did."

"These papers are from two years ago." Matt handed them back to her.

"He refused to sign them. Said we weren't getting a divorce. We had a huge fight. I took everything that was mine, and I left. I wasn't asking for alimony or any of our joint property. I just wanted the marriage over. I had an attorney working to dissolve the marriage without his signature; Marlon was adamant he wasn't going to sign it. But between legal fees and the fees the investigator charged, I couldn't afford to pursue the divorce without his cooperation. I had hoped now that enough time had passed, he'd be reasonable and sign."

Matt kept his eyes on her face. "Did he say why he wouldn't sign?"

Hope let out a harsh laugh, a sound he hadn't heard from her before. "No. But I know why. It's the same reason he tried to have me killed. It comes down to money. He didn't care about anything else."

Matt realized she meant every word. He picked up the file folder.

Hope leaned back on her hands. "Most people

would ask me why he wanted to have me killed."

Matt scanned the papers. Articles of a murder over two years old. Court transcripts. Photos. "I know what the detective knew. I spoke to him over two weeks ago. He said your husband was charged with murdering his girlfriend. That you were a witness to a violent argument, but then retracted your statement. He said your husband's lawyer made accusations that you'd faked your attack to drive suspicion away from yourself. Why did you recant?"

Hope's hands were shaking. "I didn't recant. I couldn't remember."

Matt flipped through additional papers. Medical records from two years ago with Hope's name on them. "Are you going to make me read these? Or will you give me the short version?"

Hope leaned over the papers he was holding and glanced at them. "Neurologists report. Prolonged oxygen deprivation. Permanent brain damage. Loss of memory. Loss of motor function, especially in the hands."

Matt looked into her eyes. Tears hovered as emotions came back to her. "How long is prolonged?"

Hope wiped her eyes. "Hard to say. Too long. In the police report, you'll find I was found in an alley. I don't remember the attack. I don't know who did it. I'm told that it's not unusual. But I couldn't testify in court to my previous witness statements because I couldn't remember witnessing anything. People thought I was faking it. Or that I lied."

"What did you witness?"

"Police records show I witnessed an argument between Marlon and Miranda. From what I gathered, Miranda was one in a long line of girlfriends. In the bottom stack, you'll find lots of social and gossip columns about his girlfriends. I found three, not including Miranda. If I knew about them, I don't remember."

Matt skimmed the medical records. His gut clenched as he read. "I can't imagine what that must be like."

Hope gently took the report from him and put it on the stack of papers by her side. "Part of me is glad. From what I have been able to piece together, I think I'd rather not remember. But I don't remember much of anything. I don't remember Marlon. I don't remember his son. I don't remember my mother. I think you get the picture."

Matt couldn't comprehend that. "Nothing? What about when you told me you had competed in cross-country riding?"

Hope glanced down at her hands. "Pictures. A few ribbons. I was a very good rider in my teens and twenties. I have what I call ghost memories. Little snippets that drift through my thoughts from time to time. Usually, something triggers them. When I mentioned it to you, I could see myself with a golden mare with a black mane and tail, and my long hair in braids. I think I was in my early teens."

Matt wanted to keep her talking. He sifted

through the other papers. "What other ghost memories do you have?"

Hope shook her head. "Not many. Not pleasant ones, anyway. I remember an argument with Marlon before I was attacked. It's why I think he attacked me. Or rather, had someone else do it. I was holding Sawyer when Allie brought him to your trailer, and his voice just came at me."

"What triggered it?"

Hope dropped her chin to her knees and wrapped her arms around them. "I was thinking about Sawyer. How nice it was to hold him. That I would have liked to have had a child. Then I could hear Marlon yelling at me when I told him I was pregnant. That I'd better get rid of it, or he would."

Matt dropped the papers he held. "You have a child?"

Hope wrapped her arms tighter around her legs, hugging herself. "No. The baby died. I had no oxygen, so the baby had no oxygen. It was tiny. Barely even there. I don't know if it was a girl or a boy. I don't remember being pregnant, but it's in the papers you're holding."

Matt kept reading and found the record; just a quick mention of it as if it were unimportant. Pregnancy terminated; spontaneous abortion due to the death of the fetus. "Hope, I'm so sorry."

Hope just shook her head. "Just one of many memories I don't have anymore. My life started two years ago. By reading those papers, you know everything I know about myself."

Matt kept scanning the piles. He came across a letter from an attorney about a land inheritance. He scanned it. "You said you inherited this property?"

"I did."

He had just been thinking about this land and Allie inquiring about it. "This land was held in a trust. Allie inherited the retreat and built the ranch. She wanted to buy this land but couldn't find out who owned it or who would inherit it. She just knew her aunt had owned it, as well as the other property."

Hope took the stack and shuffled through. "Held in trust until I turned thirty-two. The lawyer told me my aunt didn't want the land to go to a kid. Apparently, in her mind, thirty-two is when you're not a kid anymore. Allie's inheritance came after she was already thirty-two, so her land was never held in trust."

Matt got to his feet. He'd thought she looked somehow familiar. Looking at her through a new lens, he could see a resemblance. The hair was a little redder. She was shorter, but she had the same build, and her mouth and cheeks were the same as Allie's. It was the turquoise eyes that threw it off. "How are you related to Allie?"

Hope stood, tucking her hands into her back pockets. "Guess I should get it all out now. Allie is my half-sister. Her mom married my dad not long after she divorced Allie's dad. I have a copy of their marriage certificate. I came along a few years after their marriage.  The last photo I have of her was from the year I turned five.  I found her obituary when I went looking for her.  I found a copy of Allie's birth certificate after I left Marlon inside an old box."

Matt started pacing.  "Allie is going to flip out."

Hope came into his path.  Her pain-filled eyes held his.  "I'm not sure I should tell her.  I don't know if she knows about me.  I didn't want to come into her life and disrupt it.  She's happily married, and she just had a baby."

Matt closed the distance between them.  He pulled her into his arms and held her.  "You don't know Allie.  She'll be shocked.  But she'll be thrilled."

Hope laid her head on his chest for a moment before easing away.  "I'll take your word for it.  I don't think her husband will be."

Matt glanced at the papers on the ground.  "What else, Hope?"

"What?  Is it not enough?"

He simply waited for her to reply.

Hope shuffled her feet.  "Nothing else.  At least, not that I know of.  I talked to Trey today.  I need to go to L.A.  I told him I wanted to sign whatever I needed to sign to decline the money I'm entitled to in my prenuptial agreement."

Matt was confused.  "You want to decline the money?"

Hope nodded.  "Marlon was Jaclyn's husband.  Not mine."

Matt's voice was soft when he spoke.  "Hope,

you're the same person."

Hope's eyes darkened. "That is where you are wrong. I am not the same person. Jaclyn was spoiled and selfish. She didn't work. Her friends were superficial at best. Trust me, I met a few of them when I left the rehab center and moved back in with Marlon."

Matt was startled by the vehemence in her voice. "You need to cut yourself some slack."

She bent and pulled out a picture. She thrust it at him. "What do you think of her?"

The photograph was of a woman who only slightly resembled Hope. Only her eyes gave her away. Her hair was in a sleek black bob, not a hint of red. Her black suit was fitted to her frame. Her unsmiling mouth was painted a deep red. This woman looked cold and distant.

"That is Jaclyn." Hope grabbed another one and handed it to him.

It was a picture of Hope hugging Trixie and smiling. She was outside a vet's office. Her hair was a little longer than it was now, but he could see the slight freckles on her face, bare of makeup. She wore a loose t-shirt, jeans, and sandals.

Hope dropped her hand. "That is Hope. That's who I choose to be."

Matt understood what she meant. He touched the ends of her short curls that framed her face. "I like Hope just as she is."

* * *

Hope touched the soft smile on his lips. "I like Hope too. And this Hope wants to forget about Marlon. Forget about what she's learned about her past. As far as I'm concerned, Jaclyn died. I mourned her for a time. I wondered what she had been like. If the pictures and the stories were all that there was to her. I like to think that had her life been different, she might have been a different kind of woman. One more like Hope."

Matt bent and set the photos on top of the folder. "So what is the next step?"

"I go back to L.A. Sign the papers, collect my stuff that Trey has, and get back here as fast as I can. This land isn't much, but it's mine. One day I'll tear this house down and build a new one. I'll have a garden and a garage. Maybe a small orchard like Allie. I'll have a fenced-in area for Trixie and another dog to play in."

Matt took her hand and pulled her down to sit. "Sounds like a good plan. But Hope, you can't keep living outside."

She felt her defenses rise. "Yes, I can. It's not ideal. I wish I could afford to bring in a trailer, like yours. Or a smaller one. But I still have medical bills to pay, and now new ones. I just paid the property taxes and the inheritance tax. Maybe by winter. Had Jaclyn had a job and money of her own, I might not be in this predicament. No one will give me a builder's loan. I just hope I can hold onto my job long enough."

Matt touched her hair again. "You know, if you ride the trails and take campers on overnight trips with me, you'd get paid more."

Hope's eyes narrowed. "Only with you?"

Matt shrugged. "No, not just me. Though I like your company. We did spend three days on a mountain together."

Hope found she could laugh. Her muscles relaxed for the first time in days. "You were asleep for most of it. But I get your point. It's a deal."

Matt held out a hand. When she took it, Matt didn't shake it like she thought he would. Instead, he pulled her closer and set his lips lightly on hers. She raised her other hand and cupped his cheek.

Matt shifted and deepened the kiss. Hope knew she should pull back. She knew it was too soon after all that had happened between them. But she'd been alone for so long. She knew instinctively she could trust him. Matt made her feel good. Made her feel desirable. Made her feel like a real person—a woman with more than an empty past.

Matt released her. "When are you leaving for L.A.? I'll need to take time off to go with you."

Hope opened her eyes. "What?"

Matt rubbed his thumb over her lower lip. "You're not going back alone."

Hope scooted away. "You're not coming with me."

Matt scooted closer. "In case you forgot, last time you were in L.A. someone tried to kill you. If it was your husband, that doesn't mean whoever he paid isn't still around."

Hope gaped. "For what purpose? Marlon is dead."

Matt slapped his hand on the tarp, anger flaring in his eyes. "Murdered no less. Strangled the same way you were. The way his girlfriend was. You're not going alone. If I have to tail you, I will."

Hope relented. "Fine."

Matt's eyes narrowed as his eyes held hers. "Good. Come on, let's pack up your stuff. You can sleep in my spare room on your air mattress. Or you can sleep with me. But I can't promise that if you sleep with me, I'll keep my hands to myself."

Hope appreciated what he was trying to do for her. She really did. But she couldn't. "You can come with me. Honestly, I don't want to face my past alone. But I can't move in with you."

"I'm afraid I'm not going to give you a choice in this either. Jeremy heard there was another woman strangled. It's not safe for you to be out here alone. If they catch who did it, then you can move back here if you feel you have to. I'm not insensitive to what you're trying to do. I applaud it. But it's either you move in with me, or I pitch a tent with you. Your choice."

"And if I choose a tent?"

"Then we'll both be spending a lot of time outside together. Both of us are experienced campers. But I've got a toilet that flushes and hot water."

Hope picked up her folder and clutched it to her

chest.  "You'd do it too, wouldn't you?  I should choose a tent."

Matt waited.

"Was another woman really killed?"

Matt got to his feet. "Yes.  Come on.  I'll help."

Hope focused on breaking down her camp instead of thinking about a dead woman.  Matt helped pack up her car.  One day everything she owned wouldn't fit in her car.  She whistled for Trixie, who was off wandering.  She spent a good part of her day patrolling the perimeter.

Matt rubbed Trixie's ears before opening the car door to let her into the passenger seat.  "I'll be right behind you. You can park outside my trailer."

Hope looked at him before climbing inside.  "I hope you know what you're getting into."

"Deep water, no doubt.  But it's my choice."

Hope just hoped he could swim.

Chapter Fourteen

Hope hated L.A. She knew it wasn't fair to the city. But as horns blared on the congested freeway and the smog hung heavily over the skyline, Hope longed for the canyons and mountains back home. She wasn't sure when Utah became home, but over the past months, it had.

She was glad Matt was with her. He'd gone behind her back and bought airplane tickets. He'd gotten Jeremy and Allie to agree to watch the dog while they were gone. They'd only be in town for two days, but as far as Hope was concerned, that was too long. They'd flown in this morning and would meet with Trey and sign papers. She would then go through the boxes Trey had for her and ship back what she wanted to keep, if anything. They'd fly out tomorrow morning.

Matt glanced at her. "You okay?"

Hope made a face at her reflection in the glass. "I was not a fan of the airplane. And I'm not a fan of L.A."

Matt smiled at the face he saw her making. "L.A. has its charms. The freeway isn't one of them. I guess you don't remember if you've flown before."

Hope leaned back in her seat. She was grateful Matt was driving. "Let's just say I've had a lot of firsts since waking up in the hospital two years ago. I know I've flown before. I had pictures of me and Marlon on vacation in the early years of our marriage. I've been to Paris, London, and Venice. I had a few pictures of Shanghai too. I don't remember going to any of those places, except maybe a few fleeting memories of Venice."

Matt gently took her hand. "Maybe you'll go back one day. Make new memories."

Hope squeezed his hand. "Maybe. But I don't know if I've visited other states. So I keep thinking one day maybe I'll take a road trip. You know, when I'm old and gray, get an RV, and see the country."

Matt released her and put his hands back on the wheel as he changed lanes. The GPS said they were close to the lawyer's office Trey said to meet him at. "You can mark L.A. off your list. Though I wouldn't mark off the state. There is a lot of beautiful country to see in California. You could take a drive through wine country."

"I don't know if I like wine, but it still sounds fun. I drove through some of it on my way to Oregon."

They were now in downtown traffic. Hope was watching buildings and people pass by as Matt drove through the crowded streets. They passed a stadium. A memory tried to surface. She tapped the window. "Basketball?"

Matt glanced. "Yes. Lakers home stadium. Been here?"

Hope leaned her forehead on the glass. "I don't

know. I just know it's basketball."

"I've never been. I like to watch basketball. Fast-paced and lots of action. I played a little in junior high and high school when my grades were up. Jeremy and I have gone to see The Jazz in Salt Lake City. Allie hates basketball, so we'll do a guys' weekend."

"Does Jeremy play? You told me you grew up in a foster home with him."

Matt pulled onto a smaller street. "Jeremy is terrible at it. I tried to teach him, but he's got two left feet. His scholarships were all academic. He's smart, but he was like me back then, a bit restless. He changed majors as often as I changed jobs until he dropped out. He never did go back, and I figured going to college was a waste of money for a guy like me."

"I have an associate's degree in liberal arts. As far as I know, that's as far as I went. I have a diploma in my stack of papers."

Matt pulled into a parking deck. "How long were you and Marlon married?"

"Including the last two, ten years. Let's get this over with."

Hope and Matt walked the few blocks to the lawyer's office. It was on the sixteenth floor of a massive office building. She didn't like elevators, so she leaned into Matt as they rode up. When the door opened, there were double glass doors that led into an open-air office. The carpet was a dove gray, the reception desk was made of solid wood, and there was a sitting area with real art, not prints.

Hope took a deep breath. "Jaclyn Turner to see Trey Turner, please."

"I have instructions to take you back."

Hope snagged Matt's hand, pulling him along. She didn't know if he planned to wait in the reception area, but she found she couldn't do this alone. Her heart was pounding, and she was afraid she might hyperventilate.

Matt bent down and spoke softly into her ear. "Deep breaths. You seem to like Trey. I'll be right here."

A tall man rose from behind a black lacquer desk. His hair was salt and pepper; his three-piece suit was expensive. A gold watch peeked from under the cuff of his crisp white shirt.

He came around and embraced her. "Jaclyn. It's so good to see you. I'm glad you were able to make the trip so soon."

Hope pulled away when he held her longer than she was comfortable with. "You look well."

If he noticed her pulling away from him, he was too polite to say so. "Who's your friend?"

Hope took a step back to Matt's side. "This is Matt Henney, a friend of mine. He is also part owner where I work."

"I wasn't expecting you to bring a friend, but your friend is welcome."

Matt shook Trey's hand when offered. "Given

what happened to her and your father, she shouldn't be traveling alone."

The man's black brow rose. "I could have met her at the airport. But never mind that. We'll go to the conference room."

Hope followed him, Matt right behind her. "You must be doing well. These are lovely offices."

Trey held the door open for them. "I suppose you don't remember being here before. Not that you were here often. My partners and I have done well. Dad and I could never have worked together. I've got the papers ready to sign if you're sure you want to sign them. I don't suppose you've changed your mind?"

Hope shook her head and took a seat. "Had he signed two years ago, I wouldn't have been entitled to anything. This is how it should be."

Trey shook his head, his feelings on the matter clear on his face. "You always did have a higher moral compass than Dad or me. If I left Gloria, she'd take me for every cent. I figure it's a good thing that will never happen."

"How is Gloria?"

"She's good. She's waiting for us at a nearby restaurant. She took the afternoon off when I told her you were coming in. I thought about siccing her on you to get you to accept the money you're more than entitled to, but I also know once you've dug in your heels, there's no budging you."

Hope read through the papers Trey set in front of her. There was a list of assets that she was also relinquishing. "What is this?"

Trey leaned over her shoulder. "There is a box of some particularly expensive jewelry in your bedroom safe. About fifty thousand in cash, as well as some stocks and bonds. As far as I could ascertain, they were birthday and Christmas gifts from Dad. There is a particularly beautiful emerald necklace you left behind, with a matching cocktail ring."

*Everyone will know you belong to me.*

Hope shuddered. "Keep it."

Trey just shook his head again as she continued to read. Trey read down the list. "The car you took is yours to keep. Any clothes in the house you left, you may also take. I had them boxed up. They don't do me or Gloria any good. She's got a good six inches on you and a lot less curves."

Hope noticed Matt's lips purse at the personal comment. She ignored the comment and kept reading. "I'll take whatever you boxed up."

"Let's see. In your bedroom, there is some furniture. I wasn't sure what you wanted to do with that. It's yours if you want it. Then there was a box in your closet. I'll send it along. Otherwise, that was it. The rest of the contents in the house were either Dad's or joint property, which you're relinquishing."

"I don't have anywhere to put furniture. I'll just take the boxes." Hope took the pen Trey handed her. She had difficulty holding the small pen but legibly signed her legal name on the contract.

Trey noticed. "Whitfield? You're using your

maiden name?"

"For over a year.  I didn't think you held any illusions about me and your father."

Trey took the pen from her fingers.  "No, I guess not.  But at least it's over with."

Hope folded her hands on the table.  "The FBI said he was strangled.  He was found six months ago but only recently identified.  You and your grandfather didn't file a missing persons report?"

Trey kept his eyes down as he slid the pen into his pocket.  "I haven't seen him in a year.  He started acting strange.  Talking about how someone was stalking him; that it was payback for Miranda.  I thought he was feeling guilty that he had made Miranda a target, or I don't know, maybe drinking too much.  The only thing I was sure of was that he hadn't killed Miranda.  But he wasn't quite the same after you left.  I told the FBI when they questioned me that I didn't know he was missing.  I've gone a year without talking to him before.  Now, Grandpa, that's another story.  He's evading the question.  Claims he talked to him, and that he hasn't been missing for six months.  But to be honest, I'm not sure how much Grandpa remembers these days.  There are a lot of holes in his memory, either convenient or real.  His doctor says he's got dementia, and it is progressing.  So perhaps he doesn't know the last time he talked to Dad."

Hope pushed the contract away and rose.  "Harris doesn't know I'm in town, does he?"

Trey picked up the contract and folded it in half. "I didn't tell him. But he knows you're here. But you won't be here long enough for it to matter. You did say you were flying out tomorrow, right?"

Hope felt every muscle tighten as she gave him a jerky nod. Harris had made it a point to come by the rehabilitation center. He'd been her only visitor, besides Marlon. He had threatened her. He had grabbed her, shook her, and called her all sorts of names because she was the one testifying against Marlon. She never wanted to see him again. The quicker they got back to their hotel, the better she'd feel. But he mentioned Gloria. "Gloria is waiting for us, you said?"

Trey flashed his straight white teeth. "Yes. We should go. She's going to wonder where we are. She booked a table at your favorite restaurant."

Hope refrained from reminding him she wouldn't remember. Both Marlon and Trey had thought the memory loss was temporary. Like some temporary form of amnesia. "I'm sure that will be lovely."

Hope wrapped her arm around Matt's as they left the building. Trey kept up the conversation as they walked the few blocks over.

Trey held the door. He saw Gloria and waved. A woman almost as tall as Trey rose. Her platinum-blonde hair was up in an elaborate twist. Her makeup was applied to enhance every feature of her beautiful face.

When they got to the table, Gloria embraced Hope.

"I was surprised when Trey said you were coming into town. I'm glad to see you. You're looking great."

Hope doubted it. The woman was sleek and polished. Hope wore a calf-length floral dress she had gotten at a thrift shop somewhere in Idaho. But good manners had her thanking the woman and taking the chair Trey held out.

"Ah, Mrs. Turner. It's been too long." A man dressed in a black suit came to the table. "We're glad to have you grace us with your presence."

Hope cringed inside but plastered on a fake smile. "Glad to be back."

The man gushed. "I'll have Anton get you your drink, and our chef will make your favorite."

The man took everyone else's drink order. When the drinks arrived, Hope took a swallow and then struggled not to choke on it. The bitter drink burned as it went down.

Thankfully, she didn't have to say much. Gloria was bent on recapping everything she'd missed in the last two years. She was soothed by Matt's hand on her thigh during the meal. She hated dining in public. The pasta dish set in front of her was delicious, but she wished she had a big spoon to scoop it up. Her fingers struggled with the fork.

When dessert was set in front of her, she sighed in relief. The chocolatey dessert was decadent and, thankfully, was served with a spoon, so she didn't struggle with it quite as much.

Trey took the check when it arrived. "I had your

boxes delivered to your hotel."

Gloria sipped her cocktail. "I was so hoping you'd stay with us, but I understand. Marlon's death had to have been a shock, despite your separation."

Hope saw the emerald and diamond ring flash on her finger.

Gloria saw where she looked. "I hope you don't mind. When Trey said you weren't going to take possession of the jewelry Marlon gave you, I couldn't resist."

Hope pushed the rest of her dessert away. "You're more than welcome to whatever is there. I'm sorry, but I'm tired. It's been a stressful week, what with learning of Marlon's death."

Gloria sympathized. "I'm sure. I don't know what I would do if something happened to Trey."

Hope made some sort of sound that satisfied Gloria. She rose, and Matt's hand settled on her back.

"You have a lot of nerve. You're the reason my son is dead." A tall man stormed to their table.

"Grandpa. Be civil."

The white-haired man had spittle on the corner of his lips as he descended on them. His suit was wrinkled as if he'd slept in it. His wrinkled skin was scrunched up in anger. He kept coming at them.

Matt pushed Hope behind him. "Back off."

The man sneered at him. "So you're the man she left my son for. You bastard. She killed my son. Mark my words, you'll be next."

The patrons in the restaurant watched in

fascination as Trey tried to calm the old man. "Grandpa, Jaclyn wasn't responsible for Dad's death. The FBI will find out who is."

Harris Turner shoved Matt, but Matt didn't budge. The man pointed at Hope. "You'll regret killing my son."

Trey took Harris's shoulders and forcefully guided him out of the restaurant, Gloria following on his heels. Hope gripped Matt's arm. Her eyes pleaded with him.

Matt squeezed her shoulder. "Let's get out of here."

Matt guided her out of the crowded restaurant. He could see Trey and Gloria struggling to get the man into a car. Thankfully they were headed in the opposite direction. Hope couldn't resist looking back one last time. The old man was glaring at her. She turned and let Matt block her from his view.

* * *

Matt unbuttoned the top button of his shirt. "I can see why you left. Trey is as phony as they come. Gloria too. If Marlon was anything like them, I'm surprised you didn't leave years ago."

Hope took a seat on the bed by the window. Her gaze was steady on the view of the city. "Jaclyn was just as phony. I don't know what was in that drink, but my head is still spinning."

Matt set his hands on her shoulders. "This time

tomorrow, we'll be back home, and you won't ever have another reason to come back here."

Hope laid her hands over his. "I should see what's in those boxes."

Matt rolled up his sleeves and set one of the four boxes on the table. "Anything in here you don't want me to see?"

Hope shook her head. "I can't imagine what could be in these boxes that would be worse than what I already told you, or what you already know. I don't know what's in these boxes, but I doubt there is anything terribly embarrassing in there."

The first box was the largest. Inside were clothes. Hope pulled out a few garments. "I see why I left these behind."

Matt pulled out a very short black lace nightgown that still had the price tag on it. "I don't know; this one might look good on you."

Hope blushed, snatching it from his hands. "What else is in there?"

Matt dug through. "Nothing else strikes my fancy. Just some shirts and skirts I can't picture you wearing."

Hope glanced inside the second box. "Shoes."

Matt set the box of shoes next to the box of clothes. "Any boots or anything in there? The boots you wear at work could use an upgrade."

Hope dug through. She pulled out a pair of fur-lined boots. "These would have been great in February when I got to Utah."

Matt took them from her and set them in a keep pile. "No fuzzy slippers to go with the nightgown?"

Hope gave him a dirty look. "You have a one-track mind."

Matt held up his hands. "Hey. Don't blame me. You bought it."

Hope opened the third box. "And clearly, I never wore it. This is just doodads and knickknacks. I didn't want any of this stuff when I left."

That left one smaller box. Inside were piles of papers and notebooks. Matt flipped through them. "You used to journal. A lot."

Hope took the one he was holding. She read a few pages and tossed it. "Like anyone cares what I ate for breakfast."

Matt wasn't so quick to dismiss them. "What if there is something in them? Something that might point to who or why you were attacked?"

Hope's hand paused over the box. "You think I might have journaled something like that?"

Matt flipped through the pages of one of the journals at the bottom of the box. "You had great handwriting. 'Marlon is out again with his girlfriend. I forget which one. The man doesn't know how to be discreet.'"

Hope stood up. "What else does it say?"

Matt cleared his throat. "'Perhaps I should take Trey up on his offer. An affair with him has to be better than climbing into bed each night with Marlon.'"

Hope slapped it from his hands. "Oh, God."

Matt slipped his arms around her. "That doesn't mean you were having an affair with him."

Hope placed her hands on her hot cheeks. "What if I was? What if that was why he wasn't happy to see you with me? Maybe he wanted to pick back up where we left off?"

Matt picked up the journal and put it in the box. "We'll take these back with us. I can read through them if you don't want to. Just remember, this isn't you anymore. That's what you said, right?"

Hope reluctantly nodded. "Right."

"Then there is nothing in them that should be shameful or embarrassing to Hope. These belong to another woman."

Hope opened her suitcase and started piling the journals inside. "What a way to throw my words back at me."

Matt came up behind her. His chest brushed against her back. His arms slipped around her waist, bringing her flush against him. "We'll worry about these later. For now, why don't you go take a hot shower? We can watch television and get some sleep. Our flight leaves at ten."

She nodded and headed to the bathroom, taking a nightgown with her.

Matt kept his eyes on her until the door closed behind her. He took a deep breath. He was wading in deep waters; there was no doubt. He was feeling protective of her. He wanted to keep at bay anything or anyone who might want to hurt her. He'd wanted to throw the journal when he'd read Jaclyn's comments about sleeping with Trey. It had not gotten past his notice, and apparently not Hope's either, that the man was territorial where Hope was concerned. Matt had seen the surge of jealousy in the man's eyes.

Gloria had seemed oblivious. She'd spent over an hour gossiping about every person Jaclyn had known. Hope's eyes had glazed over, but Gloria hadn't noticed. But Trey's eyes had been on her all through dinner.

Matt changed into a pair of flannel pants and a t-shirt. He turned the television on and lay on top of the covers of the bed closest to the door. Hope had immediately gone to the bed by the window. He knew he was railroading her a bit. He'd booked the flight without her knowledge. He'd set her air mattress up in his office, and while she'd been sleeping, he'd been planning.

He wanted to get her past out of her life as fast as possible. He'd booked the flight and had informed Hope they were leaving. She'd called Trey on his phone and told him she was on her way. He'd forced her to let him come with her. He'd forced her to come stay at his trailer. But he couldn't force her into his bed. She needed to come to him.

Figuring that wasn't about to happen anytime soon, Matt told his unruly body to forget the black lace nightgown and the vision of Hope's lush body inside it.

It was twenty minutes later when Hope came out of the bathroom. Her hair was pinned up and she'd changed for bed. His tongue almost fell out of his mouth. She wasn't wearing the black nightgown, but the nightgown she had on revealed a bit of skin on her chest. Her nipples weren't visible through the fabric, but he could imagine them. The gown shouldn't be sexy. But it clung to her hips and bottom as she turned the bed down and slipped under the covers.

She tucked the covers up over her chest and under her arms. "What are we watching?"

Matt glanced at the screen. "Apparently, the weather."

She turned onto her side. "Thank you, Matt."

He turned so he faced her. "For what?"

Her eyes were serious. "For you being you."

"You're welcome." Matt rolled onto his back and pretended to watch the television. He flipped through the channels, not landing on anything that could hold his attention with Hope in the bed across from him. The only reason they were sharing a room was that he knew if he had booked two rooms, she'd have insisted on paying for hers. He'd seen the dump of a hotel she booked in town, and there was no way he was going to sleep in a dumpy hotel in L.A.

After an hour, Matt shut off the television, ignoring the too-soft mattress under him. Over the years he'd learned to sleep wherever and whenever he had a chance.  Apparently, so had Hope.  Her eyes were closed, and her breathing was even.  Tomorrow they'd get back on a plane and they'd go back home.  To his home.  He told himself he had plenty of time to figure out his relationship with Hope.

Chapter Fifteen

Matt woke when he felt the bed dip.  Hope slipped under the covers next to him.  The gap in the curtains told him it was almost morning.  They'd have to get up soon and head to the airport.

His voice was gruff when he spoke.  "Hope?  Are you okay?"

Hope leaned up on her elbows.  She nodded.  She straddled his waist and slipped her hands under his t-shirt.  When she pushed it up over his chest, he sat up so she could remove it.  Her soft hands drifted over his shoulders, down his chest, and her nails lightly scraped over his nipples.  His morning erection throbbed against her thigh.

Hope didn't say anything, her turquoise eyes on his.  She took his hands in hers and brought them to the hem of her nightgown that had ridden up.  She guided his hands under the fabric to her breasts.  His fingers closed over her flesh, kneading and plucking her nipples.  Her eyes stayed on his, and still she said nothing.  Her fingers went to the waistband of his drawstring pants and pulled the string to loosen them.  Her fingers slipped under the fabric, cupping him as she bent down to kiss him.

Matt kept his hands on her breasts, using the strength in his arms to keep Hope from collapsing on his chest.  Her hips shifted and she rubbed herself against him.  He watched as her eyes drifted closed. Matt sat up, stripping Hope of the nightgown, leaving her naked.  He could see the rise and fall of her chest in the darkness of the room.  He lifted her and laid her on her back.  He stood and stripped his pants off. Her eyes were once again on his.

Matt silently cursed for a moment.  He didn't say anything; he didn't want to break the spell.  He went to his suitcase, found the condom he was looking for, and rolled it on.  Hope was where he'd left her.  She opened her arms and thighs to him as he came back over her.  He kissed her while pulling her back to her knees.  He slipped beneath her and pulled her thighs around his hips.

Hope moaned as she took him in her hands and guided him into her body.  She eased herself down until they were hip to hip.  He sat up, pulling her deeper onto him.  He used the pillows to prop up his back and guided her hips into the rhythm that they needed.  Her breasts were crushed to his chest as her hips rose and fell against his.  He slipped his tongue into her mouth, mirroring the rhythm of their bodies. He felt her climax, and he swallowed the mewling sounds she made.  He pulled her tight against him and followed.

Hope was limp against his chest, her breathing slowing.  She kissed the side of his neck as she wrapped her arms around him.  She let out a deep exhale.

They lay that way for a time.  Hope pulled away just enough so she could see his face. "You're another first."

It took Matt a moment to realize what she meant. Matt kissed her softly, wanting to offer her whatever it was she needed from him.  This woman had been through so much in the past two years.  He was the first man she would remember being with.  It was a bit humbling; she'd chosen him.

Matt eased her off him, stripped off the condom, and tossed it in the nearby trash.  He settled her against him, the sweat on their bodies drying in the cool air of the room. "We have to get up soon."

Hope kissed him with soft, lingering caresses.  She looked into his eyes as she pulled away.  "I'd say I don't want to get up, but I want to get the heck out of L.A."

"How about we take a hot shower and get some breakfast before we head out?"

Hope slipped out of bed.  Matt was right behind her, grabbing another condom as he herded her to the bathroom and into the shower.  He knew she saw what he'd grabbed when she blushed. He adjusted the spray so that it hit his back.  They each took their turn washing up.  When Hope had finished rinsing the conditioner out of her hair, Matt rolled on the condom and soaped up his hands.  His hands found and lingered on every curve of her body. When Hope was arching against him, her hands grasping at him, he lifted her until her legs were around his waist.  He braced her against the shower wall as water poured over them.  He tested the readiness of her flesh until she was begging him to take her.

Matt sealed her mouth in a deep kiss as he lifted her onto him.  He drove into her, losing all sense of time.  When her cries were echoing off the shower walls, he drove into her one last time.  He almost collapsed under the force of his orgasm.  He used his weight to keep both of them upright.

Matt heard the shower turning off as Hope found the shower knob.  Matt carried her out of the tub, releasing her to her feet as they dripped water all over the floor.  He grabbed a towel and dried her off.  He wrapped her in it, lifted her so he could carry her to the bed, and set her down.

Matt went back to the bathroom and grabbed a towel for himself.  He briskly dried off.  When he came out, Hope was still sitting in her towel where he'd left her.  She had tears in her eyes.  Afraid he'd hurt her or triggered a bad memory, he crouched in front of her.

"Are you okay?"

She smiled at him through her tears.  "I'm fine. Overwhelmed."

Matt sat next to her and pulled her into his arms. She pressed her cheek to his chest.  She didn't shed any tears, just took a moment to hold him.  Matt held her until she stirred against him.

She pulled away and wrapped the towel tighter to keep her body covered up.  "Breakfast?"

Matt got up. "Breakfast."

* * *

Matt dumped their things in his living room. It was mid-afternoon, and there was a lot of work to do around the ranch. The work never truly was finished, and that was the way Matt liked it.

Hope dropped onto his couch. "Where do you get all this energy?"

"You don't have to come with me. I'm just going to check in with Jeremy and Allie. But we do need to go get Trixie. You can come back here and take a nap if you want."

Hope climbed to her feet. "No. It's fine. I'm used to being busy. Sometimes I'd nap at the hotel, just for the novelty of sleeping in a bed. But to be honest, I think my air mattress is more comfortable than those old beds."

Matt would bet. He grabbed their suitcases and took them back to his room. He emptied his and put his things away.

Hope trailed behind him. "Just because we slept together again doesn't mean we have to share a room if you don't want me in here. I understand if you don't."

Matt dumped the contents of her suitcase on his bed and put the suitcase in his closet. "If you want to sleep in the other room, I won't stop you. But it seems like a waste of energy to make me come get you and carry you in here to make love to you again. I don't think your twin air mattress would hold up."

Hope blushed a deep pink. "I'm just saying that I'm sure you hadn't planned on me moving in with you like this. And things have been a little strange between us. I understand if you want your private space."

Matt came around the bed. "I'd throw you on the bed and show you what I think of that idea, but I don't think I could get it up after this morning. So let's put your things away, put those journals in my office, and get back to work."

Hope took a step backward toward the door. "Sounds like a plan. My legs are like rubber after this morning."

Matt made space for her clothes and dumped her toiletries in the bathroom. He followed her out of the bedroom, pausing to put the journals on his newly purchased desk. He brushed a kiss on her lips as she tipped her head to his when he came closer. "You tempt me to see if I have the same stamina I had in my twenties, but we should go."

Hope agreed with him. "Let's go get Trixie."

Trixie greeted them first when Matt opened the front door and hollered. Jeremy wasn't far behind.

"I wasn't sure when you'd be back. How did it go?"

Matt took Hope's hand and made her come inside. "As awkward as I thought it would be. We're both happy to be back. Hope wants her dog back, and I thought I'd see where I'd be most helpful."

Jeremy yawned as he rolled his shoulders. "I need to go check on the foals. Both are doing fine, but I've got the vet coming out to check them over. Why don't you come with me? Hope, if you could, would you sit with Sawyer? Allie is sound asleep on the couch. Sawyer kept us up half the night. He's asleep in his bed right now, but I doubt he'll stay that way."

Hope came further into the room. "I can watch him until Allie wakes up."

Jeremy waved toward the kitchen. "Help yourself to whatever. There is a television in the den if you want to relax. Sawyer's room is the first door on the left down the hall."

Matt kissed her and followed Jeremy outside.

Jeremy shook his head. "I take it you two kissed and made up."

Matt shoved his hands in his pockets. "Remember when I told you someone tried to kill Hope?"

Jeremy nodded. "Not something one can forget."

Matt stopped, and Jeremy turned to him. "It was bad. I saw her medical records. She has no memory of who she was. She has neurological damage that affects her motor skills. The man came damn close to killing her."

Jeremy swore. "You're serious? No memory at all?"

Matt rocked on his heels. "She says she has ghost memories. Little flashes here and there. Sometimes you can see when she has one. Her skin turns white and her breath catches."

"I guess that explains the hands and her difficulty doing simple things like making a bed."

"I watched her tie her shoes and sign her name. She has to focus on the tasks as if her life depends on it."

The men resumed walking to the barn. "So what's the plan, Matt? I know you have one."

Matt told him what he'd told Hope. "I'd like her to start taking trips up the trails regularly. And I'd like to take her on some of the overnight camping trips, with an appropriate pay increase. She agreed."

Jeremy glanced up at the sky. "Before or after you resumed your physical relationship? Anyone standing near the two of you can see it."

"Before."

Jeremy opened the door to the stables. "I hope you know what you're doing, no pun intended."

"Don't I always?"

Jeremy just shook his head at him. "No. But that never stopped you before."

* * *

Hope heard Sawyer fussing and went to the bedroom. The baby was on his back, his face scrunched up. She was careful when picking him up and settling him in her arms. He wasn't thrilled that she wasn't his mother. She spoke softly to him until he settled. She found his pacifier in the crib, and she picked it up as she took a seat in the rocker.

"I hope you're not hungry. I'd hate to wake your mother."

The baby accepted the pacifier and stared at her.

She stroked the soft skin of his cheek with her fingertip. "Aren't you a sweet one? I think I can manage a diaper change. What do you say?"

Sawyer yawned around the pacifier, but his baby-blue eyes stayed on her face.

Hope managed to change his wet diaper while Trixie watched. Hope gazed down at the baby, tickling his belly as she redressed him. Feeling more confident, she picked him up and settled him on her chest. She played with his fingers while his eyes drifted closed.

"He's such a sweetheart when he's not crying." Allie was pulling her hair into a ponytail as she came into the room.

Hope managed not to jump when Allie spoke. "Jeremy and Matt are at the stables checking on the foals."

Allie yawned and dropped into the rocking chair. "He worries over them almost as much as Sawyer. When did you and Matt get back?"

"After noon. I can go and let you be."

Allie waved that away. "I rarely have a woman around to talk to. Jeremy is not the most communicative. He learned to be seen and not heard growing up."

Hope handed Sawyer to his mother and sat down on the armchair that was in the room. "Matt told me he and Jeremy grew up in foster care."

Allie looked down at her son. "They did. That's where they met. They ended up in a group home when they had to leave the foster home where they met. By then, they were older and harder to place. Matt was the more outgoing one. And compassionate. He was a great medic. In the field, he did what needed to be done. But when he was around the locals, he took his time with them and talked to them. He made people trust him so that they weren't afraid."

Hope wanted to hear more. "Matt said he introduced you and Jeremy."

Allie glanced at Hope. "You don't mind if I nurse him while we chat, do you?"

"I don't mind."

Allie settled Sawyer and relaxed in the rocker as she nursed him. "Jeremy was so quiet. I didn't think he liked me, to be honest. He had this way of looking at me like he could see right through me. The day he kissed me, I was shocked. It showed on my face because he apologized. Had I not grabbed him and kissed him back, he might have run and not come back."

Hope glanced at her hands. "Why not Matt?"

Allie kissed the top of Sawyer's head. "We weren't meant to be. He was attractive; still is, as I'm sure you've noticed. All that golden hair and those hazel eyes of his. I was his superior, and he was off-limits. But to be honest, it was never romantic between us.

Even if Jeremy and I had not been attracted to each other, it still would never have happened between us."

Hope relaxed in the chair. She was exhausted, but pleasantly so. "How did they end up in foster care?"

Allie switched sides. "Matt doesn't keep it a secret. Jeremy doesn't like to talk about it. Both of their dads were alcoholics, and their mothers walked out. Jeremy's dad was violent with him. Matt's dad was negligent. I don't think Matt's dad even knew he had a son most of the time. Matt doesn't talk about his dad much. He might as well have been raising himself. Matt transitioned more easily than Jeremy. Jeremy was too smart for his own good, and he used school as an escape. Matt hated school and didn't like structure or being told what to do. It took him a while to settle into the routine of the army, but it did him good to learn to take orders and not always fight them. But when we both got out, he found solitary jobs where he had control. I'm happy he finally bought in. He'll be much happier here. Maybe he'll settle down, find a nice woman, and get married."

Hope felt her eyes closing. "It does sound nice, doesn't it?"

Allie was silent as Hope fell asleep.

* * *

Matt flipped the steaks on the grill. Allie was playing with Sawyer on a blanket on the grass. Jeremy was sitting at the patio table going over some paperwork. When he and Jeremy had gotten back to the house, Allie was in the living room with Sawyer. Hope had fallen asleep in a chair in the nursery. It hadn't surprised Matt. He doubted she had slept well, and these past few days had been stressful.

Allie laughed as she tickled Sawyer. "You never did say where you found Hope."

Matt closed the lid of the grill. "That's a whole other story, one I should let Hope tell you."

A soft voice came from the sliding glass door. "Sorry, I fell asleep."

Allie patted the blanket beside her. "Come sit. Your neck probably has a kink in it from falling asleep the way you did, but I didn't have the heart to wake you."

Hope straightened her t-shirt and kicked off her sandals before she took a seat. Trixie came and lay down next to her, her head in her lap waiting to be petted. "I fell asleep on Matt last night too. I'm just tired."

Jeremy flipped the ledger book closed. "Where did Matt find you?"

Hope rubbed Trixie's fur, seeking comfort from the dog that was her constant companion. "Last year I was going through some papers. I had a few stacks I'd taken with me when I left Marlon, but I hadn't gone through them. But one night I read through them. I did some research and found an obituary. It was my mom's."

Allie spoke when Hope stopped. "I'm sorry about

your mom."

Hope buried her fingers deeper in Trixie's fur. "After what happened to me, I don't remember her. I don't have any memories from before."

Allie made a strangled sound. "You don't have any memories? Matt said that you had been attacked. Is that why?"

Matt encouraged her to continue. "It's okay, Hope."

Hope smiled slightly at him and turned back to Allie. "Yes. I wasn't breathing. There was permanent damage. But it's okay. Really, it is. I've gotten used to it. Anyway, I was curious about her. I found my birth certificate. I also found a copy of another one. I took it to my lawyer. He found that a trust had been set up and that I was one of two beneficiaries."

Jeremy stood so fast that the chair tipped. He came closer, his eyes on Hope.

Hope shrank back at the animosity she could feel coming off him in waves.

Allie turned to Jeremy. "What?"

"The property next door was being held in a trust. We couldn't find the owner."

Allie turned back to Hope. "You own the property next door? The one with the crumbling house?"

Hope swallowed the lump in her throat. "Crumbling is a nice word for it. I learned an aunt on my mother's side had passed away, leaving the property to her sister's two daughters. The larger, more valuable parcel she left to the oldest daughter.

But for some reason, she decided to leave the smaller parcel to the younger daughter she'd never met. It was held in trust until I turned thirty-two a few weeks ago."

Allie's hand flew to her mouth. "Oh, my God."

Hope pulled her knees to her chest. "I have a copy of your birth certificate if you want to see it."

Allie grasped her husband's hand when he came up behind her. "Are you telling me that my mother had another child? You're my sister?"

Matt watched the emotions play over both women's faces. He had an urge to offer comfort to both of them. Allie was staring at Hope like she'd never seen her before. Hope looked like she expected to be tossed out any second. But he stayed where he was. They had to work this out between them.

Hope turned her eyes to her feet. "Half. I didn't know what to say. Or how to say it. When I got here, I was desperate. I needed a job. When I saw the property and how it was thriving, I felt like an intruder. So I applied for a job. Then I saw you were pregnant. I had no place here. I had no business intruding in your life. But when Matt found me living on the property, he put two and two together, same as you."

Allie's eyes were filled with tears. "My dad said she had remarried, and that she wasn't coming back. Dad and I were doing just fine without her. She made both of our lives miserable when she was with us. I never sought her out. I only know she died because my father found out from a mutual friend. Her sister had already passed when I learned about Mom. There was no other family, not that I knew of. I only saw my aunt a few times after Mom left. I just assumed there was no one else."

Hope kept her eyes on her feet. "I only know dates. My parents got married a few years before I was born. My dad died years ago. I married Marlon right after he died. Mom inherited everything when my dad died. She was still named as his beneficiary, even though they were divorced. I don't know what happened to her or her house. I couldn't find any records. From what I was able to piece together, she left when I was five or so. She came back, claimed her inheritance, and disappeared again."

Allie wiped her tears. "The same age I was when she left us."

Hope looked up at her through her lashes. "I have some pictures of her. You look a lot like her."

Allie rocked Sawyer, who started fussing. "So do you."

Jeremy looked at Matt. "The steaks are burning."

Matt swore and took the steaks off the fire.

Allie stood so she was standing beside Jeremy. "My ever-practical husband."

Jeremy took Sawyer from her. "One of us has to be."

Hope got to her feet. Trixie rambled off to sleep in the shade.

Allie broke the silence, giving Hope a watery

laugh. She hugged Hope and then stepped back. "It's going to take some getting used to. I never had a sister. Just a brother."

Hope knew Allie meant Matt. She glanced over at him. "I never had either."

Matt set the steaks on the table and took Hope's hand. "Let's eat. We can worry about the rest later."

They all took a seat and shared their first family meal.

Chapter Sixteen

A loud bang on the front door woke Matt and Hope from a sound sleep. Matt pressed his hand on Hope's shoulder. "Stay here. I'll answer it. Jeremy and Allie don't knock."

Hope got out of bed and pulled on some clothes. She heard Matt talking to someone, a male. She heard her name, and her stomach tightened.

Matt's voice rang out. "Hope. Come on out."

Hope saw Agent Parks standing in Matt's kitchen. Her eyes darkened as she realized there could be only one reason why he was here. "Who?"

"I need you to come with me, Mrs. Turner."

Hope took a step closer, her arms wrapped around her waist. "Am I under arrest?"

"Right now, I just need you to come with me."

Matt came to her side. "She at least has the right to know why."

The man tipped his head and turned his eyes her way. "Your father-in-law was murdered while you were in L.A."

Hope's shoulders sagged, torn between relief that it wasn't Trey or Gloria and fear that she was a suspect. "I was only in L.A. for a day."

The man took a step closer. "A whole restaurant of people saw the confrontation between you and your father-in-law. You and your stepson are the last two people to see him alive."

Matt intervened. "Hope was with me the entire time. We were on a plane the next morning. There is no way she could have killed him."

"You're her alibi again? You two are awfully close."

Hope felt her temper slip. "We're having an affair, Agent Parks. We spend a lot of time together. He came with me to L.A. I signed some legal papers and had lunch with Matt, my stepson, and his wife. Harris showed up uninvited. Matt and I went directly back to the hotel after Trey and Gloria got Harris into a car. I assume he was going home."

The agent nodded to the chairs. "Perhaps we should sit then. Mrs. Turner, there are a whole lot of deaths surrounding you. You can't believe it's a coincidence."

Hope held out her hands. They trembled some, and not just from fear. "I am not strong enough to have strangled Harris or Marlon. Nor the woman in the woods, or whoever that poor woman was a town over. I'm sorry Harris is dead. I know he had to have been grieving his son's death."

The chair creaked as the agent leaned back. "What of Miranda Grieves? Were you strong enough then?"

Hope stumbled over the question. "I suppose. But why would I do that?"

Parks shifted his weight. "She was having an affair with your husband, Mrs. Turner."

Hope's temper flared again. "It's not Mrs. Turner. It's Hope or Ms. Whitfield. Your choice."

Parks seemed to be coming to some sort of conclusion. He leaned forward. "All right, Hope. I'm not inclined to believe you murdered all those people. I can't think of a motive as to why you would have killed those two women you didn't even know. Or even Harris Turner. But I can think of reasons for Ms. Grieves. I can think of a couple of reasons for Marlon."

Matt kept his eye on the agent. "Did you question Trey Turner?"

The man replied. "Yes. His wife said he was home all night. After they put Harris Turner in his car and instructed his driver to take him home, they made a stop at the office and then went home. Spent a night in, which sounds like a rare occurrence for the couple."

Hope tucked her hands between her knees. "I can't believe he was strangled."

The man continued. "He wasn't strangled. He was shot. Two times in the chest."

Matt interrupted. "That doesn't sound like our guy."

"You would be right. Four women strangled with one survivor. One man strangled. One man shot. If these crimes were random, Harris Turner's murder would be investigated as a different perpetrator. Now I wouldn't rule anything out at this point, but I've got murders spanning from Los Angeles to Utah.

And I'm sorry, Hope, but you're right in the middle."

Hope was going to be sick. "I need a minute."

She tried to remain calm as she walked toward the bathroom. She had to lean against the sink to keep her legs from giving out beneath her. She waited until the queasiness in her stomach subsided. She opened the bathroom door but hovered in the doorway. She could hear Matt's voice.

"She's a victim in all this. And she was with me before she found Natalie Gerber. And I was with her when Harris was shot. You read her records. She doesn't remember anything. Even if she had known before her attack what tied the crimes together, she couldn't tell you today."

Agent Parks's voice was low but clear. "There was some question as to whether or not she remembers more than she claims. Local police had questioned her after her attack, and her statement was that she couldn't remember anything. But prior, she had testified she saw her husband arguing with his girlfriend. Then suddenly she can't remember, and he walks free. Marlon was in police custody when Hope was attacked. Trey has an alibi. Harris didn't have one, but there was no evidence to suggest he was the perpetrator. Memory loss is something easily faked."

Matt leaned back and could see Hope in the doorway. "Are you okay?"

Shen nodded, still wobbly but stable enough. She didn't bother to refute the agent's words. "So now what?"

"I'll verify your alibi that you and Mr. Henney went straight back to the hotel. If you did, you'll be on camera."

Hope grabbed the back of Matt's chair. "Now I wish we had mailed a box home. We would have had the postage stamp."

Matt reached over his shoulder and put a hand over hers. "I assume you're not taking her in."

The agent got to his feet. "No. But I would suggest Hope does not go anywhere without someone with her. I would advise you the same. A gun changes the game."

The agent saw himself out.

Hope let Matt pull her around and onto his lap. "What are you thinking?"

Matt wrapped his arms around her waist. "I think we need to get to work. He's right. Neither of us goes anywhere alone."

Hope tried to wriggle off his lap, but he held firm. "You mean I don't go anywhere alone."

Matt tapped a finger to her nose. "That's what I said."

"So we just go back to work?"

Matt released her. "For now. Then I think we should go through those journals."

"Is it weird I don't want to know about myself? I mean, anyone else in my position would likely have taken them with them and read through them all, trying to remember or understand who they were."

Matt tucked a curl behind her ear. "I think I

understand.  If I woke up with no memory, and Marlon Turner was the first person I saw, and the dysfunction of his family, I wouldn't want to know either.  I'd have done what you did.  I'd have left."

Hope cupped his face in her hands.  "You always seem to know the right thing to say."

Matt brought her face to his.  His lips lingered on hers.  "It's one of my many charms."

Hope giggled against his lips.  "You have lots of charms.  Too many.  You're a dangerous man, Mr. Henney."

Matt nibbled at her lips.  "I'm tempted to show you one of my charms right now.  You passed out on me last night.  Again."

Hope's fingers went to the buttons of his shirt. "Do you think the boss will mind if we're late?"

Matt scooped her up and carried her to his bedroom.  "Why don't you convince me not to fire you for being late, Ms. Whitfield?"

Hope pulled him down on top of her and did just that.

* * *

"You look happy."  Allie popped into the barn. Sawyer was sleeping in a harness on her chest.

Matt stopped whistling and faced her.  "I am. Where's Jeremy?"

Allie came to stand next to him and admire the new foal.  "He needs to go up on the ridge.  He thinks there might be some teenagers hanging out up there."

"He needs help?"

Allie rubbed the mare's nose. "He says no. But I say he does."

Matt set the brush down. He glanced over at Hope, who was in with the goats. Trixie was becoming a fixture at the stables, and she was walking the perimeter of the fence, keeping her eyes on Hope and the goats.

Allie looked where Matt was looking. "I still can't believe she's my half-sister. My dad had no desire to remarry. He had a few girlfriends from time to time. He loved the ladies, but he said he was done with marriage. I didn't give much thought to what my mother might have done after she left us. Sounds like she did the same thing to Hope and her dad as she did to me and mine."

Matt gave her a side hug. "Who knows? You might have some other siblings out there."

Allie hugged him back. "I hope not. I do find it odd that of all the women you've known, the one you fall hard for is my half-sister. Like it was meant to be."

Matt squeezed her shoulder and let her go. "I always thought that about you and Jeremy. What were the chances that the two people I'm closest to in the world would fall for each other and get married? And now Sawyer."

Allie turned and leaned against the stall. "Do you think it's in the cards for you and Hope?"

Matt was starting to hope so.  He was drawn to Hope, had been from the moment he'd laid eyes on her. "She's already living with me."

Allie's eyes were on Hope as she started heading their way. "Does she know that?"

Matt put the rest of the tools away and grabbed his saddlebags that he kept full of supplies.  "I'll tell you what I do know.  I'm the first man she's been with since she left her husband.  Before really.  When she told me her husband didn't matter, it was because he truly didn't.  She didn't consider herself a wife.  He was a stranger to her.  I've never stomped on a woman's feelings before Hope, and I don't plan to again.  I don't know what is in the cards for us.  Time will tell."

Allie followed Matt outside.  "You've got plenty of it.  You and Jeremy be safe.  Hope can come home with me.  She should be done with work soon."

Hope came to the fence.  "Everything okay?"

Matt saddled his horse.  The gelding was getting on in age, but Matt loved his spirit.  "I'm going to go up the trails with Jeremy.  He thinks some teenagers might be partying up there."

Hope rubbed her hands over her arms.  "At least it's not the other two.  Hopefully, these are run-of-the-mill troublemakers."

Matt certainly hoped so.  He leaned over the railing and kissed her roughly.  "Allie is going to hang around.  I'll meet you back at Allie's when Jeremy and I are done."

She pulled back before he could kiss her again. "Okay. Be safe."

He gave her a salute before mounting Jax and heading off. Matt had to keep himself from looking back. He found Jeremy waiting for him at the base of the trail they rarely used. The terrain was rougher than most of the other trails, and this one ended at a cliff. "I see you obeyed and waited for me."

Jeremy urged his horse forward. "I've learned that when Allie takes a certain tone, you have two choices. You can do as she wants, or you can sleep alone. I prefer not to sleep alone."

Matt brought the horse alongside Jeremy's. "So you think teenagers have been partying up here?"

Jeremy pulled down the brim of his hat. "No. When I passed through here yesterday, there were some tracks. I came this morning, and there were fresh ones. I told Allie I thought it was kids because I didn't want her to worry. But the cliff at the top of this trail gives you a clear view of the area. You can see our house and your trailer, as well as most of the retreat cabins and stables. If you walk to the east at the top of the ridge, you can see Hope's property. And if my sense of direction is right, you can climb down the other side on a man-made path on horseback, head north, and get to the cliff where that woman's body was found. You wouldn't even have to carry the body. Lay the body over a saddle and lead a horse straight to it."

"Did you call the police?"

Jeremy nudged the suddenly reluctant horse to continue up the trail. "I didn't. I know that an FBI agent was at your trailer this morning. Hope didn't kill those women. I doubt she could if she tried. You know better than anyone that choking a person to death isn't as easy as it looks on television."

Matt's horse was starting to balk. "Something is spooking the horses."

Jeremy's sharp eyes scanned the area. "Could be a large predator came through here, but I don't see anything that would alarm the horses."

Matt did the same. The horses kept going up the trail, their anxiety easing the further up the trail they went. Matt relaxed a little. Both he and Jeremy knew not to dismiss the horses' instincts.

As they came up the hill, Jeremy pointed to a trail that led down. "You can see hoof prints. That trail keeps going to a stream. Cross that stream and keep heading east; you'll come through the woods that back up to the old house on Hope's property. When I was looking to buy the parcel, I rode around the area. It would have been easy to widen and extend the trail between the two properties. It could be widened to accommodate a horse or a truck. Our house would have been perfect up on the rise over there."

Matt could see the elevated land in the distance. It was hard to tell with the trees, but he could imagine a house there. "So a man on a horse, with a second horse with a body, could have crossed through Hope's property, come up this trail, and headed right up the cliffs. Damn. Let's hope Agent Parks doesn't figure that out. Hope might jump higher on that suspect list of his."

"What aren't you telling me?"

Matt reined in the horse and took in his surroundings, getting his bearings. "Hope's father-in-law was shot and killed not long after he confronted Hope at a restaurant where we were having an early dinner with Trey and his wife. He made quite the scene, so when the police started investigating, it wasn't hard to learn that Hope had been there. It was a favorite place of hers before."

"Before?"

Matt nudged the horse onward. "That's what Hope calls it. Before. Before the attack. Before she left."

Jeremy's horse fell into step behind him. "Got it. Before. He was shot? Not strangled?"

"Yeah. Agent Parks doesn't believe in coincidences. And neither do I. It's like someone is eliminating people around Hope."

"But he attacked Hope. To what end?"

Matt pulled up on the reins as the horse ascended the trail. It was steep, but the horse took it easily. "I wish I knew. But the two women make no sense. Hope didn't know them."

It was another hour before they reached the cliff. Matt dismounted. "Where to?"

Jeremy dismounted and hobbled the horses. "The horses can walk around the cliff on the west side. The land just keeps going up in that direction. But it will be quicker for us to climb."

Matt and Jeremy pulled the gear out. In short order, they had climbed to the top. Matt could see the top of the old house to the east. When he turned south, he had a good view of the ranch. The retreat section was further out, but the cabins and hotel were distinguishable against the backdrop of the canyons in the distance.

Matt looked over at Jeremy. "You're right. You can see straight across both properties. I think from this angle, you could see the camp Hope had set up. She had the tent more toward the middle. I'm guessing she didn't want to be too close to the old house. Who knows what's living in there? But from here, you would have seen her car parked next to the house, seen her sitting outside."

Jeremy rummaged through the leaves. He found a couple of cigarette butts, a candy wrapper, and a hole dug in the ground. "Come here."

Matt came and squatted down where Jeremy was digging up some loose dirt. There was a backpack buried. Matt stopped Jeremy from opening it. "We shouldn't touch it any more than we have with our bare hands."

Jeremy nodded and released the strap. Matt tugged out a pair of leather gloves. He opened the pack and swore. "We need to get the police up here."

Jeremy glanced inside. "Nylon rope, binoculars, a hunting knife, and field rations. Everything a man would need to catch and strangle an unsuspecting woman in the woods."

Matt reburied the bag while Jeremy called Mike. He only half-listened to the conversation. The rest of him was focused on the trees and rocks surrounding them. There were lots of places to hide.

Jeremy gave Mike their coordinates. "Yeah, the police are going to need to send a forensic team up here. Matt and I won't disturb anything else. Tell Allie we had to call the police, but don't tell her anything more than that. Just tell her Matt and I will be back as soon as we can."

Matt kept alert and scanned the area. It was quiet. For now. "Neither of us should stay up here alone."

Jeremy checked and packed their climbing gear. "Not if he's started using guns. Hand to hand, you and I could take him."

Matt nodded absently as he scanned the area. "I don't see anyone. But the horses sure were spooked. It's going to take the police a few hours to get up here unless they take the chopper."

Jeremy settled against a tree. "Cost too much for two people who aren't hurt. We'll have to wait here."

Four hours later, Matt and Jeremy stood on the outskirts while the team combed the area. The pack was photographed and tagged. The contents would be examined later. The police chief, whom they all called Sully, came to where they were watching.

"What were you two doing up here?"

Matt waved at the scene. "Looking for this."

Jeremy held a hand out and shook the man's hand. "Hey, Sully. Hope your family is well. I saw some hoof prints going up this trail at the base of my property. No one is supposed to be up here. Today I saw fresh tracks. I wanted to come up to make sure there weren't any kids up here. Partying or whatnot. Instead, we found some cigarettes, wrappers, and a hole under the brush. When we saw the rope, Matt and I called you."

The man seemed to be taking Matt's measure. "FBI has been poking around. Someone on your staff, I believe. A Haley or something."

Matt gritted his teeth. He had a feeling the man knew her name. "Hope Whitfield. And yes, she works for the Waters Ranch."

The man popped a piece of gum in his mouth. "You bought in this past spring, right? I heard about it from the Mrs."

Jeremy set a hand on Matt's shoulder. "I can vouch for him. He's been my friend for decades, as well as Allie's."

The man smiled, showing his missing eye tooth. "Allie always was a good judge of character. She'd have made a great cop had she been inclined. The way the FBI tells it, Hope Whitfield is tied to the strangling death of a woman in L.A."

Matt's eyebrows furrowed. "That's all he said? A woman in L.A.?"

The man continued chewing. "The first time he showed up. Now he says the same thing happened to her husband. When she found Natalie Gerber's body, that clinched it in his mind."

Matt figured he'd finish the story for the agent. No doubt he'd be back once news of this found its way to his desk. "Hope's father-in-law was shot two days ago. Hope can't have killed him because she wasn't in L.A. at the time. Or if she was, we were boarding a plane. And she can't have strangled Natalie because she was with me at the time."

The man moved the gum to the other side of his mouth. "I heard rumors that you two are shacked up."

Jeremy interrupted. "Enough. Look. Hope is tied to all this. We all know it. But she didn't kill those people. I'd like it if we could find out who did. We don't need any more locals getting killed, and we don't need rumors starting that we have a crazed killer wandering our canyons."

The man grunted. "That we don't. All right. I'll be making a call to Agent Parks. Not thrilled with the FBI poking around, but if these murders are all tied together, then this guy is not afraid to kill wherever the opportunity strikes. Two murders in our county are two too many."

Sully jerked his head to Matt. "Your prints on file?"

"I was in the army."

Sully straightened his hat and started heading off. "That's a yes. I'll be in touch."

Matt watched the man saunter off. "Is that the

green light for us to go?"

Jeremy grabbed their bags and gear. "Yeah. Let's get out of here. I don't like leaving the women alone."

The pair climbed back down the way they came and headed back to the main house.

Chapter Seventeen

"You had quite the artistic talent as a young girl." Matt showed Hope the page in the journal.

She made a face. "Is that a horse or a dog?"

"Could be a person for all I know. I think we can rule out that you wanted to be an artist when you grew up."

Hope snagged the journal from him. She glanced at the date written on the glittery unicorn cover. "I was eight. Cut me some slack."

Matt sifted through a few more. "You were in love with a boy named Robbie. Robbie Shane Monroe."

Hope laughed at the face Matt was making. "Is that your impression of a twelve-year-old girl in love?"

"Come on. You wrote some deep stuff here. You were going to get married, raise horses, have four children, all girls, and live in a mansion."

Hope scrunched her nose. "Four daughters, huh? I think I'll stop at two, regardless of gender. And I'll skip the mansion. If I'm going to raise horses, I'd rather do it in the country. At least I didn't want to be a princess or something equally useless."

Matt set the journal with the rest. He picked up the next one. He read a little, then handed it to her. "This one is nice. You should read it."

Hope turned the notebook around. "'I named my new mare Butterscotch after my favorite candies. She's my favorite present ever. Grandpop said it was because I was his favorite granddaughter. I can't wait to ride her in the next competition.' At least I didn't try to draw her. A few pages over, I wrote I won my first blue ribbon, all thanks to Butterscotch."

Matt set a few more to the side. "This one was before you got married. You seemed happy and excited."

Hope pointed to the toss pile. "I doubt there is anything in there worth reading. Try maybe five years ahead."

Matt sat across from Hope as they continued reading. "Here is your first mention of Marlon having a girlfriend. It doesn't seem like you're surprised. You wished her good luck with him."

Hope's hands dropped in her lap. "I bet if you keep reading, you'll find mention of a few more. I don't know how long Marlon's relationship with Miranda went on."

Matt shook his head. "I don't know how he kept them all straight. You mentioned quite a few in here."

Hope was no longer listening. She touched the pages of the journal she was holding with her fingertips as if she could summon the memory. She put her head in her hands and began to cry.

Matt quickly set the journal aside. He scooted across the floor, so he was next to her. She turned to him and buried her face in his throat. He picked it up.

"Oh, Hope.  I'm so sorry.  I didn't even think about this."

Hope's hand fluttered over the journal.  "I was so happy.  I don't know why.  I mean, I obviously knew about all or most of Marlon's girlfriends.  How could I have been so happy to be pregnant?  How could I have let him get me pregnant after all those women?"

"Maybe you were tired of waiting to start making those four girls since it didn't work out with you and Robbie.  You wanted to have a family one day, and he was your husband."

She wiped the tears from her cheeks.  "Sorry.  It just sort of hit me.  I guess I should be glad I didn't bring a baby into the world after this mess.  I don't know how I would have supported the two of us.  I could barely support myself."

Matt wiped the last of her tears.  "Losing a dream hurts.  The child was a part of you, and I have no doubt you'd have done whatever you had to do to support the two of you.  One thing I've learned about you is that you're not afraid to take the hard path."

"I was only ten weeks when I was attacked."

Matt picked up the journal she had set down.  "Given the date of your attack, this was written two weeks prior."

"Do I say anything about telling Marlon?"

Matt read through.  "You weren't going to tell him.  You were going to leave."

Hope snatched it from him and read it herself.  "I was going to leave him.  I was planning it when I knew he'd be out of town. He must have found out. I remember him yelling at me. I don't think my mind made that up."

Matt folded his hand over hers, closing the journal. "I don't think it did either. The baby was likely the reason for the attack."

Hope cleared her throat. "Go back one journal. According to all the papers I have, Miranda was strangled before I knew I was pregnant. There are pictures of me at his arraignment. The prosecution used my testimony as part of their reason for arresting and prosecuting him. I have the transcripts."

Matt grabbed the manila folder she had brought out. "Here we are. His DNA was found on her body. Not enough on its own, since they were having an affair. Her mother said the relationship was over, and that he must have attacked her daughter and forced her. That would be hearsay. A friend of Miranda's told the police a similar story. But you told the police you saw them argue the night she was killed. You heard him threaten her. Put that all together, and you have a case. Not a slam dunk, but probable that he was the killer."

Hope found the journal with the dates she was looking for. "Here."

Matt skimmed through. "'Marlon has a new girlfriend. Miranda Grieves. She's a lovely woman; I can see what he sees in her. I have to ask what she sees in him, though. Probably what I saw.'"

Hope grabbed it when he clearly wasn't going to keep reading it to her. "'Stability. A nice home. Not a bad deal. After Dad died and he proposed, I thought we made sense. I should have known better. He was twenty years my senior. He'd been married twice, but he only had Trey, so I thought it could work. I wish Miranda the best of luck.'"

Matt took it from her. "Just like the others. Let's see. Here."

Hope leaned over his arm. "'Marlon hit her. I thought he was going to strike her again when he grabbed her shoulders, shook her until she was crying, and resumed yelling. He had been so angry. I couldn't hear what Miranda was saying, but Marlon yelled loud enough for the dead to hear. Apparently, he doesn't like it when the Gucci shoe is on the other foot. Miranda has a lover. Wonder who it is? Marlon likes to huff and puff; we certainly fight enough. But tonight it seemed different. He threatened to kill her. She stormed off. He followed her. I didn't see where they went.'"

Matt turned the page and read the next section. "'I suppose I should be glad I came to my senses and didn't take Trey up on his offer of an affair. All I could picture was Gloria, his new wife. Like father, like son. I doubt Trey will be faithful to her. He told me he loved her when I asked him why he married her. But he said he loved me too, but I was out of his reach. I guess after he found out about Miranda, I was fair game. Oh, well. It wouldn't have worked. I don't love Marlon, and I don't see how I could love Trey. They're too much alike.'"

Hope closed her eyes in relief. "I guess that answers that question. For Gloria's sake, if not my own. It's not like I would have remembered having an affair with him anyway."

Matt grabbed a blank page and ripped a strip off, bookmarking the page where Hope had mentioned witnessing the fight. "And for my peace of mind. I didn't like the way Trey looked at you. I guess he was looking at the one that got away."

"Noticed that, did you? I may not remember him, but I know what lust looks like."

Matt pulled her over so that she straddled his waist. "Does it look like this?"

Hope tipped her head to the side. "Maybe. I think so. I can't be sure."

Matt rolled so that she was on her back beneath him. "How about now?"

Hope wriggled under him, pressing her hips up against him. "I'm not sure. I think you need to work a little harder."

Matt stripped off her shirt. "If I get any harder, this will be over."

Hope grabbed at the waistband of his pants. "We can't have that now."

Matt didn't bother taking off the rest of their clothes. He stripped Hope's pants and underwear to her ankles, grabbed the condom out of his back pocket, and stripped himself only enough to get it on.

Hope bit his neck, and he lost it. He gripped her hips and surged into her.

Hope moaned and bit his chest through his work shirt. Her hands gripped his butt as he drove into her. It wasn't but moments before he felt her convulse under him. He buried his face in her hair and followed.

Hope kissed his neck where she'd bit him. "We keep up this pace, we might kill each other."

Matt rolled onto his back. Hope struggled to get her legs out of her jeans. When she was naked, she sat on the carpet. He stripped off his clothes and the condom. He picked her up and carried her to the bedroom.

It was dark in the bedroom even though the sun hadn't fully set. Matt set her on the mattress. "Hope?"

Hope scooted back so she could sit. Matt sat down at her feet. "I'm not going to like what you're going to say, am I?"

Matt ran his palm over her calf and up her thigh. "I like having you here. Allie thinks it's meant to be."

Hope shivered at the feel of his rough palm on her skin. "Meant to be? Like forever?"

Matt's fingers curved around her hip as he leaned into her. "Yeah. Like forever."

Hope wet her lips. "We don't know each other well enough for that. She doesn't know me."

Matt came to his knees, one of his slipping between hers. "I know you well enough. We're not kids. I realize that I'm the only man you remember being with, but I think if you dig deep down, you'll know this is different. More."

Hope groped for her words. "I can't imagine it being like this with anyone else."

Matt pushed his advantage. "I can tell you it's not. I have memories of the women I've been with. But when I'm with you, I forget all about them. It's just you and me."

Hope bit her lip, her eyes unsure as she looked up at him. "Do you love me?"

Matt started to say yes, then stopped. Her lovely turquoise eyes were looking into his. Her eyes demanded the truth. "I could. And I think you could love me."

Hope slipped out from under him. She took out a nightgown and put it on. "I can't talk about love while naked."

Matt smiled at that. "That's the best time."

She looked at him over her shoulder. "Like I said, if we keep up this pace, we're likely to kill each other."

Matt got up and pulled out a pair of flannel pants. He pulled them on but didn't bother with a shirt. "Okay, we have clothes on."

Hope took a seat on the opposite side of the bed. The side where he slept. "Okay. So you think you could love me, and I could love you. But we're not there yet. What does that mean?"

Matt sat down. "I don't know. The last woman I was in love with was when I was in my early twenties."

Hope crossed her arms over her chest. "And what did you do?"

Matt shrugged. "Nothing. We lived together for a while. She got tired of me being deployed all the time and found a man she liked better."

Hope huffed. "That's not very helpful. I don't remember being in love. I assume I loved Marlon. I mean, I married him."

Matt climbed over to her. He kissed her upturned mouth. "Step one is you stay here with me. Step two is we learn more about each other. Step three is we fall in love. Step four is we get married. Step five is we raise horses and make babies. How does that sound?"

Hope held his face away from hers when he would have kissed her again. "That's the big plan?"

"Hey, I didn't add a mansion to the list. And I didn't specify how many babies, and I included the horses. I think that covers your big romance with Robbie."

Hope burst out laughing. "You're going to base our relationship goals on those of a twelve-year-old?"

"Twelve-year-old Hope was smart and practical. And she knew what she wanted. I can work with that."

Hope leaned back into him and let him kiss her. "Step one is good. I think we're almost done with step two. We learned more about me tonight than I wanted to know."

Matt slipped his hands under her nightgown,

finding her naked flesh.  He leaned into her until she was once again on her back.  "Let's see how much progress I can make on step three."

* * *

In the morning, they went back to the journals. Hope had made breakfast while Matt finished sorting through them.  Hope had also made a point of picking up the clothes they'd left on the living room floor. Trixie was on a pillow, her head lying on her paws.

"Your dog is bored."  Matt found a dog toy and threw it.  The big dog went running after it, bumping into things as she went.

Trixie brought it back, her eyes full of doggy excitement.

Hope came into the living room, hands on her hips.  "She's not used to being inside.  Why don't you take her outside to play?  I can finish up here.  I don't think there are any more earth-shattering secrets in them.  The only secret is why I documented my entire life."

Matt was tugging with the dog, the muscles in his arms flexing as the dog used all her strength to try to get the toy from him.  "There are a lot of them.  You were six when you started and thirty when you stopped.  The bigger question was why you didn't keep doing it."

Hope watched with growing admiration as Matt held his own in the game of tug.  "Too hard.  My hands hate holding a pen.  It took me weeks of therapy to be able to use my hands again to write my name or tie my shoes.  And I didn't have a laptop or a phone, so I couldn't type my thoughts."

Trixie won the game when she finally wrestled the toy from Matt's grasp.  "Man, your dog is strong.  I'll take her outside.  Then we should call Agent Parks. He might be interested in your journal entry on the day you saw Marlon arguing with Miranda.  You might not remember, but it's your handwriting, and that would be easy to prove is yours."

Hope nodded as she picked up another journal. Matt grabbed Trixie's toys and took her outside. Hope set the journal in her lap, unsure of what to do next.  But it wasn't the journal she was worried about.

She could love Matt.  Probably did.  He was so easy to be with.  She'd moved into his trailer, and it was like she'd always been here.  They had already established their daily routines.  They got up, she made breakfast, and they headed off to work.  That routine would change a little since she would now be going with him on trail rides and camping trips.  But then they would come back to his trailer, Matt would fix dinner, and they would talk, read, or watch television.  Then at some point, Matt would turn to her, and they would go to bed.  She was already addicted to him.  Each night as they relaxed, anticipation of the night to come filled her.  And he delivered on all the lusty promises he made her, whether with words or a look.

Trixie was already gravitating toward him. Her bed was now on the floor in his bedroom. The dog bed was on Hope's side of the bed. And wasn't that the kicker? She had her side of the bed.

They just fit.

Hope opened the journal back up. The answers to her past weren't in these journals. She didn't document who attacked her or who was responsible for her lost memories. The more she read about the eight years of her marriage, the more she was glad she couldn't remember. She didn't want those memories mingling with the new ones she was making.

Hope gave up on the journals and set the ones from her childhood years that she'd keep on the coffee table. The rest she picked up. The one Matt bookmarked, she set on the kitchen table. The rest would eventually go in the trash. She only hesitated to toss them now in case the police or FBI wanted to see them for some reason.

Twenty minutes later, Matt came in sweaty with a very happy Trixie dancing around him. Hope was up to her wrists in dishwater. "I wasn't sure what to do with those journals."

Matt picked up the one with the paper tucked in it. "I left a message for Agent Parks. I also left a message for Sully. He's likely to show up first."

Hope finished up the dishes and turned to see Matt taking pictures of the pages. "So now what? We go about our day like there isn't some crazy person out there?"

Matt tucked the journal in a drawer. "Not much else we can do. The murders have been heavily publicized. We've alerted all our staff to be on guard. So unless Trey or Gloria turn up dead, we've done all we can."

Hope shuddered. "I hope it doesn't come to that."

"Same. Come on. We're riding trails today. Friday we'll be taking our first overnight group out."

Hope dried off her hands and grabbed her bag. "I've gotten way too used to sleeping in a bed."

Matt wiggled his eyebrows at her. "Don't worry, we can share a tent. I make a great bed."

Hope brushed her lips against his. "That you do. But a lumpy one. All those muscles of yours."

Matt curved his palms around her bottom. "Complaining?"

Hope removed his hands. "Nope. But you'll have to finish that thought later. The horses are waiting."

Chapter Eighteen

Hope was up to her neck in bubbles when she heard voices in the living room. It was Jeremy, so she relaxed. She hated to admit it, but she was still getting used to being on horseback so much. As far as she'd been able to tell from the journals, she hadn't spent much time, if any, on a horse after Butterscotch died. Her leg muscles were protesting a week's worth of riding. She closed her eyes and sank further into the water.

There was a brief knock at the door. "Jeremy has mail for you. Meggie sent you a letter. Someone else did too, postmarked from L.A. Looks like maybe your lawyer's office. Allie invited us over for dinner if you want to climb out of there and go."

Hope sat up. She smiled at what the little girl might have written to her. "Be out in a few minutes."

"Want some help?"

If Jeremy weren't in the living room, she might. "No."

Matt's laughter faded as he walked away.

Hope soaped up and washed her hair. She rose from the tub and dried off. She pulled on fresh clothes and fluffed out her wet hair. As she was putting moisturizer on her face, she stopped. Some memory was niggling at her, but it wouldn't stick.

Miranda's face flashed before hers.

*I'm sorry, Jaclyn.  I wasn't going to tell you.  It's over between me and Marlon.  You were one thing, but I saw them together.  I can't believe he would stoop so low.  To hurt his son like this.*

Hope jumped when she heard Matt calling to her.

"Did you fall asleep in there?"

Hope shook off the memory.  She opened the bathroom door, tucking her blouse into her jeans as she went.  "Came close."

Jeremy acknowledged her with a brief nod. "Let's go eat.  Allie is experimenting in the kitchen again."

Hope told Trixie to stay.  "Is that good or bad?"

Matt took her hand as he led her to his truck. "Usually good."

Jeremy headed toward his.  "Meet you there.  I need to make a brief stop."

Matt helped Hope into the truck.  "I forgot to give you the letters."

"I can read them later.  It's sweet that Meggie would write to me."

Matt got in and drove them the short distance to the main house.  "I hope she and her mom are doing okay. Jeremy said her father took off after the boys were arrested."

Hope wasn't surprised.  "He wasn't going to win any Father of the Year awards, that's for sure."

"No.  Meggie and her mom will have a rough time, but any woman who goes up into the mountains in search of her stepsons, despite what they did, is tough.  I hope she doesn't bear the burden of what those two boys did."

Hope hoped not too.  "Maybe she'll start a new life with her daughter somewhere else."

Matt laid a hand over hers.  "Just like you did."

Hope turned her hand over to hold his.  "I didn't have much choice.  Neither does Mrs. Edgerton.  But if she's smart, she'll get divorced and wash her hands of those two."

When they got to the house, they found Allie in the kitchen.  Sawyer was in his swing.  Matt picked him up.  "He's getting so big."

Allie glanced at Matt holding her son.  "I know. Jeremy is convinced that now is the time to get him a pony.  I told him to give it a few years."

Hope joined Allie in the kitchen.  "At least.  Can I help?"

Allie handed her a spoon.  "Just stir.  Everything is almost done.  I wanted to have you over now that I've had some time to process the fact we're related."

Hope kept her back to Allie and stirred the pot. "It was a shock for me to learn I had a sister too. Especially given the circumstances.  But I found the birth certificate copy in a box buried under others, so I don't think I knew about you before."

Allie tossed some pasta in the now boiling water. "I certainly didn't know about you.  I called my dad. He was surprised, to say the least.  She had so little interest in raising me; he found it hard to believe she'd have gotten pregnant again."

Hope's fingers trembled on the spoon. "Do you want proof?"

Allie stood beside her. "No. I believe you. And you inherited that property, which means you have to be related to my aunt regardless. From what little you know, it doesn't sound like our mother was all that interested in you, either. But I thought you might like to see some old pictures."

Hope wanted to say no. She'd already spent a lot of time going down memory lane with her journals. But she did want to get to know Allie better. As far as she knew, Allie was her only living relative. "That would be nice."

Matt came over. "It smells good."

Allie gave Matt a knowing look. "Just a new spaghetti sauce recipe."

Matt walked the baby around the kitchen when he started fussing.

Allie took over the sauce. "Hope, why don't you drain the pasta? There's oil in the cabinet to the right of the sink."

Hope was watching Matt with the baby. He looked so sweet with him. She grabbed the pot handles with the potholder and carefully carried the pot to the sink. But when she went to tip it, her hand gave way and the pan dropped, splattering hot water. She turned on the sink and ran cold water over her burned hand.

Matt quickly transferred Sawyer to Allie. He

took her hand, seeing the deep red scald. "That's going to hurt."

Matt led her to the table where he held out a chair for her. She took a seat, her hand throbbing. He left and came back with supplies. She let Matt tend to her hand, and when he was done putting salve on it, she watched him bandage it up. "You sure do come in handy."

Matt wiggled his eyebrows at her. "I'll show you later."

Allie was apologetic as Jeremy came in. "I'm sorry. I wasn't thinking about your hands."

Hope's eyes caught Jeremy's. She didn't see the derision she was used to seeing there. She relaxed a little. "It happens. I've burned myself a few times over campfires or cut my hand cutting fruits and veggies. The therapist I saw at the rehab center told me I had to keep trying. But it can be hard to make my hands do what I want them to do."

Jeremy took Sawyer, and Allie finished getting dinner on the table. "Matt here is the best one to patch you up."

They ate dinner, and Jeremy and Matt left to go over some paperwork. Hope found herself alone with Allie.

"I took all the photo albums out. Our mother left most of her things behind when she left. I also did some digging and found a picture of our aunt and a few other women in the family. The auburn hair is dominant in the women on our mom's side."

Hope carefully sifted through the photos one-handed. Allie told her what she knew about each photo. Hope couldn't help but smile at the pictures of Allie as a child. She had freckles on her face, just as she did now, had her hair in braids, and wore a pair of overalls.

Hope held the picture up to the light. "We looked a lot alike at this age. I have a picture of me holding a blue ribbon with my horse Butterscotch, my hair in braids. I had on my riding gear. It's the only picture from my childhood I have. I had it tucked in one of the keepsake boxes in my bedroom at Marlon's house."

Allie leaned over to look at it. "Mom was gone by then. Our Aunt Julie took this one. She was our great aunt. She had a brother, but they were estranged. But he had a daughter that she kept in touch with. I think that's where Mom went when she left, to go stay with her cousin. I have a picture."

Hope's heart stopped and then picked up speed. "Miranda."

Allie flipped the picture over. "Yeah. She was about the same age as Mom. I never met her."

Hope's thoughts raced. "No. You don't understand. This is Miranda."

Allie looked confused. "Do you know her?"

Hope sifted through the photos but didn't recognize anyone else. She turned her head toward the hall. "Matt!"

Matt immediately came into the room at her

tone. "What is it?"

She thrust the picture at him. "It's Miranda."

Matt looked confused for a second, then his eyes widened. "Marlon's Miranda?"

Hope nodded vigorously. "That's her. I have her photo in my files."

Allie rubbed her hands on her jeans. "What do you mean, Marlon's Miranda?"

Hope wrapped her bandaged hand around her waist. "The woman he was having an affair with. The one he killed."

Jeremy trailed behind. "You're saying that the woman Marlon killed was your cousin?"

Hope rubbed her forehead where a headache was forming. "I wouldn't have known. I mean, I didn't read anything in my journals that mentioned Miranda other than the affair."

Matt took the photo. "It can't be a coincidence. Marlon had to have known she was related to your mother."

Jeremy came to stand behind them. "It makes a little sense. Allie, when your mom took off, she could have gone to stay with Miranda. Maybe Miranda kept track of the family after your mom took off."

Hope thought of the memory earlier. She shivered. What were the chances she'd recall that conversation hours before finding out Miranda was a cousin? Hope closed her eyes, trying to bring the memory back. "Miranda knew something she shouldn't. She told me that it was over between her and Marlon. That she didn't know how he could hurt his son like this."

Jeremy came around to stand by Allie. "Hurt his son like what?"

Hope wanted to scream in frustration. "I don't know. Just that she'd seen 'them' together. But I don't know who she saw Marlon with or why it would hurt his son."

Matt set the photo down. "Likely Gloria. Maybe Marlon was having an affair with Gloria; Miranda found out, so Marlon killed her to keep it a secret."

Jeremy agreed. "Makes sense. I looked into the news reports. Miranda was an attorney. I bet if we looked, we'd find Miranda was the one who filed the divorce papers for your mom to divorce her two husbands. Given that Marlon, his dad, and his son are all lawyers, they probably knew one another or traveled in the same social circles."

Hope pulled her knees to her chest. "Why try to kill me? If it was some weird love triangle, I wasn't a part of it."

Matt disagreed. "You were going to testify in court that you saw them fight. You wrote it in your journal. So you knew about the affair, and you knew about the argument."

Hope shuddered. "But I didn't see him kill her."

Jeremy came around so he could look down at her. "And that's when Marlon's attorney and the press had a field day turning the tables, suggesting you were the one who killed Miranda in a jealous rage, and your attack was staged.  Those rumors were rampant, and you didn't refute any of them."

Hope thrust her bandaged hand out. "I can't have strangled Marlon.  Whoever strangled Marlon had to be the one who tried to kill me.  And those other two poor women.  I can't even lift a pot, much less strangle a man."

Matt eased her closer to him.  "Unfortunately, there are ways you could do it.  And the police and the FBI know it.  The trick isn't strangling so much as subduing your victim.  You would have had to incapacitate them, and there was nothing in the photos we saw of any other violence.  No head trauma that we could see.  It's possible drugs or a taser, but if that were the case, Agent Parks is keeping it to himself."

Hope leaned on him.  "So we have my journal and a cousin who had an affair with and was killed by Marlon.  I'm guessing we have to make a call to the police."

Matt stroked her hair.  "I'll call Sully.  He can take the journal into evidence, and we can tell him about the family relationship between you and Miranda.  Allie can corroborate it."

Jeremy glanced at Matt.  "I don't like Allie getting involved in this.  I'll be sure to tell Sully to be discreet about it."

Hope could understand and appreciate his protective instincts.  Frankly, Hope wanted to run.  She couldn't shake the feeling that there was a target on her back.  And in turn, possibly putting a target on anyone around her.  She shivered again as fear gripped her.

Matt helped her to her feet.  "You're tired.  We'll call Sully in the morning."

Jeremy and Allie walked them to the door, and Jeremy followed them out.  "Keep your eyes peeled. Hope wouldn't recognize her attacker, assuming she knew who it was when it was happening.  People around her are turning up dead."

Matt glared at his friend.  "Not helpful.  But we all need to keep our eyes open."

When they walked inside Matt's trailer, Hope was at a loss as to what to do.

"Don't even think about it."  Matt closed and locked the door.

"Jeremy is right.  People around me are dead. Miranda, Marlon, and Harris.  Trey and Gloria had better be on guard.  And so should you, Jeremy, and Allie if it gets out that Allie is my half-sister and that I'm living with you."

Matt took her into the kitchen and fixed her a cup of tea.  "You're just tense."

Hope wanted to swear.  "And what of the two women?  They had nothing to do with me, and yet they died the same way.  The FBI wouldn't be here if they didn't think it was the same person."

Matt pushed the warm cup into her non-bandaged hand.  "If it's the same person, he likely developed a taste for murder when he killed

Miranda."

Hope stared at the dark liquid. "It's starting to look like Marlon didn't kill Miranda, doesn't it?"

Matt urged her to sit and drink her tea. "I don't know. I'm not an investigator, but if we assume the same person killed all the victims, then Marlon is off the list. But if we assume Marlon did kill her, then he hired someone to kill you; that person could have killed Marlon, and those two women after you survived the attack."

"Harris too."

Matt shook his head. "Not necessarily. He was shot."

Hope set the cup down. "My head hurts, and so does my hand."

Matt opened and handed her Meggie's letter. "This might cheer you up before bed."

Hope leaned over, grabbed the other letter from her attorney, and set it aside. "'Dear Hope. I hope this finds you well. I've been scared since Mom and I got out of the mountains. But we're settling into a new home. My brothers are in jail, and I'm sorry for what they did. Mom tried to keep it from me, but all the kids at school knew about it. But you saved me. And I heard you saved your friend, Matt, too. I want to thank you for finding me and getting me back to my mom. She has no one else. Be safe, and Matt too. You're both my heroes. Love, Meggie.'"

Matt took the letter and there was a picture of a smiling Meggie, her arm in a cast. "Glad she's okay.

Kids can be cruel."

Hope managed to tear open the letter from her lawyer. She frowned at it. "They said a package was delivered to their office addressed to me. The letter says they didn't open it, as they are no longer managing my case, but, as a courtesy, they forwarded it to me."

Matt saw it was mailed to Hope Whitfield, care of Waters Ranch. "Maybe something about your Aunt Julie's property. Or maybe from Trey about the papers you signed."

Hope couldn't imagine what else there was to say as far as Marlon or Trey were concerned. She opened the letter. A slip of paper slid out.

Matt picked it up. "It just says 'You're welcome.'"

Hope pulled out two large photographs. She screamed as they slid from her fingers onto the table. It was pictures of Marlon. Dead.

* * *

Sully handed Matt and Hope each a cup of coffee. It was after midnight, but Matt figured the caffeine couldn't hurt, and Hope was shivering. She had been shivering the entire drive to the police station. She was still in shock. Seeing the photos when the FBI agent had hit her with them cold was a lot different from receiving a note from the person who likely killed Marlon.

Sully had the photos and the note. He had bagged them to be sent to the crime lab for fingerprints or any other evidence. Matt's prints were on file, but Hope's had not been. She was still rubbing the ink from her fingers. Matt stilled her hand. If she rubbed any harder, she'd likely take skin with the wipe.

Sully picked up the journal. "I read the reports. The D.A.'s office ultimately dropped the charges. The D.A. was worried he would be found not guilty and not be able to retry the case. Investigations were ongoing up until a year ago. Marlon Turner was a well-known figure. There were rumblings about a potential political career, though none of that was corroborated. Trey Turner denies it. But in the course of the investigation, it was discovered that Trey and Marlon were not exactly close. Father and son were estranged from what the detectives could ascertain. Trey had also been investigated in the murder of Miranda Grieves. His wife alibied him, and the police couldn't figure out a motive anyway."

Matt watched Sully's face as he read the journal. The man gave nothing away. "What did Agent Parks have to say?"

Sully turned the page. "More than I particularly wanted to hear. My guess is that I'll have the FBI and the State Bureau of Investigation on my doorstep in the next day or two. Agent Parks wasn't exactly a fount of information, but he's been busy. He tied two more murdered women to our perp."

Hope gasped. "What?"

Sully set the journal aside. "Digging turned up a body in Northern California with the same M.O. Another body was found in Oregon."

Hope blindly grabbed Matt's hand. "When?"

"California was eighteen months ago. A Debbie Ripton. Oregon was eleven months. A Lydia Bancroft. Then came Natalie Gerber and the other victim, Betsy Hargrove. I don't suppose you knew any of them?"

Matt pulled her against him. He could see tears in her eyes as she struggled to process what they had just learned.

Hope couldn't get any words out. She shook her head.

Sully leaned against his desk. "They look like you."

Hope jumped in Matt's arms, but he kept her in her seat. "Was that necessary?"

Sully's eyes hardened. "Miss Whitlock is tied to seven murders. She would have been eight. I read her statement to the FBI. Hope was in both of those states when the murders occurred. Within miles. DNA on the first body in California rules Hope out as the killer. DNA was male."

Hope found her voice. "There was DNA evidence? What kind?"

Sully folded his arms over his chest. "The kind only a man can leave behind."

Hope turned even more pale. "She was raped?"

Sully set his hand on the folder next to him. "No. None of them were. But his DNA was there just the same. Forensic results said the man tried to clean her up but left traces behind. He didn't make that same mistake again."

Matt stroked Hope's hair. "What about Miranda Grieves?"

"No DNA except Marlon's. A few fibers were found on her body, but not much else. She was strangled, but the killer used his bare hands. A partial print was obtained, but it was too smeared to use in court."

Hope's hand went to her throat. "The police told me I was strangled with the strap of my purse, not hands."

Sully considered that. "It's not as easy to choke a victim with your hands as it is with a rope or tie. Could be Miranda took too long, and the killer perfected his method. Or your purse was handy. Can't say either way."

Matt kept Hope in the circle of his arms when she tried to pull away from him. "So what is the next step?"

Sully tapped the photos in plastic. "We see what the state lab can find. We already alerted the public, though we will again. Hope doesn't go anywhere alone. Best case, the killer will go after surrogates again. Worst case, he tires of his game and goes after her directly. Carry a gun on you and learn how to use it."

Matt rose. "I know how to use one."

Sully nodded. "Army. Medic if I recall."

Matt gripped Hope's hand. "I'd rather heal people than shoot them, but I hit what I aim for."

"Good. I'll keep the journal. It doesn't say much that we don't already know, but it at least corroborates the story that circulated at the time of Miranda Grieves's murder."

Hope cleared her throat. "I was talking to Allie Waters. It's a bit complicated, but she's my half-sister. We learned last night that Miranda was our cousin."

Sully stopped in his tracks. "You were related to the victim?"

Hope quickly continued. "I own the property to the east of the Waters's property. I inherited it from an aunt. I learned from some family records that Allie Waters was my half-sister from our mother's previous marriage. She inherited the retreat and a huge parcel of land. I inherited the land next door. Allie didn't know about me, and I only just learned about her. She was showing me some old family photos. One of them was her cousin, Miranda. It's the same Miranda."

"Huh?" Sully took a few notes. "Not sure it matters, but something to consider. Miranda wasn't in line to inherit the property?"

Matt didn't like where that line of questioning was going. "You'd have to check the trusts. But Julie Cleary, Allie and Hope's aunt, left her property to her two nieces. Miranda was the daughter of Julie's brother."

Sully took a few more notes. "Odd she didn't leave anything to the other niece."

Hope rubbed her chilled arms. "If I ever knew, I don't remember. Our working theory is that our mom left Allie's dad and went to stay with Miranda. Miranda was an attorney. I'd have to check the files I have to see who the attorney on record was for my mom's divorce from my dad. But it seems awfully coincidental that my husband had an affair with my older cousin. I don't know if Marlon would have known Miranda was my cousin, but maybe he met her through my mom."

Sully's tone was skeptical. "And you have no memory?"

Matt saw Hope grit her teeth. "She has no reason to lie. Can we go?"

Sully set his notebook down. "You can go. I assume neither of you are going anywhere. Just be alert. And keep that gun with you, like I said. You all are isolated out there."

Matt kept his arm around Hope as they went to his truck. He boosted her in. He didn't like the paleness of her skin. He turned on the heat when he climbed in. He could see goosebumps on her arms, and she'd been rubbing her arms on and off since they'd left his trailer.

Hope closed her eyes. "I don't know what to do. He's been following me. Why send the photos care of the lawyer? He probably knew where I was the whole time."

"I don't know. I want to see all of the files from your private investigator and all the papers from your lawyer. We have to be missing something."

Hope rubbed her tired eyes. "I can't imagine what."

Matt ticked off his thoughts. "Why did Marlon refuse

to divorce you?  He had plenty of female companionship.  How did he find out about your pregnancy?  You didn't tell him.  I assume you would have been careful to conceal it since you were leaving him.  Why would Trey outright suggest an affair?  Not very subtle for a guy who seems like a smooth talker.  Did Gloria know?  You said they were newly married, and that Trey claimed to be in love with his wife, but also with you.  How does Miranda being your cousin change the narrative?  Why didn't she stand to inherit any property?  Was there a rift between your aunt and her brother?"

Hope held up a hand. "Matt. Stop. I don't know."

"I wonder if Allie knows why Julie didn't leave Miranda an inheritance."

Hope's head rolled against the seat to look at him. "Maybe she inherited something else.  I don't know.  But if she did, it wasn't land.  I couldn't find anything in any of the papers from the lawyer.  But like you, I'm not an investigator.  And if the man I hired to find Marlon knows anything else, he certainly isn't going to tell me unless I pay him what I owe.  Perhaps not even then.  He was pretty ticked off when I told him I couldn't pay him."

"Let me look at what you do have.  Then we can contact him if I think he might know more."

Hope sat upright. "You are not paying that bill."

Matt touched the tip of his finger to her nose. "You're cute when you're mad."

Hope slapped his hand away. "I mean it."

Matt shrugged.  "I know.  You might be the only person I know who would turn down a big fat alimony check out of principle.  If Jeremy were to step out of line, Allie would take him for everything he has, right after she kicked his ass.  She's a lot tougher than she looks.  A lot like her sister."
Hope crossed her arms over her chest.  "Flattery will get you nowhere."
Matt just grinned at her.  "We'll see."

* * *

Jeremy finished looking over the printouts.  "You're right.  The guy is a crook.  How much did Hope pay this guy?"

Matt paced behind his friend.  "She won't say.  One thing I do know is that it was more than she could afford."

Jeremy tossed the papers from the investigator onto the desk.  "Her lawyer was more thorough, at least when it came to putting together her divorce papers and a title search on the property before she signed the papers.  The law office handled a lot of the paperwork for her.  There is no record of Hope trying to claim her mother's estate.  No will surfaced.  Thankfully no other relatives came out of the woodwork.  I've advised Allie to see what good old Cheryl was worth.  As far as I'm concerned, whatever that woman had, Allie and Hope should take possession. Assuming there was anything of value."

Matt didn't care one way or the other.  Hope had made it clear she wanted nothing to do with her past, not even the money she was entitled to.  "Hope said her mother was the recipient of her father's estate.  There are copies of papers in Hope's legal files that Marlon filed on Hope's behalf, but it doesn't look like Hope ever signed them."

Jeremy sifted through the other pile.  "No doubt Marlon was steamed Hope didn't sign them.  Her father had a lot of money, and Hope could have contested his will given the divorce.  I get the feeling Marlon likely married her for what he thought would be her inheritance.  Still would like to know why Hope married him, but from what we've gathered, her husband had a great love of money.  I saw the picture of that monstrosity he called a house in Hope's files."

Matt had understood why Hope would never want to set foot in that house again.  Monstrosity was an apt description.  "I'm not sure what to do now.  Hope won't let me help."

Jeremy gave Matt an odd look.  "You're going to let that stop you?"

Matt had no choice but to relent.  Hope had sworn she'd leave if he didn't leave it alone.  She didn't want him digging any further into Jaclyn's life.  She said the county, the state, and the Feds were looking for the man who strangled those women.  It had to be enough.  At least in her mind.

Jeremy leaned back in his chair and gazed at the ceiling.  "I know a guy."

Matt knew that look. "What guy?"

Jeremy turned on his computer and started searching for a file. "An investigator."

Matt looked over his shoulder. "Why would you need an investigator?"

Jeremy pulled up a document. "Samuel Gentry. He's out of Virginia. I hired him before Allie and I got married. I had him locate my dad."

Matt skimmed the letter. Jeremy's dad had been killed in a one-car crash outside D.C. "That was good news. You never said anything."

Jeremy jotted down the contact information. "It was for my peace of mind. I didn't want the old man ever showing up on my doorstep. He did the world a favor when he killed himself in that crash. Going to tell me you never looked for your dad?"

Matt rolled his shoulder. He hated to admit that it still ached. "I did. But he wasn't hard to find. Never moved out of that dump he calls a house. His name is still on the property taxes."

"I'm going to call him. We'll turn this all over and see what he can dig up. If you want to stay out of it, be my guest, but this affects my wife too. Hope might want to try to bury this, but I don't believe that has or will do any good. Her past is hell-bent on catching up with her. I won't have my family caught in the middle."

Matt knew Hope was going to be livid. "Call him."

Chapter Nineteen

Hope gaped. "You did what?"

Matt tried to take her hand, but she jerked away. "Look, Hope. Jeremy is right. What if this guy comes after Allie? It's not just about you anymore. Five women are dead. Your husband and father-in-law were also casualties. Whoever he is, he's not going to stop."

Hope stalked off to the bedroom. She started pulling her stuff from the drawers. "I meant it. I should never have come here. If I'm not here, he won't be here. I can protect my family too."

Matt took both of her hands in his. She pulled, but he was stronger than she was. She wanted to yell at him. To lash out at him. Matt, Allie, Jeremy, and even Sawyer were in danger because of her. Because she came here. She had such hopes. She'd finally have a home of her own. She thought she'd figured out why her life had been spared, but all she'd done was bring a killer with her. No, she hadn't known. But now she did.

Hope yanked harder. "Let me go."

Matt scooped her up and sat her on the bed. "Running isn't the answer. You know that. You ran for two years. He'll just follow you. And until we know why he killed Miranda, we can't know if Allie would be safe if you left. Let Jeremy's guy look into it. It can't hurt. And I can't let you leave. I won't."

Hope got to her feet and threw her arms around his neck. "I really hate you right now."

Matt kissed the side of her neck. "I know. You're not alone anymore, Hope. I'm not afraid to admit I've gotten used to having you around. I've spent a lot of time alone on the road. Sometimes the loneliness was more than I could bear. When I came here, I didn't expect this. Expect you."

Hope pulled back and cupped his cheek. "I didn't expect you either."

Matt folded up the clothes she'd yanked out of the dresser and put them back inside. "At least you didn't start with the closet."

Hope sat back on the bed. "We have a group of campers we're supposed to take out today."

"We do, and there is no one else to take them. Jeremy will be with Allie. Allie is too tired to argue about being kept inside. We'll take the group out. Likely it's safer for both of us at the remote campsite."

Hope didn't bother to refute his logic, though she knew he was well aware of the hole in it. She knew the killer's belongings had been found up on the plateau between the two properties. Whoever he was, he wasn't unfamiliar with the area. She still got the creeps when she thought of him watching her. How many times had he been sitting up there, watching her bathe, cook, or sleep?

Matt started packing up clothes for the two of

them. "Pack up Trixie's stuff and enough food for a couple of days. We'll bring her with us."

Hope shook off her disturbing thoughts and did as Matt asked. Within the hour, they were going over the guidelines with a group of eager campers. The group wasn't an experienced one, but she didn't mind. It made her feel useful to be able to teach the groups about surviving in the wilderness. As they did when they were leading groups out on the trails, Matt took the lead and Hope brought up the rear. Trixie went back and forth between them. They were now almost at camp. After they'd been dropped off at the start of the trail, they'd hiked the trail for four hours toward the campground.

When they got to the campground, there was a collective groan of relief. Bags were dropped, and several people took a seat on the wooden logs near where the fire would be built.

Hope watched Matt as he organized the group after letting everyone take a brief rest. The group pitched their tents. Hope helped a few people get theirs erected, and while her hands weren't cooperative, she was able to guide the campers on how to do it themselves. She saw Matt pitch a tent for the two of them. It would be a tight fit, but Matt assured her she and the dog would fit in it with him. Looking at it, she had her doubts.

They spent the afternoon fishing. Hope didn't even try to figure out how to use the rod, and Matt didn't press her. She simply sat back and watched the group of ten learn how to fish.  Today the fish were biting, and Hope knew there would be plenty for dinner.  On their way back to camp with the bucket of fish, Matt pointed out several edible plants surrounding them.  Hope found herself as much a student as the group.  Plants were gathered to go along with their meal.

The conversation around the campfire during dinner revolved around how gross cleaning fish was. Matt winked at her when she agreed, but they all could agree that the fish was delicious.  Matt had shown the group how to spit roast the fish over the open flames.  Dinner was supplemented with biscuits from the retreat's kitchen, as well as plenty of fresh fruit and vegetables.

Darkness had barely fallen when the campers retired to their tents.  It had been a long day for the inexperienced group.  Hope could admit to being tired herself, but she still helped Matt get the camp ready for the morning, banking the fire and piling supplies nearby.

Matt came up behind her and massaged her shoulders.  "You look as tired as they do."

Hope leaned into his hands.  "I don't know if I've hiked that far before.  I might need those magical hands of yours on my legs."

Matt nipped her neck.  "Magical, huh?"

Hope gripped the back of his thighs when his hands covered her breasts.  "You need to stop that."

Matt started to walk her to their tent, his erection

pressed against her bottom as they walked back to chest. Matt held the tarp and Trixie made herself comfortable. Hope dropped from his arms and crawled in. Matt moved Trixie until she was lying in front of the tent flaps at their feet.

It was a tight fit, but Hope managed to get undressed and yank her nightgown over her head. She tucked her boots in the corner and tried to relax. Unlike the tent she'd been living in, there was no air mattress. She wriggled, trying to find a comfortable spot.

Matt stripped and then smiled at her as he pulled a condom out of his bag. Hope felt her body flush. She pressed her hands against his bare chest when he crawled toward her. Her voice was a whisper. "There are people outside this tent."

Matt eased her onto her back, pushing her nightgown to her waist. "Then you'll have to be very quiet, won't you?"

Hope watched as Matt rolled the condom on. He was already fully aroused. She felt her body respond in turn. Her breasts tightened, and she knew the second he saw her nipples bead against the fabric. He knelt between her thighs, his hands smoothing their way over her belly to her breasts. He didn't uncover her but slipped his head under her nightgown. She could see the bare skin of his back as he suckled and laved her breasts. She gripped his head through her gown, biting her lower lip to keep silent. When he released her breasts, he kissed and bit the skin on her belly.  She felt his tongue tracing the path his hands had taken.  His torso was between her thighs when she realized his intent.  Knowing there was no way she was going to be able to be quiet, she shoved her fist against her mouth.  She caught his satisfied smile as he slid lower and bent his head between her thighs. She bit her fingers hard enough to leave a mark as he kissed and licked her flesh.  It wasn't long before she felt herself convulse around his tongue.

Matt released her, pushing the nightgown to her neck.  He settled between her thighs, stroking her wet flesh.  She kept her fist where it was as he eased himself into her body.

He whispered in her ear.  "I've been wanting to do this to you all day."

Hope could barely move; she was limp beneath him.  He rode her until she once again started to respond to him. When her legs were wrapped around his waist, he quickened his pace.  She bit his shoulder, leaving the same marks there that she'd left on her fingers.  Matt's fingers slipped between their bodies and stroked her until she came.  She felt him bury his face in her neck as he found his release.

Afterward, the only sounds were their breathing. Matt rolled off her, but Hope couldn't move a muscle. She felt his hand tug her nightgown back over her body to her knees.  He stripped off the condom and pulled on a pair of shorts.

Hope was still dazed when she rolled onto her side.  She used his bicep as a pillow.  She kissed his rib cage. "Matt?"

He pulled her thigh so that it draped over his. He yawned, and his entire body relaxed. "Yeah?"

Hope looked at the marks on her fingers. "I think I might have finished step three."

Matt's body tightened beneath her, and he tipped her chin up so he could see her face. "I knew I finished step three when I let Jeremy call that investigator. I knew you'd be mad. But I'm not about to let anything happen to you, Hope. If I'd had to tie you to the bed to keep you there, I would have."

Hope rolled onto her back. "I'm not sure if I should smack you for that or kiss you."

Matt leaned over her, his forearms keeping him balanced above her. "I love you, Hope. You can smack me or kiss me. You could do pretty much whatever you want to me, and I'd let you."

Hope lifted to give him a soft kiss. She then rolled him onto his side and snuggled back up against him. "I love you, Matt."

* * *

Hope was alone in the tent when she woke. She could hear voices outside. She sat up, pulled her knees to her chest, and laid her chin on her knees. She was in love with Matt. And he said he was in love with her. She grinned and released her legs, excited to begin the day. She found her bag and pulled out fresh clothes.

Matt glanced her way as she emerged from the tent, and Hope smiled shyly at him. She wound her way around the camp for some privacy. Trixie followed. She petted the dog as she went a little deeper into the woods. It was cool this morning, though Hope knew temperatures would rise as the day went on. They weren't at a high enough elevation to avoid the hotter temperatures. Hope took a moment and washed up. Trixie was happily sniffing around.

Hope was on her way back when she heard shouting. She ran back to the camp. A man was sitting on the log, rocking himself. The other campers were huddled around him.

Hope ran to Matt. "What's wrong?"

Matt held her to him for a moment. "His wife is gone. He said she went off on her own a little while ago and hasn't come back. We need to organize a search."

Hope crossed her arms over her body as Matt called in a missing person. She looked over at the group.

Matt laid a hand on her shoulder, his voice soft as he spoke. "We have to assume the worst. I want you to take the group back down the mountain. I'll stay here and wait for the search party."

Hope's throat closed as Matt started packing up the gear. She didn't want to consider what might have happened to her. Matt addressed the group. The husband refused to leave, but the others did as

Matt said.

Hope had all her gear packed by the time Matt had gotten the group to do the same. He came back over to her. "Stay together. Follow the path straight down. No one goes off on their own, not for anything."

Hope nodded. "Be careful."

Matt kissed her briefly. "Same goes for you."

Hope gathered the group, called Trixie, and they started down the trail. She tried to stay focused on her job and on getting these people back to the safety of the retreat. Four sweaty hours later, Mike met her at the path of the trail.

"Thank goodness you made it back down."

Hope let the employees waiting for them take the campers back to the retreat. "Is the search team up there yet?"

Mike led her back toward the main house. "They should be there soon. The men are on horseback and will make better time. Matt gave strict orders I'm to send you straight to the main house. Jeremy and Allie know what's going on. Sully arrived an hour ago with an FBI agent, the same one that was hanging around and asking questions a few weeks ago."

Hope wiped the sweat off her brow. "Thanks, Mike. Could you take Trixie with you? And if Matt calls, you can tell him I followed orders."

Mike nodded, took Hope's bag of dog supplies, whistled for Trixie to follow, and left her to make her way to the house. She knocked, not comfortable going in without Matt. She heard Allie's voice tell her to come in. Hope opened the door and let the screen close behind her. The house was quiet. She figured Sawyer was napping.

Hope kept her voice low as she made her way into the main living space. "Allie? Jeremy?"

Hope continued toward Sawyer's room. She saw Allie sitting in the rocking chair, holding Sawyer to her chest. Her eyes were filled with fear. Hope jumped when the bedroom door slammed behind her.

Hope was shoved forward and landed at Allie's feet. She turned to see a gun aimed at her head. Her eyes tipped up to see Gloria glaring down at her. Hope got to her knees.

"Just stay there." Gloria pointed the gun at Allie. "I don't want to hurt anyone. Except you."

Hope remained on her hands and knees. "Gloria. I don't know why you're doing this, but you can let Allie and Sawyer go. I'm the one you want."

Gloria kicked her in the stomach, then shoved her over with her foot. "I don't want you. Trey does. And Marlon did. Even the old man would have tried to get into your pants if he thought you'd let him. Though he wasn't always one to ask. Frankly, I don't know what any of them saw in you."

Hope clutched her stomach and stayed where she was. "I never wanted Trey."

Gloria waved the gun at Allie. "Take the zip cuffs from the bag over there and bind her wrists behind her back. Do as I say, and you might make it out alive."

Allie kept Sawyer in her arms but went to the bag lying across the room. She took the cuffs.

"Hands behind your back, Jaclyn. I don't have all day."

Hope got to her knees. She looked over at Allie. "Do as she says, Allie. For Sawyer."

Allie got the cuffs on her and gently tightened them. She turned pain-filled eyes to Hope. "She shot Jeremy and locked him in the pantry."

Hope glanced at Gloria and then back at Allie. "I'm so sorry, Allie. I never should have come here."

Gloria yanked Hope to her feet. "Got that right. All those poor innocent women died because you didn't have the courtesy to die two years ago."

Allie clutched Sawyer to her. "You tried to kill Hope?"

Gloria snorted in derision. "Hope. Jaclyn. All the same. I should have just shot you. But I did learn my lesson. Harris went down so easily I almost felt sorry for him."

Hope wasn't surprised at either confession. "What about Trey? You killed his father. His grandfather."

Gloria shoved her toward the door. "Now that is a story I should let Trey tell you."

Allie rushed forward but stopped when Gloria swung the gun at Sawyer. "You've got a decision to make. You can try to save Jaclyn. Or you can save your husband. Assuming he hasn't already bled to death."

Hope shook her head at Allie as she backed out of

the room. "Tell Matt—"

Allie nodded when Hope's voice choked.   "I promise."

Hope felt the gun press into her back as Gloria pushed her toward the front door.  Hope saw Allie run to the kitchen.  She prayed Jeremy was still alive.  If anyone could save him, it was Allie.

Gloria kept shoving her, guiding her toward the back of the boulders.  "I was surprised to learn you had a sister.  Of course, that piqued Trey's interest.  No doubt he'll find his way back here one day."

Hope spun, shoved her shoulder into Gloria, and tried to make a run for it.  Gloria tackled her from behind.  With her hands tied as they were, her face smacked the ground on her way down.  She tasted blood as she spit dirt and grit out of her mouth.

"That was exciting.  In the truck."

Gloria yanked on Hope until she was once again standing.  Hope didn't have an easy time climbing into the back seat.  When she was inside, Gloria waved the gun at her.

"Lie down. We're taking a ride."

Hope couldn't see much from the back of the truck. "Why are you doing this?"

"That is the question.  Trey and I made a pact.  It's just the two of us from now on.  But for that to happen, a few people had to go."

Hope twisted her hands beneath her, trying to get her hands out of the cuffs.  Her skin was raw, and the cuffs didn't loosen.  "I don't understand."

Gloria glanced down at her. "I wanted Marlon. Trey wanted you. But we both ultimately wanted the same thing. Marlon's money."

Hope felt bile rise in her throat. "So you tried to kill me because of Trey?"

Gloria stepped on the gas and the truck sped down the paved road. "It was this odd kind of domino effect. I only met your mother once. The story goes Cheryl hooked up with her cousin Miranda when she decided to divorce your father. Your father hired Marlon to represent him in the divorce. Marlon was in Boston at the time. You met Marlon through your father. Years later, you married Marlon when your father died. Marlon figured he'd get a big chunk of the old man's estate when he married you. He bought a mansion in Los Angeles, mostly to piss off his dad who'd been practicing law there for decades. But it turns out your dad left it all to his bitch ex-wife. Marlon was furious. But he also knew when you turned thirty-two, you'd inherit a big chunk of property. He figured he could have the best of both worlds. He screwed everything in skirts that let him, and you didn't seem to mind."

Hope tried to look out the window to get her bearings, but all she could see was rocks and pine trees. "I got that impression."

Gloria glanced back at her again. "Marlon knew about the inheritance because your father told him. I guess Cheryl told him. Cheryl was using Miranda to try to figure out how she could screw you and Allie out of it. Unfortunately, Julie died, and Allie got her parcel of land. Yours was in a trust."

"Now it's mine." Hope rolled onto her side and continued twisting her wrists.

"You can keep trying all you want; you won't get free. But in the meantime, let's finish the story. Cheryl died and no one cared. You didn't. Once again, Marlon was cheated because you refused to sign the documents to claim your mother's estate. So he reached out to Miranda. He knew from handling your father's divorce that Miranda was a blood relative. Miranda came out to Los Angeles and Marlon started an affair with her to try to convince her to claim Cheryl's estate. Miranda was more than happy to after she realized you weren't. She wasn't particularly worried about Allie. No one had seen or heard from her in years. And she had her inheritance. But then Miranda caught Marlon and me in bed together. She made the fatal mistake of telling you about our affair. See, it was okay for her to screw your husband, but not okay for me to."

Hope stilled. "You killed Miranda."

Gloria laughed. "Nope. Like I said, it was a domino effect from the very beginning. Marlon killed her, just like you thought. Strangled her with his bare hands. What he didn't count on was Trey witnessing it. Marlon made all sorts of excuses. Trey swore he'd keep silent. And he did, for a time."

Hope thought it made a sick sort of sense. "He protected his father."

Gloria nodded as she turned onto another road. "You made accusations against Marlon. Trey kept his mouth shut. I did the same. Then Marlon told me you were pregnant."

Hope froze. "He told you?"

Gloria slammed her hands on the steering wheel. "Marlon was going to prison for murder. Once he was locked up, Trey and I figured you'd get a divorce, and we'd take possession of the house and Marlon's belongings. But that baby changed everything. That baby would get Marlon's money. That baby would live in the mansion surrounded by all of the Turner family heirlooms. That baby would get everything that should have been mine."

Hope struggled to sit up. "You killed my baby."

Gloria swung onto a gravel road fast enough to send Hope flying into the door. "You never saw it coming. I grabbed your purse, swung the strap around your neck, and pulled with every muscle I had. You fought me. Managed to scratch me up pretty good. I'm sure my DNA is sitting in some tubes somewhere with your name on them. We were walking home from dinner, and I dragged your body deeper into an alley. A nurse found you. A nurse! Can you believe it? Marlon was released because his wife was attacked the same way Miranda was killed. After the press and Marlon's lawyer had a field day trashing your reputation, you disappeared. Hell, Trey helped you."

Gloria slammed on the brakes and jumped out of

the truck.  She came around, opened the truck, and grabbed Hope by the hair.  She pulled hard enough that Hope had to use her legs to propel herself out of the truck the rest of the way so Gloria would let go. The air was knocked out of her when she hit the ground.

Gloria pulled several strands of Hope's hair from her fingers.  "Good old Trey.  He still couldn't get you out of his mind after you left.  At first, he would hook up with women who reminded him of you.  But you know what?  He liked watching Marlon strangle Miranda.  The first time he strangled a woman, it was a woman who looked just like you.  There were others.  Agent Parks is right about that.  Trey would get a glimpse of you, find a woman, screw her a few times, take her out somewhere, and strangle and dump her.  And you know what?"

Hope rolled to her knees.  "What?"

Gloria pointed the gun at her.  "That's exactly what he's going to do to you."

Chapter Twenty

Matt and the other searchers continued to look for the missing woman.  His body was focused on the task, but his mind was on Hope.  Mike had assured him that Hope had gone straight to Allie and Jeremy's house.

Matt wiped the sweat from his face.  He heard shouting from several yards over.  He tightened the straps on his pack and quickly made his way over.

Andy, one of the workers at the ranch, waved him over. "She's down there."

Matt came to the cliff's edge.  A blonde woman sat on a slim ledge.  He could hear her cries from where he stood.  He let out a pent-up breath.  She was alive.  In a precarious position, but alive.

"I can't climb that, but I know you can." Andy kept his voice soft and calm to not alarm the woman below.

Matt dropped his bag.  He never left without his climbing gear, and he quickly and efficiently set up a rig to hoist her up the cliff.  He just needed to climb down, get her in the harness, and get them both off that ledge.

It took Matt a few minutes to get everything together.  He heard the satellite phone ringing in his backpack but ignored it.  He needed to focus on the woman and get her to safety.

With Andy's help, Matt set up the pulley that would lift the woman. He carefully made his way down the cliff. It took him several minutes and carefully placed feet before he made it to the ledge. There was no room for him to stand or sit beside her. He used a hammer and placed a few strategic bolts and anchors to hold him while he got her into the harness.

The woman was shaking from head to toe; she tried to latch onto Matt. "A man dropped me down here."

Matt stabilized her while he let her cry out her fright. It would be much easier if he could get her to take a few deep breaths. He spoke softly to her and explained to her how he was going to get her up the side of the cliff. After a couple of minutes, the woman relaxed her grip on him.

Matt kept talking to her as he got her into the harness. "Your husband is up the hill. He's been frantic since you disappeared. He said your name is Nancy."

She hiccuped. "Nancy Reddick. We came here to learn how to camp. We have a four-year-old son. Rick has dreams of taking him camping when he's older."

Matt cinched the harness, hooked the carabiner to the rope, and fastened a knot. It wasn't pretty, but it would hold her weight. "You tell him he can take girls out camping too. My fiancée, the woman who I came up here with, is an excellent outdoorswoman."

Nancy closed her eyes as Matt eased her off the ledge and her weight settled into the harness. "The pretty redhead?"

"That's the one. Now my friend Andy above is going to start pulling you up. I'll be attached to the rope next to you and I'm going to climb up the way I came down. We'll go up together, okay?"

Both Matt and Nancy were drenched in sweat when they reached the top. Rick was waiting for her. Matt unhooked his gear while Nancy and Rick reunited. Once the pair were willing to release each other, Matt helped Nancy out of the harness.

Andy nodded him over. "Sully and that FBI agent have arrived."

Sully came and gently asked Nancy to tell them what happened.

Nancy's voice shook as she told them how a man had attacked her. He'd grabbed her by the neck and dragged her further into the woods. She'd tried to fight him, but he choked her until she passed out. When she came to, he had her dangling over the ledge by her arms. Then he dropped her.

"He said that if Matt didn't find me first, he'd be back to finish the job."

Matt turned to Sully and Agent Parks. "Her description sounds a lot like Trey Turner."

Agent Parks nodded to the trees away from the group. "I got an interesting call from our forensic lab. They reprocessed the DNA found on the body of the first strangling victim, and while it wasn't a match to Marlon Turner, it was a familial match."

Matt's hands fisted. "Let me guess, his son, Trey."

Parks gave a nod. "I don't have Trey's DNA, but I guarantee you it will be a match. Marlon Turner had no other sons that we're aware of."

Matt wanted to find him and tear him apart. "He's the one who tried to kill Hope."

Parks tucked his hand in his pocket. "Actually, he's not. DNA found on Hope was female."

Matt took a step closer to the agent. "You didn't mention that before. I don't think Hope knows."

"Miss Whitfield was not cooperative with the investigation after her attack. She took off shortly after. My guess is no one contacted her. There is no match to the DNA. No suspects. She already knew it wasn't Marlon, since he'd been in custody. If she ever wondered who it was, she never asked."

"It doesn't make sense." Matt turned to look at Nancy, who was still talking to Sully.

Parks came to stand beside him. "Marlon had dozens of girlfriends. It could have been one of them. Marlon could have convinced one of them to kill his wife. But Miranda Grieves's murder went cold. The police were sure Marlon killed her and were even more convinced once the DNA on Hope came back as female, but Marlon knew the law inside and out. When Marlon was killed, strangled no less, the number one suspect was his wife. Hope wasn't easy to find. Instinct said she didn't kill him. But instincts can be wrong. It took me a while to find her."

Matt knew where Hope had been. But it hadn't been until she started working for the Waters that she was found. "Her employment records."

Parks nodded again. "Before Hope, I questioned Trey myself, but his wife alibied him. She's been his alibi more than once. She was his alibi when Harris Turner was shot. She was his alibi when Hope was strangled. She was his alibi when Marlon was killed. It would take a sick sort of wife to stand by a husband while he murdered people. Or maybe he let her be his alibi because he didn't want to admit his wife might have killed."

"You think Gloria tried to kill Hope."

"I do."

Matt jogged over to Sully. "Can we get a couple of officers over to the Waters's house? Hope is there, and if it's Trey who attacked Nancy, she could be in danger."

Sully held up a satellite phone. "That was Allie Waters. Gloria Turner shot Jeremy Waters, held Allie and her son hostage, and took Hope."

Matt's knees buckled. He grabbed the phone. "Allie!"

Allie's voice came over the line. "Matt. I'm sorry, Hope is gone. I couldn't stop her from taking her. I had to help Jeremy."

Matt leaned into his training. "Is Jeremy alive?"

"He is. He lost a lot of blood. I'm in the ambulance now. He's getting fluids and they've stopped the bleeding. I don't think he'll need a transfusion, but he's weak. The small-caliber bullet is lodged in his ribs."

"I know I don't need to tell you, but you and Sawyer don't leave that hospital until we find Hope."

Tears came over the line. "I couldn't stop her, Matt."

"I know. Sully is here and so is Agent Parks. We'll find her." Matt hung up.

Sully came up and laid a hand on Matt's shoulder. "We're too short-staffed in these parts for me to tell you to stay out of it. I'm dividing everyone up. If Gloria Turner had taken her into town, someone would have seen her. I have both Gloria's and Trey's pictures on the wires. Within the hour, everyone in town will be on the lookout. You know this area better than anyone. Where would they go?"

* * *

Hope sat huddled in the darkened interior of the old house. She closed her eyes to shut out the rats that were sniffing around and climbing on her legs. The rats smelled the blood on her wrists. The cuffs weren't going to come off, so now she focused on the rats. Close to panic as she felt their sharp teeth bite through the thin denim, she continuously kicked them off her to keep them from getting near her face. She wanted to scream, but Gloria had gagged her. Her muffled sounds didn't make it past the dirty confines of the room.

Gloria's voice came through the rotted wood of the walls. "We have to hurry. No doubt her boyfriend will figure out where we've stashed her."

Trey came through the door. "Jeez, Gloria."

Hope tried to kick Trey as he reached out for her. He slapped her hard across the face, grabbed her under her arms, and yanked her to her feet.

Gloria stood outside the house, her eyes alert to their surroundings. "Use the truck."

Trey tossed her over his shoulder. His hands ran up her legs and over her backside. "This is going to be so good."

Gloria opened the door to the back seat. "Just be quick. And she had better be dead when you're done. We had a deal."

Trey set her on her feet. He smiled down at her, his hands caressing the spot where he'd hit her. "You should have taken me up on my offer all those years ago, Jaclyn."

Hope screamed behind the gag as he lifted her onto the seat of the truck. He climbed in, and Gloria slammed the door behind him. The window was down, so she peeked inside.

Trey kicked the door, causing Gloria to jump. "I don't need an audience."

Hope closed her eyes so she wouldn't have to see what he was doing. She felt his hands on the buttons of her shirt. Tears seeped through her lashes.

Trey's voice was filled with excitement as his

hands closed over her throat. "You were always the most beautiful woman to me, Jaclyn. When my father refused to divorce you, I knew I had to kill him. Kill him the same way he killed Miranda. I felt his life leave him. I'd never experienced anything like it. Then I came to look for you. You were free of him; you just didn't know it yet."

Hope's eyes flew open when his hands squeezed her throat. She thrashed as she struggled for breath.

"Then you showed up with him. You're mine. You've always been mine. Your boyfriend is going to find you dead in that house. You should have come alone. We could have been together. It didn't have to be like this. But Gloria, she won't let you live. I either take your life, or she does. I want to be the one who feels the life drain out of you, Jaclyn. Just like I did with those other women."

Hope tried to scream again. Trey, his hand loose now on her throat, untied the gag. She coughed as air filled her lungs. "My name is not Jaclyn anymore, Trey. You can't kill her. She's already dead."

Trey slapped her again, this time hard enough to split her lip. "Shut up. Shut up!"

Hope struggled beneath him. "You lost her a long time ago. My name is Hope. Hope Whitfield. I live in Utah. I own this property. I'm going to get married and raise a family here."

Trey ripped open her shirt the rest of the way. He then lifted only far enough so he could get to the button of her jeans. "I'm going to take you, Hope. I'm going to kill you, Hope."

Hope screamed as Trey's body jerked and fell on top of hers. She felt something hot and wet soaking into her clothes, oozing over her skin and under her back.

"Hope!" Matt's voice filled the truck.

Hope realized Trey wasn't moving. His body was yanked off hers, his face a bloody mess. She saw his blood pooling all over her. She screamed again. She felt arms come around her and lift her from the truck. Matt's face filled her vision, and he held her to his chest, pressing her face against his shirt. She felt the ties on her hands being cut. Despite the pain in her arms, she wrapped her arms around Matt's neck. She felt his arms under her legs as he lifted her.

"I need a blanket or a towel or something. I need to get this blood off her."

Hope stood docilely as Matt stripped her shirt off. He removed his own and wiped the blood off her skin. She dropped her arms to her sides, a numbness coming over her.

Matt caught her as she collapsed in his arms.

* * *


Matt paced the emergency room. It had taken almost an hour to get her to the hospital. She'd woken in the ambulance, but all she had done was cry and fight the paramedics who were trying to treat her. The paramedic was hesitant to give her a sedative until they were able to ascertain what had happened. In the end, the paramedic gave her something to calm her. They had tended to the wounds on her wrists, taped the cut on her lip, and cleaned several wounds on her legs.

Matt had seen a lot in his career as a medic. He knew a rat bite when he saw one. His stomach physically ached at what she had been through. Bruises were forming on her cheeks; he had seen bruising on her stomach once the blood had been completely wiped off her, and she'd been assaulted.

Matt wished he could have been the one to take the shot that ended that bastard's life.

Allie came rushing in. She threw herself into Matt's arms. "Oh, Matt."

Matt gently guided her to a seat. "Where's Jeremy?"

Allie pressed her face to his shoulder. "He's in surgery. I don't know what I'd do without him."

Mike came in behind them, holding Sawyer. "He's going to be all right. The doctors are going to patch him right up. Jeremy is one tough S.O.B."

Allie released Matt. "I know. He'll be fine. He has to be."

Matt rubbed Allie's back when she turned to face where he knew Jeremy was undergoing surgery.

Allie turned her head toward him. "Where's Hope?"

Matt scrubbed a hand over his face. "She's being treated. I'm not family, and I'm not her husband.

They won't let me in."

Allie shot to her feet. "I'm family, dammit, and they'll have no choice but to let me see her."

Matt almost laughed as Allie marched herself to the reception desk. Allie's tone was very much that of the commanding officer she had once been. Matt shook his head as Allie followed a staff member to the back.

Mike handed Sawyer to Matt. "I need to get back to the ranch. Guests are freaking out; the police have been everywhere. The hotel managers were trying to calm the guests when I followed Allie in the ambulance. But since you're here, I should get back. And you let Miss Hope know that Trixie is in good hands."

Matt shook the offered hand. "There's a raise in this for you."

Mike slapped him on the back. "I'm holding you to that. Try to rest, if you can. I'm sure Miss Hope will be fine. She's one tough lady."

Matt knew she was. But he didn't know what she'd suffered at the hands of Gloria and Trey. It would be a long time before she forgot this day.

It was half an hour later when Allie came back out. "She's awake. She gave the staff permission to let you in. Says you're her fiancé."

Matt smiled. "We're at step four in our relationship."

Allie didn't quite smile back. "Step four?"

Mat kissed her cheek. "Yep. Wait until you hear

what step five is."

Allie brushed her lips against his. "I can't wait to find out. Jeremy is out of surgery. He's mad enough to spit nails. Gloria Turner is in police custody, but you can bet your boots that when he's released, he's going to make a personal appearance at the station."

Matt gave her a quick hug, then handed Sawyer over to her. "I'll join him. In the meantime, I'll see how Hope is doing."

Allie halted him. "She's bordering on panic. She's been through a trauma. And not her first one. She's going to need your strength."

Matt squeezed her arm and headed back. He lightly knocked on the glass and slid the curtain slightly open. Hope was lying in the hospital bed, her skin almost as white as the sheets.

Hope sat up. Her eyes filled. "Matt."

Matt came, dropped the rail, and sat beside her. When she started crying, he gently guided her face to his chest. She sobbed, soaking his shirt. He couldn't make out what she was saying, but in the end, it didn't matter. Whatever happened, he'd be there for her.

Hope pulled away and pressed her fingers over the wet spot on his shirt. "He's dead, isn't he?"

Matt brushed back the damp curls from her cheeks. "He is."

Hope swallowed. "Gloria?"

Matt's fingers went to the bruises forming on her throat. "Jail. Oh, Hope."

Hope jerked back when he touched her throat.

She pulled her knees to her chest. "Not yet."

Matt stood. "As much time as you need. I'll be here."

"How did you find me?"

Matt pulled up a chair and sat. When she didn't pull back, he took her hand. "I found the missing woman. Alive. She was hugging the side of a cliff when the searchers found her, and I got her off the cliff. Sully and Agent Parks both showed up. Parks had evidence that Trey was the one who killed that woman in California. He didn't say so, but my best guess is that Parks has been watching Trey and Gloria for a while."

Hope squeezed his hand. "You saved her."

Matt turned her hand over in his and stroked her fingers. "She was a distraction. I stayed on the mountain to look for her, while Gloria lay in wait for you to return."

"You knew they took me back to the house."

"It's where he watched you."

Hope shuddered in revulsion. She pulled her hand out of his. "He sat up there and watched me. It was probably part of some sick fantasy that he would kill me there."

Matt tried to tread carefully, but it hurt him to see her like this. Her shirt had been torn, but she'd still been wearing her jeans, though they had been unbuttoned. It made him sick to think of Trey's hands on her. "You want to tell me what happened?"

Hope rolled onto her side, turning away from him.

"Nothing.  He was going to kill me.  You found him. The police stopped him."

Matt came around the bed.  "If he assaulted you—"

Hope grabbed the cup of water from the table and threw it at him.  "Leave me alone!"

Matt felt his eyes sting as Hope began to cry again, this time curling up in a ball, her back to him.  He felt useless.  Impotent.  He didn't know how to help her. The woman he loved most in the world was hurting, and he was helpless to stop it.

* * *

Hope was eventually taken to a room where she fell into a fitful sleep.  Matt knew the antibiotics and the anxiety medication were helping.  But before she had fallen asleep, she had told him to leave.

So Matt did as she asked.  He'd spent a restless night on his couch before he made his way to the barn and got to work.  Mike had canceled Matt's camping and climbing trips for the rest of the week.  Given what had happened, he hoped the guests understood. But Matt could see riders on the trails, so he got back to work.  He cleaned out the goat pen and fed and watered the horses before mucking out the stalls.

Allie found him later in the day.  "Hey.  Jeremy is home.  He's grumbling about being stuck in bed, so I told him I'd send you his way.  Maybe have some guy talk."

Matt set the pitchfork against the wall.  "Glad to

hear he's grumbling."

Allie opened the barn door and Matt followed her out. Allie glanced up at the bright blue sky. "Me too. I've never been so scared in my life. Jeremy, being Jeremy, is taking it all in stride. Once he was convinced Sawyer and I were not hurt, he was ready to get back to work. But as his nurse, I'm making him rest."

Matt pushed his hat further down on his head. "I wish I could say the same for Hope."

Allie bumped her hip against his. "I stopped in and saw her. She's feeling better. She asked if you would come back tonight. The doctor is going to keep her to make sure she doesn't develop a fever or an infection from the rat bites. The antibiotic is doing its job, but he wants to be sure."

Matt stopped. "She told me to leave, Allie."

She patted his cheek. "And now she's asking you to come back."

Matt glanced down at her. "You have that look on your face."

Allie continued toward the house. "Which one? I have a lot of them."

"The superior one that says I'm being an idiot."

"Ah. A personal favorite. Go talk to Jeremy. Then take a shower and go see Hope. I promise she'll be glad to see you."

* * *

Hope had tuned out a lot of what Agent Parks had been saying to her. When he'd shown up, she at first had optimistically hoped it was Matt knocking at her door. She'd been so rude to him yesterday. She'd treated him horribly. But she had been reliving the days when she'd been in the hospital after her attack. When he touched her, she felt disgusted. She felt confused. She felt another man's hands. And she sent him away.

"Miss Whitfield?"

Hope turned back to the agent. "I'm sorry. I wasn't listening. Your man is dead. Gloria admitted Trey witnessed Marlon killing Miranda. Gloria also admitted to attacking me in an alley and shooting Harris. And Trey admitted he killed his father and those other women. It's over."

The agent took a seat. "It is. But it will live with you for a long time. We can't charge Trey for what he did to you. But you can tell your story. Get it off your chest. And Gloria can be charged as an accomplice and a willing partner in the crimes."

Hope adjusted the blanket around her chest. Her hands dropped when Matt came in. Her eyes held his. "He said he was going to kill me. That he'd made a pact with Gloria. That either he would do the deed, or she would. Gloria kidnapped me and drove me to the house. She tied me up there. My wrists were bleeding, and the rats were everywhere. I tried to scream, but I was gagged. I don't know how long I was there. But then I heard Gloria tell Trey they had to hurry up. He was going to assault me and strangle me. He hit me. And again. He choked me until I couldn't breathe. But someone shot him before. Just before."

Matt came further into the room. "I wish it had been me."

Hope's lips trembled. "I'm glad it wasn't. You're not a killer, Matt. You're a healer."

Agent Parks cleared his throat. "I think that should do it."

Hope halted him when he would have left. "Did Gloria say why?"

The agent glanced at Matt and then back to her. "The simple answer is jealousy. You have what she wanted."

Hope's eyes softened as she looked at Matt. "Do I?"

Matt came to sit beside her. "You do."

The agent slipped out of the room.

Hope grabbed Matt's shirt and pulled him to her. Her lips found his. She sighed into his mouth when he kissed her back. When her IV beeped at her, she withdrew.

Matt straightened her arm. "You're kinking your hose."

Hope grinned at him and then laughed. She laughed until her eyes watered, and her stomach hurt. "I love you, Matt."

* * *

Matt held Hope as they left the police station. They'd both given their statements. Gloria was going to plead out.

"Is it weird I sort of feel sorry for her? She's grieving the death of her husband." Hope put on a pair of sunglasses.

Matt shrugged, but Hope knew he had no sympathy. Sully had said it had been difficult to get much out of Gloria since she'd been arrested three days ago. Mostly she cried in her cell and refused to talk to anyone. She eventually lawyered up. She had admitted to everything she had told Hope. That and more. Jealousy might have been the emotion. But Hope knew it was pure greed that drove them. Gloria wanted Trey to stop coveting Jaclyn. Trey wanted Gloria to keep her mouth shut. They were going to spend the rest of their days living it up off Marlon's money. Little had either of them known that Agent Parks had been closing in.

"It is weird. But it's also okay. You can feel sorry for her if you want to. I'm just amazed that the two of them thought they could come here, kill you, and go back home like nothing happened."

Hope took his hand as they headed to her car. She had adamantly refused to get in his truck. Her outburst had shocked both of them. Allie had picked her up from the hospital, not Matt, so she hadn't been confronted with his truck until that morning. Matt had simply steered her toward her car. She knew the fear would pass in time, but for now, Matt did what he could to help ease her anxiety. He kept his touches light, stayed on his side of the bed unless she sought him out, and treated her with care.

When they got home from the police station, Jeremy and Allie were waiting for them. Sawyer was playing with toys on a blanket.

Matt closed the door. "So what do we owe the pleasure?"

Allie patted the spot next to her for Hope to sit. "Jeremy got a phone call from that investigator."

Hope groaned. "I don't want to hear what he has to say."

Allie gave her a brief hug. "You'll like this."

Jeremy interrupted. "Just the facts, Allie."

She nodded. "Right. So the investigator was digging into the files on the trust. Now we know from what Gloria confessed that she knew who I was to you. And she knew about the trust. The one outstanding question was why Marlon refused to divorce you."

Matt leaned against the wall. "Facts, Allie."

She made a face. "Right. Turns out that this particular parcel of land used to lease out mineral rights back in the day. Your property, the ridgeline that marks the boundary of your land and the government land, used to be mined."

Hope's brow furrowed. "Mined for what?"

Allie laughed. "Gold. Can you believe it?"

Hope was confused. "You're saying there's gold on

my property?"

Allie patted Hope's knee. "Not anymore, or at least, none that has been dug up. But when Aunt Julie died, the money from the lease went into an account that was tied to the property. From what the investigator could tell, the mining company's lease was up six years ago. Right around the time I inherited my parcel. But the lease money has been sitting in an account earning interest for years. Aunt Julie never spent it. She left it in the account."

Hope wasn't sure what she felt. "Marlon knew about the money in the account, didn't he?"

Jeremy chimed in. "He did. And he saw dollar signs. You were to inherit the property in two years when you walked out. If he could stall you long enough to take possession, he would have fought you in court for his share."

Hope shook off her mood. "Or kill me like he did Miranda and inherit it. Figures. That explains that. Anything else?"

Jeremy shook his head. "Most of what he found we already know, either from the police or from Gloria's confession. I have the report if you want to read it or add it to your papers. He sent the information for the bank with it. The account goes with the land, so the money in it is yours. You'll have to pay additional taxes on the income, but you, Hope, are now a wealthy woman."

Hope took the paper and choked. "Is that a real number?"

Allie laughed. "It is, dear sister. Interested in buying into a ranch?"

Epilogue

Hope watched as the last of the old house was cleared away. The road between her property and the Waters's property had already been widened and paved. Where the old house stood would now be a meadow. Hope wanted to let the land grow as nature had intended it to. A fencing company would be coming in a couple of weeks to install a new fence around the old homestead.

Matt waved at her from where he was talking to the contractor who was overseeing the building of their new home. Hope picked up the skirt of her new sundress and made her way over.

Matt kissed her as he wrapped his arm around her waist. "Blueprints are done. We'll spend the fall and winter in our trailer, but we should be able to break ground and get started before the ground freezes."

The man handed her the final drawings. "I think you'll like the changes, Mrs. Henney."

Hope took the drawings. The beautiful two-story home was exactly as she had imagined it. There would be high ceilings, wood floors, beautiful archways, an eat-in kitchen, three and a half bathrooms, and five bedrooms. Hope had plans for all of those bedrooms. Matt let her take the lead on the house, rarely offering his opinion. He refused to touch a penny of her money. So it had been up to her to add extra space to the garage, add a small greenhouse, and a backyard patio.

"These are perfect."

Matt thanked the man, and he left. He pulled Hope into his arms. "Allie is in heaven right now. The expansion of the farm onto your section of the property is going well. I'm still not sure why the two of you decided we need more animals. Are you sure you don't want to build stables on your property?"

Hope had already explained. "No. I'm now one-quarter owner of the Waters Ranch. Adding to the stables is my contribution. You did say step five was to raise horses and make babies."

Matt lifted her higher against his chest so he could kiss her. "So I did."

Hope nibbled his lips. "I do have one small change I'd like to make."

Matt's fingers bunched up her skirt, and he trailed his fingers over the back of her legs. "What's that?"

"I decided I do want the four kids I planned when I was twelve."

Matt lifted her so that her legs were circling his waist. "Well, then. We'd better get started."

Hope agreed and laughed as he carried her to the tent she'd insisted he set up. This one was triple the size of her old one and had a real mattress in it. They'd already spent a few nights inside it.

Trixie came in and lay on her bed, ignoring the two humans as they did what humans do.

<u>From The Author</u>

Hope and Matt.  Their romance was a whirlwind for me.  I lost count of days, but it took less than a month to write their first draft. Something about the couple drove me to finish it. It was outlined. It was researched. But then nothing. I started and then stopped at a few hundred words in. Then I rewrote Chapter One, and it simply flowed from there.

I love romances where the couple are pitted against Mother Nature. Snowstorms, deserts, jungles, frigid mountains, rain, or mud slides. I'm not picky, though I love a good trapped in a blizzard story. Forced proximity is a favorite trope of mine. My favorite line is when Matt asks Jeremy what is the opposite of a damsel in distress. Whatever it is, that is what Matt was. I loved the role reversal, especially when everyone thinks Hope is helpless. But in the end, Matt does save her in typical hero fashion.

If you enjoyed the book and would like an email of my next release, please sign up for my newsletter @ elizabeth-castle.com/contact. You can also follow me on Facebook @ facebook.com/elizabethcastle.romanceauthor.

Also, if you enjoyed this book, or any of my other titles, please consider leaving a rating at your favorite retailer, Goodreads, and/or Bookbub. And if you have the time, a text review would be lovely. Indie authors rely on readers like you to tell others how much you enjoy their books.

Happy reading,

Lizzy Castle

Books by Elizabeth Castle

Single Titles:
   Going Home
   This Kind Of Love
   Chasing Hope
   The Babe & The Librarian (novella)
   Ghosts Of The Past

The Heart's Way Series:
   For Now and Always
   Ask Me To
   Say You Love Me
   Forever Love

All Of Me Series:
   All Of My Days
   All Of My Nights

Bennett Family Series
   This Time Love
   A Bride For David
(novella)

Cantwell Series:
   Falling Slowly
   Unraveled
   Hidden Away
   Entangled

Contemporary "Retro" Romance Series:
   Loving Jordan

Visit *elizabeth-castle.com* for newsletter signup and up-to-date releases

www.ingramcontent.com/pod-product-compliance
Lightning Source LLC
Chambersburg PA
CBHW061735310726
48969CB00002BA/315